The Complete Strategy & War Collection (Vol. 3)

Caesar's Commentaries & Frederick the Great's Instructions
— Command in the Field

A Modern Translation

Adapted for the Contemporary Reader

Julius Caesar | Frederick the Great

Translated by Tim Zengerink

Table Of Contents

Preface - Message to the Reader 1

Introduction 4

The Commentaries 9

Instructions to His Generals 146

Thank You for Reading 233

Preface - Message to the Reader

What If You Could Help Rebuild the Greatest Library in Human History?

Thousands of years ago, the Library of Alexandria stood as the crown jewel of human achievement — a sanctuary where the collected wisdom of every known civilization was gathered, preserved, and shared freely.

And then, it was lost.

Through fire, conquest, and the slow erosion of time, humanity lost not just books — but ideas, dreams, discoveries, and stories that could have changed the world forever.

Today, the Library of Alexandria lives again — and you are invited to be a part of its restoration.

Our mission is simple yet profound:

To rebuild the greatest library the world has ever known, and to translate all timeless works into every language and dialect, so that no seeker of knowledge is ever left behind again.

By joining our movement to rebuild the modern Library of Alexandria, you become part of an unprecedented mission:

• **Unlimited Access to the Greatest Audiobooks & eBooks Ever Written:**

Instantly explore thousands of legendary works—Plato, Shakespeare, Jane Austen, Leo Tolstoy, and countless more. All instantly available to read or listen, placing a complete literary universe at your fingertips.

- **Beautiful Paperback & Deluxe Editions at Printing Cost**

  Own any title as an elegant paperback, deluxe hardcover, or stunning collectible boxset—offered to you at true printing cost, delivered straight to your door. Build your personal Library of Alexandria, crafted for beauty, built for durability, and worthy of proud display.

- **Fresh Translations for Modern Readers—in Every Language & Dialect**

  Enjoy timeless masterpieces reimagined in clear, contemporary language—no more outdated phrases or obscure references. Alongside the original versions, we're tirelessly translating these classics into every language and dialect imaginable, ensuring accessibility and understanding across cultures and generations.

- **Join a Global Renaissance of Literature & Knowledge**

  You directly support expanding our library, publishing deluxe editions at true cost, translating works into all global languages, and bringing humanity's greatest stories to people everywhere. By joining today, you're not just preserving a legacy of masterpieces; you set in motion a powerful wave of literary accessibility.

Become a Torchbearer of Knowledge.

Join us for free now at **LibraryofAlexandria.com**

Together, we will ensure that the light of human wisdom never fades again.

With gratitude and a shared love of knowledge,
The Modern Library of Alexandria Team

Visit:

www.libraryofalexandria.com

Or scan the code below:

Introduction

Caesar and Frederick:
The Embodiment of Command in War

Leadership in war is never merely about tactics—it is about perception, decisiveness, logistics, discipline, and communication. It is about managing not just armies, but human emotion, terrain, ambition, and chaos. In The Complete Strategy & War Collection (Vol. 3), we study the lives and minds of two masters of military command: Julius Caesar and Frederick the Great. Both were not only military commanders but also writers of uncommon clarity. Their works—Caesar's Commentaries on the Gallic and Civil Wars and Frederick's Instructions to His Generals—are both documents of action and guides to thinking about the nature of power, leadership, and operational excellence.

These writings do more than recount battles—they reveal the psychology of high command. Caesar's firsthand narrative documents his campaigns in Gaul and his dramatic crossing of the Rubicon, while Frederick's treatise offers distilled wisdom for the generals under his rule. One is embedded in the blood and dust of campaign; the other is composed in the reflective tone of a sovereign seeking disciplined order in his military machine.

Together, they form a profound study of applied strategy. Caesar models adaptability, speed, and personal charisma; Frederick demonstrates foresight, methodical planning, and moral authority. They were both relentless, rational, and possessed of the same gift: the ability to translate complexity into clear, actionable leadership. This introduction will examine their individual approaches to command, the ethical implications of their strategies, and their enduring influence on generations of leaders across fields.

Julius Caesar:
Speed, Eloquence, and the Personal Engine of War

Gaius Julius Caesar (100–44 BCE) was one of the most influential military and political figures in Western history. His campaigns extended Roman control to the English Channel and the Rhine, reshaped the political foundations of the Republic, and catalyzed the transition to imperial rule. But perhaps even more impressive than his achievements in politics and war is the literary elegance with which he documented them.

His Commentaries on the Gallic War and The Civil War are written in clear, economical Latin prose, third-person narration, and with a consistent tone of rational detachment. Yet the simplicity of the style belies the depth of the strategy, the speed of execution, and the scale of the maneuver he commands. These works are more than propaganda; they are textbooks in applied leadership.

Caesar's campaigns in Gaul (58–50 BCE) were marked by incredible mobility, rapid adaptation, and psychological acuity. He understood how to divide enemies, exploit tribal rivalries, and use terrain to his advantage. He was as comfortable building bridges across wide rivers as he was commanding pitched battles, often resolving complex military dilemmas with daring, pragmatic solutions.

In The Civil War, we see a different Caesar: the commander fighting for political survival against the Roman Senate's forces. Here, his talent for logistics, morale management, and calculated boldness becomes even more evident. His crossing of the Rubicon is not merely a military move—it is a philosophical moment: the commitment to decisive, irreversible action. His campaign against Pompey is a masterclass in strategic momentum—how to maintain the initiative, destabilize the opposition, and dictate the tempo of war.

Crucially, Caesar was also a master of perception. His narratives not only document events; they shape them. By writing in the third person and highlighting his restraint, clemency, and reason, he casts himself as a reluctant but rational actor—one whose greatness lies in judgment as much as in power.

Through his Commentaries, Caesar becomes the prototype of the political general: one who commands both men and narrative, whose battlefield success is inseparable from his control of public imagination. His legacy is not only in the territories he conquered, but in the rhetorical and strategic frameworks that continue to define leadership today.

Frederick the Great:
Discipline, Doctrine, and Enlightened Control

Frederick II of Prussia (1712–1786), known as Frederick the Great, was both a philosopher-king and a formidable commander. His military innovations, especially during the Seven Years' War, solidified Prussia's status as a European power. Yet Frederick's influence endures not only because of his victories, but because of the intellectual rigor with which he approached command.

His Instructions to His Generals is a lucid, highly organized text that codifies the essentials of military leadership. Addressed to the officers who served under him, the work is part manual, part doctrine, and part moral code. Frederick believed that great command was founded on foresight, precision, and personal integrity. He demanded from his officers not only tactical skill, but judgment, loyalty, and unwavering commitment to duty.

One of Frederick's key messages is that generals must be prepared for the unexpected. "The art of war," he writes, "consists in always having more strength at the decisive point." He emphasizes flexibility—one must plan thoroughly, but never become a prisoner of the plan. When unforeseen circumstances arise, the capable general must improvise without panic.

Discipline, for Frederick, is the bedrock of military performance. He champions strict order in camp, clear hierarchy, and the elimination of carelessness. Yet he also tempers this with the insistence that generals lead by example. A commander must not only command well, but live well. Morality and leadership are interwoven. In his vision, the army is not only a tool of statecraft, but a mirror of national character.

Frederick also warns against pride, rashness, and self-indulgence. He believed in economy of force, in the intelligent use of terrain, and in the integration of logistics into strategy. He insists that every movement, every order, every march must serve a clear and calculated purpose.

While Caesar operated in the volatile world of personal ambition and civil war, Frederick built a disciplined state army grounded in Enlightenment ideals. His Instructions reflect a different kind of power: not charismatic conquest, but institutional stability. He is not seeking glory, but order—and in that order, the enduring capacity for military success.

Strategic Leadership Across Eras: Principles That Endure

Though separated by centuries and temperament, Caesar and Frederick converge on the essential traits of great commanders:

- Clarity of Purpose: Every campaign, every battle must serve a strategic goal. Whether it is Rome's expansion or Prussia's survival, success begins with alignment between means and ends.
- Speed and Adaptability: Both leaders understood the value of tempo. Caesar's fast marches and Frederick's emphasis on decisive points show that victory often belongs to those who control the clock.
- Control of Narrative: Caesar wrote his own history. Frederick shaped the ethical and procedural frameworks of his military.

Both understood that lasting power is as much about perception and cohesion as about raw force.

- Discipline and Morale: From Caesar's legions to Frederick's regiments, effective command depends on the cohesion and spirit of the force. Leadership must inspire as much as it commands.

- Judgment Over Doctrine: Neither man believed in rigid formulas. They valued preparation, but also recognized the need for improvisation, initiative, and trust in one's own discernment.

These insights remain urgently relevant. Whether in war, business, governance, or crisis leadership, the challenges remain the same: to make decisions under pressure, to balance vision with execution, and to lead with both confidence and conscience.

The Commentaries of Julius Caesar and Instructions to His Generals are more than historical texts—they are blueprints for real-world decision-making. They reveal that greatness in command is not only a matter of action, but of awareness. It is not only about what one does, but how one sees.

Welcome to The Complete Strategy & War Collection (Vol. 3). May the legacies of Caesar and Frederick inspire you to lead with discipline, clarity, and courage—whatever battlefield you may face.

The Commentaries

Julius Caesar

Chapter I.
Introduction.

It could be said that Cæsar's Commentaries mark the beginning of modern history. Although written nearly two thousand years ago, Cæsar documented events as he experienced them, recounting his own actions and the events he observed firsthand. He wrote about regions that are familiar to us today—such as Britain, which he invaded twice—and about peoples close enough to be recognizable as our neighbors and predecessors. His accounts bring us actual history, not fictionalized tales. The straightforward style of his narrative is perhaps its greatest strength; it convinces us that the events he describes truly took place, almost exactly as he recorded them. Cæsar describes large-scale movements across Europe that shaped the current political landscape of nations. While readers may find fascination in the great exploits of Greek heroes or the powerful words of Greek orators, it is challenging to find any direct and reliable connection between the fortunes of ancient Athens, Sparta, or Macedonia and our own time. The same can be said of the earlier history of Rome, prior to Cæsar's era.

The Punic Wars, the Social War, the lives of the Scipios and the Gracchi, or even the power struggle between Marius and Sulla, do not resonate as personally as the Gallic Wars or the Roman invasion of Britain. Through these latter events, Roman civilization was first extended westward, setting the stage for the "Bellum Civile" (Civil War), which initiated a long line of emperors, whose legacy extends almost to our own time. These events lay the groundwork for the development of nearly every European nation we know today. Admittedly, if all facts were available to us, we might trace every current political and social structure back to the earliest days of humanity. But our interest often wanes when facts become uncertain and history seems entangled with legend. While Herodotus captivates with his myths, the enjoyment we derive from his writings rarely comes from a desire to trace a direct line from his time to ours. There is a vast difference between the mythical wonders of Herodotus and the documented realities of Cæsar.

With Cæsar, there is a level of clarity that we associate with modern history. From the start, it's essential to remember that Cæsar wrote only about events he personally experienced or directed. His two surviving works, his Commentaries, are all that remain of his writings. We are told that he produced other works as well, including a poem, but these two Commentaries are the only complete texts that have come down to us. The first, consisting of seven books, describes the events of his initial seven campaigns in Gaul over seven consecutive years, where he subdued the tribes living between the Rhine, the Rhone, the Mediterranean, the Pyrenees, and the English Channel. The second Commentary recounts the details of the civil war in which he clashed with Pompey—his former partner in power, along with Crassus, in the first triumvirate—and established the empire that would later pass to Augustus after a second, short-lived triumvirate between Augustus, Lepidus, and Antony.

This little book aims to describe Cæsar's Commentaries for those who do not read Latin, rather than to provide a full history of Rome. Still, it may be helpful to begin with a brief look at the life and character of Cæsar himself. Most of us recognize the name Julius Cæsar. As children, we learned he was the first of the twelve Roman emperors whose names we memorized in school. We were taught that when Cæsar came to power, the old republican system—where two consuls, elected annually, governed Rome—came to an end. First, there were the seven kings of Rome, whose names we also know, then the consuls, and finally, the twelve Cæsars, beginning with the renowned Julius. This much we all remember about him, and we're also familiar with the fact that he was assassinated by conspirators in the Capitol just as he was about to take on the role of emperor—a detail that, ironically, seems to contradict his claim as the first of the Cæsars.

We also know Cæsar as a brilliant general, conqueror, and writer who recorded his deeds in his famous "veni, vidi, vici" style, famously proclaiming, "I came, I saw, I conquered." We're aware that he commanded a powerful Roman army and used this force to establish his own rule in Rome. He did so by leading part of his army across the Rubicon, a small river that marked the boundary of his provincial authority. By crossing it, he entered Roman territory in a manner forbidden to generals serving the Republic, setting the stage for his rise to power. This is the basic story most of us learned.

In this brief introduction to the life of the great commander and historian, there is no need to question or alter these early lessons, as has so often been attempted in recent years. Those lessons were generally correct. Here, I'll simply add a few details that, while once learned by schoolchildren, may have faded from memory over time.

Dean Merivale, in one of the first chapters of his well-regarded history of the Romans under the Empire, declares that Caius Julius Cæsar is the greatest name in history. He makes this statement without holding back, and without suggesting that it is only his own opinion. We often find such claims made by authors in favor of their heroes, and usually, we are inclined to challenge them. Yet, even though this claim is huge, it is difficult to deny. Dr. Merivale doesn't claim that Cæsar was the greatest person who ever lived. When people measure greatness, they do so by different standards. One might think a poet is the greatest, another might choose a religious leader, a third might select a thinker who unlocked nature's mysteries, and another still might see a powerful ruler as the greatest. But the names of some of these people cannot be called great purely from a historical perspective. Homer, Luther, Galileo, and Charles V. are all famous names, as are Shakespeare, Knox, Queen Elizabeth, and Newton. However, the two rulers in this list would probably be the least admired overall. But no one can argue that the poets, religious leaders, and scientists are necessarily greater in history than these rulers. Dean Merivale means that of all the people whose actions we know, Julius Cæsar did the most to change the world, and we agree that he is right.

Those we might compare to Cæsar are Alexander, Charlemagne, Cromwell, Napoleon, and Washington. For the first two, when we make comparisons to them, we do so knowing we have only partial records of what they achieved. In Alexander's time, history was still somewhat obscure, and by the era of Charlemagne, it had once again become vague. What Cromwell achieved was limited to Britain, and though he was immensely important for the British Isles, he does not appear as significant to the world at large as someone who influenced all of Europe, both in the present and the future. If Cæsar has any true rival for this title, it is Napoleon. As a soldier, Napoleon was just as remarkable, and he operated across just as wide an area. But there is an old saying that no one's fortune is truly secure until the end, and Cæsar's dramatic death on the steps of the Capitol feels more aligned with our sense of greatness than Napoleon's passing on St. Helena. Furthermore, there seem to be fewer flaws in the personal character of the Roman "Imperator" and Dictator than in the character of the French Emperor. Technically, Julius Cæsar was never really an emperor as we understand the term; his successor Augustus was the one who truly became emperor.

As for Washington, we might agree that he was perhaps the greatest of all in terms of moral qualities. He risked everything for his country, even the disgraceful death of a rebel, had he not succeeded in a venture that seemed very unlikely to succeed. He succeeded in all he set out to do. His name is the crowning one among those who created the United States, and all its people celebrate him for that. His achievements were driven by love of country, without any trace of personal ambition. But it cannot be said that his achievements were as momentous as those of Cæsar, nor that he was as powerful in carrying them out. Washington risked everything with as noble a purpose as any person could, and he succeeded, yet the deeds he accomplished are small in comparison to those of his less honorable rival for fame.

Mommsen, the German historian, describes Cæsar as a man too vast for the reach of his intelligence and ability to portray. "The historian," Mommsen writes, speaking of Cæsar, "when once in a thousand years he encounters perfection, can only be silent about it." Napoleon, too, in his biography of Cæsar, portrays him as perfect. But Napoleon's portrayal is, in reality, a way of claiming godlike perfection for his own uncle, the second Cæsar. And the perfection Napoleon describes is different from what Mommsen suggests. Mommsen wants to convey that Cæsar was flawless in his human capabilities and intelligence, while Napoleon credits him with moral perfection. "We may be sure," says the Emperor, "based on the above facts, that during his first consulship, Cæsar was driven by only one motive—the public good." However, we cannot completely accept the facts as the French Emperor presents them, nor can we fully share his confidence. Yet, most readers would likely agree that no name in history is as great as that of Julius Cæsar, and this volume will offer some account of his writings in the following sections.

He was born exactly one hundred years before the birth of Christ, into an old and noble Roman family, known for the name Julius rather than Cæsar. The origin of the name "Cæsar" is uncertain and surrounded by stories and myths. Some say it came from the thick hair of an early member of the Julian family, while others claim it's from a child of the family being, like Macduff, "ripped from his mother's womb"—with Latin words conveniently supporting these ideas. Another story says that a member of the family once kept an elephant, and that "Cæsar" sounds like the word for elephant in some Eastern language. Yet another legend, which fit well with Cæsar's Gallic campaigns, claimed that in the Gallic language of the time, "Cæsar" sounded like a phrase meaning, "Send him back." Supposedly, when Cæsar's horse once bolted and carried him over to the enemy, a Gaul who recognized him shouted "Cæsar, Cæsar!" Hearing this, the other Gauls mistook it for an order to let him go, so he safely returned. The German historian who recounts this tale dismisses it with great skepticism. Whatever the true origin, the name "Cæsar" gained huge importance due to Caius Julius Cæsar's achievements and writings. It eventually came to signify, in multiple languages, a ruler with absolute power. And although the Russian title "Czar" is said to be unrelated to the Roman word, the association is so strong that people will likely always connect the Russian Emperor's title with the Roman legacy.

Cæsar was related by marriage to Marius, the influential general who, through a mix of brutal victories and near-disastrous failures, battled Sulla for the top position in the republic. In these power struggles, Sulla represented the aristocratic and patrician faction—the side we might today call "Conservative." Marius, on the other hand, came from humble origins. He had started as a common soldier, earned his way up the ranks, and eventually became a favorite of the army and the people. If the term "Liberal" had existed back then, he might have identified with it. Like other political leaders after him, Marius's so-called "liberal" stance led him to personal power. He served as Consul seven times, securing his final election through horrific violence against his opponents in the city. He died during this last consulship.

Although young Cæsar was born into the patrician class, he succeeded Marius in leading the popular party. From a very young age—even in his teenage years—he seemed to have set his sights on the power he could achieve by skillfully navigating the political landscape.

Cæsar was highly cautious and showed an impressive level of confidence and patience. Most readers probably know the story of how the Roman Republic fell and turned into the Roman Empire after a series of civil wars that began with Marius and ended with "young Octavius," better known as Augustus Cæsar. Julius Cæsar was Marius's nephew by marriage, and Augustus was Julius's great-nephew and chosen heir. The power Marius gained almost by accident—and which Julius Cæsar pursued strategically throughout his life—was finally secured by Augustus through brutal acts of conscription and killings. These events, while perhaps fewer in number, were no less horrific than those of the French Revolution. This power, which Augustus received and held, was then passed down to the emperors after him.

When we look back at history, we often find that despotic power tends to arise from popular uprisings against authority. This happened with Cromwell, twice in modern France, and certainly in the rise of the Roman Empire. Establishing this empire relied on Cæsar's intellect, skill, and courage, regardless of whether we see this as good or bad. And when we compare the lives of Marius, Cæsar, and Augustus, who each worked toward the same end—the destruction of the oligarchy disguised as a Republic—we see that Cæsar was the only one with any true humanity. Marius, as an old man, and Augustus, as a young man, committed atrocities so horrific that they still shock readers today, even considering that these acts occurred before the influence of Christianity. Marius, along with his rival Sulla, drowned his enemies in blood. Meanwhile, Octavius—who later became the godlike Augustus—secured his position by executing close friends to appease his allies, Lepidus and Antony, in the second triumvirate. Cæsar, by comparison, is remembered for his mercy. Yet, as one reads his accounts, the sheer scale of the cities he razed and communities he destroyed can be overwhelming. He could recount the slaughter of women and children in just one line without any hint of emotion. Nevertheless, Cæsar didn't relish bloodshed. He saw it as a means to an end—an action taken without hesitation when it served his purpose. But he was not drawn to violence for its own sake. He was a calculated, cautious thinker, and could carry out orders with calm resolve when he deemed them necessary.

Cæsar also seemed to be motivated by a sense of duty and love for Rome, much like his contemporaries Pompey and Cicero. However, it's hard to say the same for those before and after him, like Marius, Sulla, Antony, and Augustus, whose actions seemed driven solely by power, greed, vengeance, personal ambition, and a belief in their own fates pushing them toward greatness. These desires existed in Cæsar as well, as they do in today's leaders, but he also carried a noble vision—

to stay true to Rome's greatness and to claim power with the hope of ensuring its empire was governed wisely. Augustus, to be fair, ruled well. And while Cæsar had little time to govern after his conquests, Augustus's intelligence can be credited with recognizing that maintaining the well-being of Rome's citizens was key to his own security.

In his early years, Cæsar rose to a high position, even though his rise was fraught with dangers. People around him were amazed that Sulla hadn't killed him when he was still young—when he could have been "crushed in the shell," so to speak. But Sulla spared him, and Cæsar advanced steadily. We learn that he was appointed priest of Jupiter at seventeen, and at that time, he was already married. He began training himself as a public speaker early on, and amid constant threats, he took up the popular cause in Rome. He served Rome in the East— likely in Bithynia—avoiding the dangers he might have faced if he had stayed in the city. He was made Quaestor and later Ædile, with the backing of the Marian party, which supported him as a rising leader they saw as their future head. Cæsar attacked and was also attacked in turn, becoming known for his "tireless harassment of the aristocracy," who tried, but failed, to crush him. Though he was young and embraced all the pleasures of youth—Sulla once even called him a "trifler"—he made sure to learn everything he needed as the head of a powerful party and as the leader of great armies. At thirty-seven, he was appointed Pontifex Maximus, the head of the Roman priesthood, which was the most honored role in the city. He achieved this despite opposition from the entire aristocracy and the candidacy of Catulus, who was the most admired and virtuous member of their party. The following year, he became Prætor, though he faced fierce opposition from those who feared him. After completing his twelve-month term, he took up the governorship of Spain, the province granted to him as Proprætor according to Republican tradition, defying a Senate decree that ordered him to stay in Rome. It was in Spain that he achieved his first major military success, winning the loyalty of his soldiers, and returning to Rome eligible for the honor of a triumph.

But there was still one more step in his political career that he had to achieve before he could reach the position he likely already envisioned for himself. To command many legions, he needed to become Consul. And in order to officially apply for this position, he had to give up his triumph. Triumphs were only possible for those acting as Generals for the Republic's armies, and as an Imperator, or General, he couldn't enter the city. Cæsar gave up the Triumph, sought the consulship in the usual way, and by doing so, allowed the people to believe he valued their service over his own personal honors. At forty-one, he became Consul. During his struggle for this office, the famous triumvirate was formed—an alliance so well-known to later generations, though it was likely less talked about among Romans at the time. Pompey, who had once been under Sulla's guidance and had been the hope of the patricians to whom he belonged, had returned to Rome after achieving several victories as Proconsul in the East. He had celebrated his triumph and thought he could retire on his honors, disbanding his army and assuming he could live quietly. However, the political environment was too chaotic for such a simple course of action, and Pompey, though he wished to step away from power, found it difficult to be sidelined by his own party. He may have thought that he could lead Rome using his influence alone, without needing the support of his legions. Seeing this, Cæsar approached him with an offer, and together with Crassus, whose wealth made him valuable, they formed the first triumvirate. Their agreement allowed them to control Rome and its provinces together. However, though it was a shared plan, Cæsar no doubt secretly aimed to take ultimate power for himself. In the years that followed, as Cæsar fought in Gaul, Pompey stayed in Rome. He was not, in truth, Cæsar's ally—their superficial friendship had ended with the death of Julia, Cæsar's daughter, who was Pompey's wife, despite him being five years older than Cæsar—but rather, he remained in cautious rivalry with the ambitious man who was training his armies abroad to eventually seize power at home. Later, after Cæsar crossed the Rubicon, as we will discuss, their rivalry became open hostility. It was, perhaps, only natural that they should become enemies. In his middle years, Pompey, as we have noted, had married Cæsar's daughter, and Cæsar's second wife was a Pompeia. But when they were younger, and each man was more committed to the politics of his own faction, Pompey had married Sulla's daughter-in-law, while Cæsar married the daughter of Cinna, who had almost joined Marius in leading the popular faction. Given these connections in their early lives, it is not surprising that Pompey and Cæsar would become adversaries, and that their joining forces with a third member in a triumvirate was a shallow compromise, designed only to buy them time.

Now, as Consul, Cæsar openly mocked the Senate and the aristocratic partner assigned to him, Bibulus, who will appear again in his account of the civil war. Throughout his year in office, he seemed to govern almost solely, wielding immense power. The Senate was compelled to follow his lead, and during this period, Pompey stood by him as an ally. We know that once prætors and consuls completed their terms within the city, they were granted authority over the Republic's major provinces, where they governed as proprætors and proconsuls. After serving as Prætor, Cæsar spent a year in southern Spain, the province allotted to him, returning victorious—though he chose not to claim his Triumph. Following his consulship, he was assigned the joint provinces of Cisalpine Gaul and Illyricum, not for the typical one-year term but for five years; Transalpine Gaul was also added to his command. This appointment gave him control over Northern Italy, Illyria to the east, and across the Alps to the west, over the Roman-established province in southern France. The Transalpine Gaul province, bordered to the north by Lake Geneva and the Swiss mountains, stretched south to the Mediterranean and westward halfway across the neck of land connecting Spain to continental Europe. This region was already under Roman control, and it was now Cæsar's responsibility to protect it and defend Rome itself from the fierce Gauls. To achieve this, he gathered his legions in the area we now recognize as northern Italy.

It seems there was no original intent for Cæsar to conquer all of Gaul. Up until then, Rome had viewed the Gauls with fear, having suffered from their incursions in the past. In earlier times, the Gauls had even invaded Rome, leaving only when they were paid a ransom. They had spread through Northern Italy, which became known as Cisalpine Gaul once conquered by Rome. Over the century before Cæsar's campaigns, Rome gradually extended its influence across southern France, with Marseilles, or Massilia—a colony of Greek merchants allied with Rome—serving as the focal point. Readers of history know well where alliances with Rome typically led. The Greek colony became a Roman town, and the province expanded around it. As the governor of Transalpine Gaul, it was Cæsar's duty to protect the region from marauding Gauls. His first Commentary recounts how he took on this responsibility.

During the fourth year of his term, while Pompey and Crassus, his partners in the triumvirate, were consuls, his command over these three provinces was extended for an additional five years. However, he would not complete the full ten years in this arena. Julia, his daughter, had passed away, creating a rift between him and his powerful ally, Pompey. The Senate demanded his recall, and Pompey, though hesitant, agreed. At the Senate's order, Cæsar released part of his army, which was sent back to Italy and soon came under Pompey's control. At that point, Cæsar decided that the Italian side of the Alps was the better place to be. The territory known as Cisalpine Gaul, just across the Rubicon, needed his attention, making it a strategic base. His second Commentary, De Bello Civili, in three books, covers the events and experiences of the civil war and documents his actions and outcomes in the years 49 and 48 B.C. His career as a general continues in three more Commentaries written by others, which, while significant, fall outside the main scope of this account and will be briefly noted. This period was followed by one final year of supreme power, marked by triumphs, achievements, and notable, if short-lived, governance. Then came his end, famously and frequently recounted, when he was struck down by allies and adversaries alike at the base of Pompey's statue in the Capitol.

It's important to add a few words about the nature of Cæsar's writings, as the purpose here is to give some insight into them for readers who may not have the chance to read the works themselves. This volume is not meant to tell the full story of Cæsar's life, as that would be to cover the history of the world as it was in his time. The term that Cæsar chose for his work—"Commentary"—has become so associated with him that anyone using it now might seem to be referring directly to Cæsar himself. In Cæsar's sense, "Commentary" essentially means a memoir. Without Cæsar's use of the term, the word "Commentary" would typically mean an addition from a critic rather than an original work by an author. Cæsar's Commentaries are personal memoirs, written by him about his campaigns, where he refers to himself in the third person, telling his story as though a scribe or secretary traveling with him were recording it. Given this, we naturally wonder if perhaps a scribe or secretary may indeed have written these accounts. There is a compelling reason to consider this: the sheer amount of work Cæsar undertook—not only in his military campaigns but also in his political life—would have been overwhelming without adding the effort required to write detailed memoirs. He was probably the most burdened man of his time, as the idea of "division of labor" was far less practiced in large matters then than it is now.

Cæsar was far more than a general. He was also an engineer, an astronomer, an orator, a poet, and a high priest. In that last role, though a non-believer in the gods of Olympus, he still had to understand the intricacies of the Roman religious system. Politically, he was constantly engaged with opposition—yet without any relief from the intense workload it brought. We've had our own examples of busy statesmen who were also writers: two prime ministers translated Homer, another wrote novels, and yet another made a name as a historian, dramatist, and biographer. But none of these men led armies while managing Parliament, nor did they face the unending demand of Cæsar's political life, where opposition rarely allowed time for rest or reflection. From the beginning of the Gallic War until his death, Cæsar was in active combat every year but one, and his successes were achieved only through his personal leadership. In the pages that follow, the reader will see that with one notable exception—the siege of Marseilles—no major achievement happened in his absence. Cæsar had to build his army himself, as well as command it. Each legion had to be raised by him, drawn together by the strength of his name and his leadership.

The extraordinary rewards necessary to inspire his soldiers to remarkable bravery and effort were handed out as if from his own resources. He was responsible for every aspect of his soldiers' tasks, and at the same time, he had to navigate the political dangers back in Rome. This required not only managing his rivals but, even more challenging, keeping his allies under control to prevent political disaster. With so many demands, could Cæsar actually have written his own Commentaries? It's likely that he gathered a great deal of material, with the help of his secretaries, which was known as the Ephemerides of Cæsar—notes or records kept daily. Could it be that the Commentaries bearing his name were crafted from these notes by a skilled and knowledgeable secretary?

These notes have stirred up considerable debate among editors and scholars. One German scholar, passionately asserting that Cæsar never wrote any Ephemerides, grudgingly concedes that someone must have recorded certain details—like distances traveled, elevations of mountains, the sizes of rivers, and the counts of prisoners and slaves. "Not even I," he says, "not even I believe that Cæsar could have kept all these figures in his head." He then goes on to argue that any scribe could have taken down such notes, and that it seems improbable Cæsar would have had time to make meticulous records while actively engaged in the field. Although the critic's indignation is somewhat amusing, his logic is sound. It's likely that these notes were compiled by Cæsar's secretaries under his close supervision; yet there is ample evidence that the Commentaries themselves are Cæsar's own writing.

The Commentaries seem to have been known to the educated Romans of the time almost immediately. Cicero, who was perhaps the most learned and certainly the most discerning critic of his day, discusses them without any question as to their authorship. It was clearly recognized that Cæsar wrote the first seven books of the Gallic War himself, whereas the eighth book was completed by another. This point alone appears to settle the matter. Moreover, there is internal evidence within the works themselves. Although Cæsar carefully maintains a third-person narrative throughout, he slips into the first person three or four times, momentarily forgetting himself. No ghostwriter, tasked with writing for Cæsar, would likely have done this. There are also personal touches in the way he tells certain details—such as his references to "young" Crassus and "young" Brutus—small nuances that a scribe would not have likely included. He also subtly conveys his pride when receiving a legion from Pompey as a token of friendship, followed by his intense dismay when the Senate requisitions that legion and another one, which Pompey then turns against him. These elements lend authenticity to the Commentaries, but they are hardly necessary; the confidence of Cæsar's contemporaries alone is convincing enough.

It appears the Commentaries were written in parallel with the campaigns, with each book likely published soon after completion. If this were not the case, it would be hard to explain why Cæsar began his Civil War commentary before completing the account of the Gallic War. The pressing demands of the civil conflict likely prevented him from finishing the last two books of the Gallic War, so he entrusted this task to his friend Hirtius, who summarized those two years in a single book. Additionally, Cæsar's descriptions of individuals who were once his allies but later turned adversaries suggest that his first Commentary was already completed and published before he started on the next one. For example, Labienus, once Cæsar's most trusted lieutenant during the Gallic campaigns, defected to Pompey's side during the civil conflict. If Labienus had joined Pompey while the first Commentary was still in progress, Cæsar almost certainly would have referred to his betrayal within that work.

The style Cæsar employed was quickly acknowledged by the foremost literary critic of his time as perfectly suited to its purpose. It's clear that Cæsar wasn't aiming for literary acclaim but was focused on delivering a vivid, concise, and understandable account of his actions. He sought a style that would capture the reader's attention through clear and effective narration. Cicero, the great critic, commented on the Commentaries, saying, "Valde quidam, inquam, probandos; nudi enim sunt, recti, et venusti, omni ornatu orationis, tanquam veste, detracto." This passage is simple to grasp in Latin, though not easily translated into English. It means something like, "I consider them very commendable; they are plain, direct, and graceful, with all the decorative flourishes of rhetoric stripped away, like a garment removed." This remark was made by Cicero while Cæsar was still alive, as indicated by the context. Cicero's praise isn't to imply that Cæsar's writings are rough or lacking elegance; the word venusti (graceful) makes this clear. In another instance, Cicero notes that Cæsar spoke with a refinement and precision of language that surpassed nearly all other speakers of his day. Given that Roman orations were often carefully composed in writing, it stands to reason that Cæsar's written style would reflect his spoken elegance.

Montaigne, for his part, held Cæsar in great admiration, saying, "I read this author with a respect that surpasses what I'd normally grant human writings, sometimes contemplating him in his own person, through his astonishing deeds, and sometimes admiring the pure, inimitable polish of his language and style, by which he outshines all other historians, as Cicero acknowledges, and perhaps even rivals Cicero himself." Montaigne, however, stretches Cicero's words a bit too far; Cicero never went so far as to claim that Cæsar surpassed him.

But Montaigne's fondness for Cæsar is evident, and he often speaks of him with great enthusiasm and reverence.

For us, who tend to clarify our ideas by using many words and rarely prioritize brevity in writing, Cæsar's tightly condensed style can initially be challenging to grasp. Reading his work demands a slow, deliberate approach until one becomes accustomed to his way of packing meaning into brief phrases. After this, though, speed reading is still not advisable. Often, he conveys what would, in English, require three or four sentences, through a single phrase with two or three adjectives or, more likely, participles. Capturing Cæsar's full meaning in English often requires three times the number of words he used. This characteristic isn't unique to Cæsar but extends to many, if not most, Latin authors—owing to the Roman penchant for conciseness, while ours leans toward expansion. However, with Cæsar, though every word is weighty, sentences themselves are often long, which soon makes it clear to the reader that skipping is impossible and rapid reading is counterproductive.

What will likely stand out most to the typical English reader in Cæsar's narrative is the sheer cruelty of the Romans—a cruelty that Cæsar himself exhibits to a shocking degree, without any sign of regret. Despite this, he gained and retained a reputation for clemency that has lasted even to this day. Assessing Cæsar's character solely on his own actions, without considering those of his contemporaries, it's hard to avoid the conclusion that he was exceedingly ruthless. He never killed for the pleasure of it, but he also didn't spare anyone out of compassion. Everything he did was calculated for political purposes; when his strategies required it, he could order widespread killing without hesitation, and seemingly without remorse, regardless of the victims' numbers, gender, age, innocence, or defenselessness. Our only explanation for this is that he was Roman, and that Romans as a whole were indifferent to human life. In their culture, suicide was a common response to unavoidable misfortune, and it followed naturally that people who could easily dismiss their own lives would also be untroubled by ending the lives of others.

Nearly all the figures mentioned in these pages met violent deaths. Cæsar and Pompey, the two most prominent, were murdered. Dumnorix, the Æduan leader, was killed on Cæsar's orders. Vercingetorix, the courageous Gallic chieftain, was kept alive only to be executed as part of Cæsar's Triumph. Ariovistus, the German, managed to escape from Cæsar, but he soon met his end, reportedly at Roman hands. The fate of the fugitive Ambiorix remains unknown, but his fellow king, Cativolcus, poisoned himself with yew-tree sap. Crassus, who had joined with Cæsar and Pompey in the first triumvirate, was killed by the Parthians. Young Crassus, an officer serving Cæsar in Gaul, chose to be slain by his own soldiers to avoid capture by the Parthians; his head was cut off and sent to his father. Labienus perished at the Battle of Munda during the final civil war in Spain. Quintus Cicero, one of Cæsar's officers, his brother the orator, and his nephew all perished in the purges of the second triumvirate.

Other fates were equally grim: Titurius and Cotta, with their army, were slaughtered by Ambiorix. Afranius was killed by Cæsar's troops after the last battle in Africa. Petreius died in a brutal contest with King Juba. While Varro lived to an old age and wrote many books, Domitius, who defended Marseilles for Pompey, was killed in the aftermath of Pharsalia. Trebonius, who led the assault on Marseilles by land, was later killed by Cicero's son-in-law at Smyrna. Decimus Brutus, who attacked Marseilles by sea, was beheaded by Camillus, who sent it to Antony as a gift. Curio, leading forces on Cæsar's behalf in Africa, charged into enemy swords and was cut down. King Juba, who defeated Curio, had a slave kill him when he failed to take his own life. Attius Varus, who had held the province of Africa for Pompey, fell later at Munda.

Marc Antony, Cæsar's leading general during the Pharsalian campaign, committed suicide. Cassius Longinus, another of Cæsar's officers, drowned. Scipio, Pompey's ally at Pharsalia, ended his own life in Africa. Bibulus, his chief admiral, wasted away and died. Young Ptolemy, to whom Pompey fled, drowned in the Nile. His sister, Cleopatra's, tragic end is well known. Pharnaces, who opposed Cæsar in Asia, was killed in battle. Cato died by his own hand in Utica. Pompey's eldest son, Cnæus, was captured and killed in Spain. Sextus, the younger son, was killed years later by a soldier under Antony. Both Brutus and Cassius, the prominent conspirators, committed suicide.

In all these events, scarcely three individuals met their end in fair battle, if even that many. The vast majority died through murder, suicide, or assassination.

The above list is filled with notable figures—primarily warriors, men who knowingly and willingly faced danger to achieve specific goals. The bloody roll call is so extensive, so close to encompassing everyone mentioned, that it almost gives the reader a dark, uneasy sense of humor. But when we turn to the outright slaughter of entire towns, to the calculated destruction of lands so that men and women would be left to starve, to the cold abandonment of the elderly, the young, and the vulnerable so they might die alone on the hillsides, to the brutal mutilation of masses of men, to cities being set aflame in passing, and to thousands drowned as casually as if one were discussing the extermination of pests—the dark humor evaporates, and only a deep sickness in the heart remains. It is then we recall how the coming of Christ changed everything and recognize that, even though terrible acts have been committed since, people today are no longer as they were in Cæsar's time.

Chapter II.

FIRST BOOK OF THE WAR IN GAUL.— CÆSAR DRIVES FIRST THE SWISS AND

THEN THE GERMANS OUT OF GAUL.—
B.C. 58.

In the previous chapter, it was noted that Cæsar didn't appear to have any specific mandate to conquer Gaul when he first took charge of his three provinces. The people of Rome still harbored a fear of the Gauls, and his responsibility was to ensure that they did not cross the Alps into Roman territory. He was also tasked with defending against invasions and preventing rebellion in that part of Gaul already established as a Roman province, though the local sympathies leaned more toward their former allies than their new rulers. History shows us that once a powerful empire begins to protect what it already possesses, it often extends its hold over more, until it controls everything in reach. This is how the British Empire expanded in India. It's how Spain established dominion over America. It's how the United States continues to expand its influence. And it's how Prussia, as we recall, recently took Nassau, Hanover, Holstein, and Hesse, all under the pretext of self-preservation. It's the same as when the wolf claimed the whole river, claiming it couldn't tolerate the nearby lamb. The compassionate reader of history may curse the ruthless, all-consuming, greedy wolf. But the reflective reader understands that, in this way— and no other—civilization reaches distant lands. The wolf, however ravenous, brings energy and knowledge along with him.

We don't have any clear insight into what Cæsar's ambitions were regarding Gaul when he was first assigned to govern the provinces. However, we might guess—and, indeed, we feel certain—that he had a plan in mind that was far more significant to him than merely adding new territory to the Republic, no matter how vast Gaul might be. Cæsar had seen enough of Roman politics to understand that true power in Rome lay in the control of legions. Both Marius and Sulla had asserted themselves in Rome with armies they had raised as esteemed generals of the Republic. Pompey, too, had led a successful army in the East, and there had been an expectation that he would use his forces similarly.

Yet Pompey, whether out of nobility, indecision, or poor judgment—depending on one's perspective—chose to disband his legions when he returned to Italy. As a result, he was left, at the very time Cæsar was planning his future course, to seek influence within Rome through an alliance with Cæsar, his natural adversary, and Crassus. Seeing this, understanding the paths to power taken by Marius and Sulla, and witnessing Pompey's diminished influence, Cæsar surely resolved that, regardless of the wars he would fight, he would keep a loyal and trained army at his command. So, when he first encountered a reason for conflict, he was already prepared. Not long into his term as proconsul, a wayward lamb came to drink from his stream.

As he describes his conquest of one tribe after another across the land he calls Gallia, Cæsar shares almost nothing personal about himself. He keeps silent on his political ambitions, his vision for Rome, and even his activities in Italy during those winter months he spent on the Roman side of the Alps, while his army wintered under the command of his lieutenants. He writes solely about the campaigns, and although he occasionally mentions the dignity of the Republic, he rarely pauses in his account to reveal the motivations that drive him. In these seven commentaries on his seven years of warfare in Gaul, only once does he refer to a personal motive. After defeating a fourth of the migrating Swiss—the first military victory he won in Gaul—he notes that he had avenged both an offense to the Republic and a personal injury. The tribe he defeated had once killed the grandfather of his father-in-law in a previous conflict.

It's also worth noting that he generally avoids speaking in the first person. When he does, it's in minor passages where the personal tone feels unintentional and insignificant. Instead of saying "I" or "me," he refers to himself simply as "Cæsar," as if the writer of the Commentary is somehow separate from the Cæsar he writes about. He sometimes speaks highly of his own actions, but in doing so, he uses a tone devoid of both humility and pride. Even when he praises his own achievements, there's no sense of boasting—he recounts his accomplishments in the same straightforward way he talks about the deeds of his generals and soldiers. He mentions without hesitation that, at the close of certain campaigns, Rome declared "supplications"— public festivals and ceremonies of thanksgiving for his victories— lasting fifteen or twenty days upon hearing news of his triumphs.

When it comes to the challenges he faced in Rome, the political obstacles that arose in his absence, he leaves us in the dark. Yet these struggles must have weighed heavily on him. Other sources tell us that his actions in Gaul were hotly criticized in Rome, where he was accused of brutal aggression against states believed to be friendly to the Republic. At one point, it was even suggested that he should be handed over to his enemies as punishment for his alleged treachery. Had the Senate decided to act on such a proposal, it's unlikely they could have enforced it. It was far easier to grant him a "supplication" lasting twenty days than it would have been to halt his momentum once his legions had come to know him.

Cæsar rarely discusses his strategic struggles in detail; however, occasionally, he lets us glimpse the challenges he faced—like when his ships were battered on the British coast, or when he had crushed the Gauls so severely that they united against him under Vercingetorix. Yet, his approach is to simply state his intentions, describe his actions, and report the final outcome—all with the fewest words possible. If a reader were to examine both Cæsar's seven books on the Gallic War and the first four volumes of Mr. Kinglake's 'Invasion of the Crimea,' they would find two excellent examples of precise word usage: Cæsar's narrative is remarkably concise, while Kinglake's is almost exhaustively detailed. And yet, each narrative is equally clear, both skillfully arranged to make the reader appreciate the mastery behind the storytelling.

Cæsar is generous with praise—whether for his lieutenants, his soldiers, or occasionally even his enemies. His enthusiasm shines through, though often in just a single word or a carefully placed epithet within a sentence designed for an entirely different purpose. He's sparing with blame; so much so that it seems he viewed some flaws, even those involving trustworthiness or bravery—or wisdom—as natural human weaknesses, and thus excusable because of that necessity. He describes the complete destruction of a legion due to the failings or possible cowardice of one of his lieutenants without uttering a single harsh word against the man's name. He also recounts how a favored tribe repeatedly broke their word to him without showing anger, simply explaining how he accepted them back as allies—not out of forgiveness, but because it served his purposes. But he can also tell us, without a hint of hesitation, how he wiped out a city with all its women and children so that other cities might learn what would happen if they resisted, refusing to bow down and become subjects under the divine hero in whose hands Providence had placed their fate and wealth.

It seems Cæsar always had confidence in himself. His words are so plain, and his awareness of his own dignity so clear, that he never has to insist he has never been defeated. His very simplicity implies that no campaign he undertakes could ever end in failure. His writing suggests that victory is so assured for him that to question its likelihood would be pointless. He feared no one, and because of this, he commanded the fear of others. He could confront his legions when they refused his call to arms and bring them to obedience with just a word. Lucan, who understood Cæsar's character well, wrote that "he deserved to be feared, for he feared nothing"; "meruitque timeri Nil metuens." He writes of himself as one might expect a god to write, secure that his divine purpose would surely prevail, never needing to question it. With Cæsar, there is always this godlike simplicity that makes his "Veni, vidi, vici" a natural expression of how he views his own approach to action. The same quality comes through in the many brief mentions of the punishments he administered. Cities are left desolate, almost as though by a wave of his hand, though he scarcely bothers to mention that his hand even moved. He tells of one Acco who opposed him, that "Graviore sententiâ pronunciatâ,"—as if there had been some jury to hand down this severe sentence, which in reality came only from Cæsar himself—he sentenced him "more majorum." We learn from other sources that this punishment involved stripping him, binding his neck in a cleft stick, and flogging him to death. After a half-sentence telling us how he forced the accomplices of the tortured chief to flee from their own country, he moves on into Italy with a dignity so imposing that he seems far too grand to linger on these small yet distasteful details. And we feel he truly is grand enough for such restraint.

It has already been mentioned that the great proconsular "wolf" soon learned of a "lamb" coming down to drink from his stream. The Helvetii, or Swiss as we now call them—those tribes living by Lake Leman and scattered throughout the hills and valleys to the north of the lake—had decided that their homeland was lacking. They believed they could greatly improve their lot by leaving their mountainous territory and moving into parts of Gaul, where they might prove stronger than the tribes already there and take hold of the fertile lands. In order to do so, the easiest path out of their own region led down the Rhone, where it now flows through Geneva into France. However, to follow this route, the Swiss would need to cross a portion of the Roman province. Here, indeed, was a case of the "lamb" stirring the waters with a vengeance. Upon hearing that these Swiss planned to "facero iter per Provinciam nostram"—"make their way through our Province"—Cæsar rushed over the Alps into Gaul, arriving in Geneva as quickly as he could.

He opens his first book with a geographical outline of Gaul. Though it may not be perfectly accurate, it provides us with a remarkably clear picture of what Cæsar wanted to convey. When he speaks of Gallia, he refers to the entire territory stretching from where the Rhine empties into the ocean down to the Pyrenees and eastward to the Rhone, the Swiss mountains, and the borders of the Roman province. He then divides this territory into three regions: the Belgians inhabited the northern part, above the Seine and Marne; the Aquitanians held the land south of the Garonne; and the Gauls or Celts occupied the intermediate territory. Having thus set the stage, he plunges at once into condemning the Swiss for their grievous offense in seeking to pass through "our Province."

He has only one legion stationed in Further Gaul—that is, in the Roman province located beyond the Alps from Rome. So, when Swiss ambassadors approach him, asking for permission to cross through the small patch of Roman land and pledging to cause no harm as they pass, he stalls for time. He tells them he can't provide an immediate answer and needs to consider the matter. He instructs them to return on a certain day—by which time he will have gathered more soldiers. Of course, when the day arrives, he refuses their request. The Swiss attempt to cross but quickly abandon the plan in frustration. They find an alternate route to exit their mountainous homeland through the territory of a people called the Sequani, securing permission to do so. However, Cæsar knows how dangerous the Swiss "lambs" could be to him and his "wolves" if they succeed in reaching the back of his province—that Roman territory which left behind the name "Provence" in modern France, until France insisted on unifying into a single nation. Moreover, certain allies of the Roman Republic, called the Ædui, ask him to come and halt the advance of these rough Swiss travelers. Cæsar is always willing to aid the Ædui, though they are a fickle and unreliable people—and, above all, he is eager for war. So he maneuvers to intercept the rear of the Swiss, striking when three parts of the people have crossed the river Arar (Saone) and one portion remains behind. This unfortunate group—since all these people belong to one tribe or mountainous canton—he falls upon and completely destroys. And in this instance, he congratulates himself for avenging the death of his father-in-law's grandfather, slain by this very tribe.

This tale of the Helvetii's attempted migration stands as one of the most extraordinary in history, told by Cæsar without a hint of astonishment. The entire population decided that, because their lands were cramped, their numbers growing, and their spirits high, they would venture out—taking men, women, and children—to seek new homes. We frequently read of large-scale migrations—like those of the

Northmen sweeping south, or Danes and Jutes coming into Britain, or people from Scandinavia crossing the Rhine. We know that it's by this method that many lands came to be populated. But we often imagine such movements as being dominated by warriors, leaving behind homes and families, with the option of returning later. These Swiss wanderers, however, had no intention of returning. Anything they couldn't carry with them, they destroyed, even burning their homes and crops so there would be no chance of turning back.

They do make significant progress, reaching as far as Autun in France—at least three-fourths of them get that far. But it's there that they face Cæsar, who outmaneuvers them on a hill. At this time, Roman power had not fully established its fearsome reputation in the area, so the Swiss almost gain the upper hand. Cæsar acknowledges, as he does only once or twice more in his Commentaries, that the battle was long and the outcome uncertain for much of it. But eventually, the unfortunate Helvetii are routed in a bloody defeat. However, Cæsar is not content to simply see them flee; he forces them back to their original territory—back to their burned homes and ruined fields—fearing that otherwise, certain German tribes might settle there and cause problems. And so, they return—at least, those who survive the ordeal. With careful attention to detail, Cæsar records that 368,000 people embarked on the expedition, but only 110,000, or less than a third, managed to make it home. Among those who perished, countless were sacrificed to honor the shade of his father-in-law's grandfather.

Following this, the Gauls begin to realize just how formidable a man Cæsar truly is. He informs us that no sooner had he concluded the war with the Swiss than nearly every tribe in Gallia sent representatives to congratulate him. In particular, one tribe, the Ædui—whom we hear much about and never quite warm to, given that they are untrustworthy allies, loyal to Cæsar only until they sense he's in difficulty—now come to request a significant favor. Two tribes, the Ædui, whose name has left little trace in modern France, and the Arverni, who are still known in the region of Auvergne, have long been in a struggle for dominance. In response, the Arverni and their allies, the Sequani, have called upon certain German tribes from across the Rhine for support. The Ædui have been on the losing end of this conflict. One of their leaders, Divitiacus, now entreats Cæsar to intervene. Would he be willing to expel these troublesome Germans, retrieve their hostages, free them from oppressive rule, and set things right? Indeed, not only are the Ædui suffering under these Germans and their king, Ariovistus, but the situation has worsened for the Sequani as well, who had invited the Germans in the first place. In fact, Ariovistus has become an unbearable menace to the eastern part of Gaul. Would Cæsar please be so kind as to drive him out?

Cæsar consents, and we are reminded of another fable—the story of the horse who asked the man for help in a fight against a stag, only to find the man mounted on his back and never dismounting. Cæsar wasted no time in taking the reins, and, once in control, had no intention of letting go.

Cæsar then explains his reasoning for accepting this commission. The Roman Senate had often referred to the Ædui as "brothers" and "cousins," and it would be unfitting for men honored in such a way to be dominated by Germans. Moreover, if these marauding Germans weren't stopped, they might develop the habit of crossing the Rhine, eventually encroaching on the Roman Province and even posing a threat to Italy. And Ariovistus was personally so arrogant that this situation needed to be dealt with. So Cæsar sends ambassadors to Ariovistus, inviting the German leader to a meeting. Ariovistus refuses to attend. If he wanted to see Cæsar, he would come to Cæsar; if Cæsar wanted to see him, he was welcome to come to him. Such was Ariovistus's reply. Ambassadors shuttle back and forth between them, and a good deal of argument ensues, in which Ariovistus, surprisingly, presents the stronger logic. Cæsar, with his characteristic simplicity, does not hesitate to let Ariovistus's arguments be fully heard.

Ariovistus reminds Cæsar that the Romans have governed their conquered tribes in their own way without interference from him,

Ariovistus, and that the Germans claim and intend to exercise the same right. He goes on to say that he is quite open to living in peace with the Romans, but asks Cæsar to bear in mind that the Germans are an undefeated people, trained to fight, and used to hardship—as Cæsar might judge by the fact that they had not slept under a roof for fourteen years. Meanwhile, other Gaulish tribes are appealing to Cæsar for help. The Treviri, whose territory corresponds to present-day Trier, are suffering attacks from the fierce, fair-haired Suevi, a people who at the time seem to have dominated what we now know as Prussia on the far side of the Rhine, driven westward by the same desire that has since characterized the region. Additionally, a people called the Harudes, coming from the Danube, are also harassing the Ædui.

Observing all of this, Cæsar realizes that unless he acts swiftly, the northern and southern German forces may join together. He gathers his supplies and advances on Ariovistus with remarkable speed.

In all his campaigns, Cæsar, much like Napoleon would later, achieved everything through swift and decisive action. He doesn't lecture us on the importance of speed in warfare or give lengthy explanations; he simply tells us again and again that he moved his army "magnis itineribus"—by very rapid marches; that he worked tirelessly day and night, and took "magno opere" measures—with much effort and utmost care—to stay ahead of the enemy. In this particular instance, Ariovistus is attempting to reach a town belonging to the Sequani, called Vesontio—known to us now as Besançon, though the name has evolved significantly. This town sat atop a hill, a natural fortress nearly encircled by a river that served as a natural moat. Cæsar notes that nothing is more advantageous in war than possessing such a naturally strong position. So he rushes forward, outpaces Ariovistus, and occupies the town.

At this point, the reader begins to sense that Cæsar is destined for almost supernatural success. We know this in advance, and expect nothing worse for him than narrow escapes. But, at that time, the Romans themselves didn't share the same confidence in him. While stationed at Vesontio, Cæsar receives news that his soldiers are terrified of the Germans. And understandably so. Though Roman soldiers had become hardened by the art of war and trained through conquests in the East, the Punic wars, and battles with surrounding nations, they were still, even up to this point, quite fearful of the Gauls. Ever since the days of Brennus, the invasion of the Gauls into Italy had struck terror into Roman hearts. The Germans, however, were even more frightening than the Gauls. Ariovistus's claim that his men had not slept under a roof for fourteen years was not merely boastful or empty; it reflected their raw, untamed nature. These Germans were a terrifying, rough, yellow-haired people whose fierce gaze was unsettling to Italians.

The soldiers were so overwhelmed with fear that they were "sometimes unable to hold back even their tears"—"neque interdum lacrimas tenere poterant." When we consider what these men later became under Cæsar's command, their initial tearful dread of the Germans seems almost humorous. And it reminds us that Italians, then as now, were generally more open with their emotions, in contrast with the reserved demeanor expected in northern countries. It's hard to imagine soldiers crying out of sheer fear. Cæsar's centurions inform him that the anxiety is so intense that the troops might outright refuse to take up arms when ordered to fight. Cæsar then addresses his officers in a speech full of bravado, full of scorn, and likely embellished with a good deal of untruth, though he uses truth whenever it serves him. Cæsar was renowned for his gift of persuasion. His words could flow "sweeter than honey" or cut "sharper than steel," just as Nestor's did. In any case, if others wouldn't follow him, he could count on his tenth legion to stand with him. He would go forth with that one legion of loyal soldiers if need be.

Though he had been commanding his forces for only a short time, Cæsar already had his elite troops, his guards, his beloved tenth legion. He knew well how to harness their strength and valor to inspire similar qualities in others.

Then Ariovistus sends ambassadors, stating that he is now willing to meet with Cæsar. He proposes a meeting on a certain plain, with each bringing only his cavalry guard, pointing out that foot-soldiers could be risky—aware, of course, that Cæsar's foot-soldiers would be Roman, while his own cavalry were Gauls. Cæsar agrees, but cleverly has men from his tenth legion mount the horses of his less-trusted allies. The accounts of these meetings, and the arguments given on each side, are quite fascinating. While we must remember that Cæsar is narrating both sides of the story, it feels as though he aims to tell it fairly. Ariovistus has little response to Cæsar's demands but speaks at length about his own accomplishments. The meeting is broken up, however, when the Germans launch an attack on Cæsar's mounted guard, and Cæsar withdraws—not before he has, however, expressed to Ariovistus Rome's grand principle of protecting her allies.

Ariovistus then suggests another meeting, but Cæsar declines to attend personally, instead sending some ambassadors. Immediately, Ariovistus captures these ambassadors and throws them into chains, leaving no option now but battle.

Due to space, the details of all these battles can't be fully covered here, and nothing particularly unique about this battle demands special focus. Cæsar describes the German tactic where their cavalry and infantry fight together, with the footmen advancing out from the midst of the horsemen and then retreating for cover. Cæsar's own men fight well, and the Germans, despite their fierce looks, are eventually driven in a complete rout back toward the Rhine. Ariovistus manages to escape over the river, saving himself, but has to abandon his two daughters and his two wives. Both wives and one of his daughters are killed, while the other daughter is captured. Cæsar had sent a dear friend as one of the ambassadors to the German leader, and, as we recall, he and his fellow envoy were immediately put in chains. During the German flight, this ambassador is recovered.

Cæsar tells us that this event brought him as much joy as the victory itself—seeing "one of the most honest men of the Province of Gaul," his close friend and guest, freed from enemy hands and safely returned. Fortune did not lessen this joy by inflicting any harm upon the man. Thrice, as the ambassador himself reported, it was decided by lot before his eyes whether he would be burned alive then or be held for a later date. Cæsar's telling of the story makes us appreciate his genuine enthusiasm, and we're glad to hear that the fellow envoy was also rescued.

When the yellow-haired Suevi hear of all this, they immediately halt their advance along the lower Rhine and hurry back to their own lands, suffering some misfortunes on the way. Such is Cæsar's growing reputation that tribes, almost in alliance with him, even dare to challenge the Suevi. Then, in his "Veni, vidi, vici" manner, he informs us that, having wrapped up two wars in a single summer, he can put his troops into winter quarters even earlier than required, allowing him to return to his other Gaul across the Alps—"ad conventus agendos"—to hold some form of session or council for governing his province, and especially to raise more soldiers.

Chapter III.
SECOND BOOK OF THE WAR IN GAUL.— CÆSAR SUBDUES THE BELGIAN TRIBES.— B.C. 57.

The man had now firmly seated himself on the horse's back, but the horse still faced a number of troublesome enemies, against whom the man could be very useful, so the horse was in no hurry to unseat his rider. Could Cæsar kindly go and subdue the Belgian tribes? Cæsar, naturally, finds reasons to comply. The Belgians are conspiring against him, believing that now, with all Gaul "pacified"—as Cæsar describes it—the Roman conqueror will surely turn his sights on them, and so they had best prepare. Cæsar proposes that they would understandably see it as a major grievance for a Roman army to spend the winter so close by. Thus, by this rationale, these Belgian lambs have greatly disturbed the waters, and the wolf must respond. He gathers two more legions, and, as soon as the earth provides enough food for his increased numbers of men and horses, he rushes off to confront these Belgian tribes in Northern Gaul.

One tribe, the Remi, immediately reaches out, insisting that they are not rebellious lambs like the others; they have never disturbed the waters. According to the Remi, all the other Belgians—and some Germans with them—are conspiring together. Even the Suessiones, their closest neighbors, brothers, and cousins, are guilty; but they, the Remi, have steadfastly refused even to approach the stream, acknowledging that it rightfully belongs to the benevolent wolf. Would the wolf kindly take them and all they possess under his protection, allowing them to be the humblest of his friends? We come to detest the Remi as we do the Ædui; but their cleverness spares them from much of the starvation, slaughter, and ruin that the other tribes endure. Among most of these Belgian tribes, we recognize the familiar names of present-day regions. The old land of the Remi is now Rheims, the Suessiones now Soissons. Beauvais is where the Bellovaci lived, Amiens is the former land of the Ambiani, Arras that of the Atrebates, and Treves of the Treviri, as previously noted. The Silva Arduenna, of course, is today's Ardennes Forest.

The campaign starts with an attack by the other Belgians on the Remi, those disloyal traitors who have sided with the Romans. There's a town of theirs called Bibrax, now a small place known as Bievre, where the Remi are besieged by their fellow Belgians. When Bibrax is close to falling—and we can imagine the dire fate that awaited the townspeople—the Remi send word to Cæsar, who is only eight miles away. They inform him that they can't hold out any longer unless he sends help. Waiting for the right moment, Cæsar promptly sends assistance, and the Belgian besiegers fall into utter confusion. They agree to retreat to their respective territories, planning to defend any tribe that Cæsar might next choose to attack. "Thus," Cæsar says, as he concludes this minor episode, "without any risk to us, our soldiers killed as many of them as daylight allowed." Only when the sun set did the killing stop, just as Cæsar had ordered.

There is no real evidence that these Belgians had any intention of attacking the Roman province or even any Roman ally, other than Cæsar's statement that they had all conspired. But regardless of any actual wrongdoing or lack thereof on their part, Cæsar is set on carrying forward his campaign until he completely subdues them. The very next day, he advances on the Suessiones and reaches Noviodunum—now known as Noyons. When the inhabitants witness the power of his war engines, they abandon any thought of resistance and ask for terms. The Bellovaci soon follow suit. Thanks to the recommendations of his allies, the Remi, Cæsar spares one city, and to please the Ædui, he spares the other as well. Yet, he still takes their weapons and demands hostages. From the Bellovaci, known as a strong and influential people, he demands no less than 600 hostages. Through all these campaigns, we can only wonder how Cæsar managed and housed so many hostages. However, it was clearly understood that any town, state, or tribe providing these hostages would face their deaths if they opposed the great conqueror in any way.

Next come the Ambiani, whose forebears of our modern Amiens surrender almost immediately. Then he encounters the Nervii, who live much farther north, near present-day Lille and a considerable part of Flanders. Cæsar had heard astonishing stories about this tribe. Unlike modern-day Belgians, they allowed no traders among them, abstained from wine, and avoided all luxuries, fearing such indulgences might weaken their warrior spirit. Unlike other tribes, they send no ambassadors to Cæsar and resolve to defend their land if possible. They rely solely on infantry in battle and lack any cavalry. To guard against the cavalry of other nations, however, they construct thick artificial hedges, nearly as impenetrable as walls.

When Cæsar faces the Nervii, he commands eight legions, and he explains how he advanced on them in "his usual manner." The Nervii had apparently received incorrect information on this approach, which led them into serious difficulties. Cæsar begins by sending his cavalry ahead, followed by six legions—all foot soldiers. After these, he moves the baggage, supplies, and all equipment required for sieges. Finally, he brings up the rear with the two most recently enrolled legions. It is worth noting here that a legion in Cæsar's day, theoretically, consisted of six thousand heavily armed infantrymen. Each legion was divided into ten cohorts, and each cohort into six centuries or groups of about six hundred men. As with modern regiments, the actual numbers likely varied. Thus, eight full legions would represent an army of approximately 48,000 infantry. Cæsar, however, does not specify the exact count of his forces here or elsewhere.

By his own account, Cæsar found himself forced into battle almost before he realized what was happening. He claims that he had to manage everything himself, all at once—raising the battle standard, giving the signal with the trumpet, recalling the soldiers from their work, summoning back those who had gone a distance for materials to build a rampart, arranging the army, giving the soldiers a short address, and finally giving the battle cry. As for his speech to them, he kept it simple, telling them only to remember their past valor. The enemy was so near and eager for battle that the Romans could barely put on their helmets and pull their shields from their covers. The confusion was so intense that soldiers couldn't reach their own ranks but had to fight wherever they stood, under whatever flag was nearest. With so many challenges—especially the thick, artificial hedges blocking their view—it was impossible for them to fight in any organized fashion, leading to moments of shifting fortune. One is left with the impression that, in this case, Cæsar was caught off guard. At times and in certain places, the Nervii seemed to be gaining the upper hand.

The ninth and tenth legions chased one tribe into a river, where they had to fight them again and drive them out. The eleventh and eighth legions, having already put another tribe to flight, were attacked at the river's edge. The twelfth and seventh legions faced similar difficulties when Boduognatus, the Nervian leader, broke into the very heart of the Roman camp. The confusion was so severe that even the Treviri—considered the bravest cavalrymen in Gaul and fighting on Cæsar's side as allies—fled back home, claiming the Romans had been defeated. However, Cæsar managed to save his army through his own daring. Seeing the dire situation—"rem esse in angusto," as he describes it, meaning the battle was in a tight spot—he grabbed a shield from a common soldier, as he had come without one, and charged into the fray. When the soldiers saw him in the midst of the fight, and realized he was watching their every move, they rallied with renewed strength, and the Nervii's advance was finally stopped.

Readers might wonder how much of this is strictly true. It reads as though it were. We might not fully understand today how one brave man, especially at such a moment, could have such a profound effect, or how Cæsar, in such a large army, could know his soldiers personally enough to call the centurions by name. Yet, the account feels genuine, as though Cæsar, too proud to boast, would not be hindered by any modern restraint from stating the truth of his actions. It's as if the goddess Minerva were recounting a moment when she descended among the Trojans.

The Nervii continued to fight but, inevitably, they were driven back in defeat. According to Cæsar, the tribe was nearly annihilated—so thoroughly that barely a trace of their name remained. We are told that out of six hundred senators, only three survived, and from sixty thousand warriors, barely five hundred were left. Then, Cæsar extended his mercy to the few who remained. He allowed them to return to their homes and even forbade neighboring tribes from disturbing them. There's little doubt that Cæsar came close to defeat in this encounter, and we might guess that the experience taught him a valuable lesson for future campaigns.

But there still remained the Aduatuci to deal with before the summer ended—a group that had aided the Nervii, who had a town of their own and were located in what is now roughly the Namur region.

At first, they put up a little resistance around their town's walls. However, when they saw the frightening siege engines Cæsar had—devices designed to reach them over their very walls—they became alarmed. They watched him construct a massive turret at a distance, laughing at its size, but as he moved it closer, looming above them, threatening them with stones and arrows, they realized they had no defense against such height. In awe, they sent out envoys to plead for mercy. Surely, they reasoned, Cæsar and his Romans must wield powers beyond human. They promised to surrender everything if Cæsar would only be merciful enough to let them keep their arms, explaining that they were constantly at war with neighboring tribes and that without weapons they would be defenseless.

Cæsar responded. As for deserving mercy, they had no claims. How could any tribe merit mercy when it stood against him in war? Yet, as was his usual practice, he would grant them some terms of grace if they surrendered before his battering ram touched their walls. But the idea of keeping their arms was clearly absurd to him. Naturally, they would need to surrender all their weapons. Just as he had done for the Nervii, he would instruct their neighbors not to harm them. They agreed and threw their weapons into the outer ditch of the town—but not quite all. They cunningly kept back a third, hiding these weapons for a later opportunity. When Cæsar entered the town, those who still had arms, along with others without, attempted to flee. A battle ensued; thousands of Aduatuci were killed, while the rest were driven back and subsequently sold into slavery. We can't help but wonder who purchased these captives and what price each man fetched on that day in the Aduatuci's city.

Then, word came to Cæsar through his young lieutenant, Crassus, the son of his fellow triumvir, that the Belgian states, from the Scheldt to the Bay of Biscay, had been brought under the Roman yoke. Even the Germans sent ambassadors to him, so convinced were they that fighting him was useless—such a deep impression this last campaign had left on the minds of the barbarian tribes. But Cæsar was in a hurry;

he had no time for ambassadors now, wishing to get into Italy. They were told they would have to return to him next summer.

Upon hearing of these achievements, Rome decreed a public thanksgiving, lasting fifteen days, in honor of Cæsar's glorious accomplishments.

Chapter IV.

THIRD BOOK OF THE WAR IN GAUL.— CÆSAR SUBDUES THE WESTERN TRIBES OF GAUL.—B.C. 56.

In the opening of the third book, we see that Cæsar was concerned not just with conquering lands but also with securing the benefits that conquest could bring. After his last campaign, when he traveled into Italy, he sent one of his lieutenants, Galba—whose descendant would later become an emperor after Nero—along with the Twelfth Legion, to spend the winter in the upper Rhone Valley. The aim was to open up an easier trade route over the Alps for merchants coming in and out of Northern Italy. This route appears to have been through the Great St. Bernard Pass, and Galba stationed his forces at Martigny, a location many people know today. However, he soon faced a violent attack from the local inhabitants of the valley, who likely didn't appreciate being told how much toll they should charge the passing traders. In the struggle, Galba and his legion were nearly overrun. Yet, when the Romans found themselves nearly out of weapons and provisions, they decided to fight their way out. They did so with such success that they reportedly killed more than ten thousand enemies, while the remaining twenty thousand Swiss warriors fled. Even so, Galba thought it best to leave the area, which proved difficult to sustain during the winter, and he retreated down the valley toward the lake and into the Roman province, setting up winter quarters among the Allobroges, a people south of present-day Lyon. While we don't know if the Allobroges were pleased with his presence, they were considered loyal at that time, though they had caused trouble in the past. Their position made loyalty to Rome almost a necessity. Whether Cæsar's commanders compensated the locals fairly for their food and supplies or simply took what they needed remains unclear. It was Cæsar's practice, however, to have the lands his army occupied support them.

When we think about the number of troops Cæsar took into unfamiliar lands and the boldness he showed in doing so, it's striking how little he says about the difficulties he must have faced. His armies likely needed supplies for as many soldiers as the British and French forces combined in the Crimean War, and unlike them, he couldn't rely on ships to carry everything. We know the road from Balaclava to the heights over Sebastopol was terrible, though short. Cæsar's route, stretching from the base of the Alps in the Roman province to the lands he sought to conquer, would have been no easier and many times longer—almost a hundred miles for each mile that caused so much hardship in the Crimea. However, Cæsar traveled lightly, with few supplies beyond weapons and essential tools, which he likely crafted along the way. His soldiers were given a daily ration of grain and some pay. Before Cæsar's time, legionaries received 100 asses a month—an as being worth less than a penny—but Cæsar doubled it. We can imagine that paying his men was not his main worry, though finding daily grain and forage for so many soldiers and horses must have been a constant challenge. He mentions these difficulties at times, but not with the frustration we associate with the struggles over coffee and supplies in the Crimea. Sometimes he waited for forage to grow, and there were necessary discussions on provisioning, yet he barely speaks of overwhelming obstacles and says nothing at all about rough roads. One advantage Cæsar had over Lord Raglan was that he was his own reporter. His soldiers certainly didn't get coffee, and if their grain wasn't well-prepared, Cæsar had no reporters at hand to broadcast their complaints to the world.

When Galba's affair was settled, and Cæsar, by his own account, believed that all of Gaul was "pacified," or at least brought under control—having subdued the Belgians, driven off the Germans, and slaughtered the Swiss in the Rhone valley—he thought he might take a brief trip into his other province, Illyricum, to see what it was like. Just then, however, he learned of yet another uprising in Gaul! Young Crassus, needing to find winter provisions for the seventh legion he was ordered to lead into Aquitania, had sent his men out to neighboring regions to gather grain. Being a well-trained young general, Crassus had already taken hostages, as was proper, before allowing his soldiers to roam among unknown and potentially hostile barbarians. But despite this precaution, the Veneti—a seafaring people from ancient Brittany, in the same area where we now find the Druid monuments of Carnac and Locmariaker—decided to detain two of his officers, who would later be referred to as ambassadors, though initially Cæsar called them prefects and tribunes. The name of this tribe lives on in the capital of Morbihan, Vannes. These Veneti, who were powerful at sea, saw no reason why they should have to give up their grain to Crassus. When Cæsar heard that his officers, his sacred ambassadors, had been detained, he was filled with both outrage and indignation, and rushed back, probably with only a glimpse of Illyricum.

Cæsar's fury over the detained ambassadors—a sentiment that extended to the Gauls themselves, who soon realized the severity of what they'd done by imprisoning these "legates," a term held sacred and inviolable by all nations—was intense. This anger, he felt, made his resolve even more necessary. It reminds us of the Spanish conquistadors, who issued proclamations (in Spanish) to native people in Venezuela and New Granada, ordering them to obey a faraway king authorized by an even more distant pope, who claimed the authority of an even more distant God. The pain in history often lies in the injustice of the wolf preying on the lamb, yet the belief remains that only through such conquest could the lamb rise above a simple, subjugated life. And Cæsar was serious about his mission.

Cæsar gives a translated summary of his reasoning for this campaign in section ten of the book: "There were challenges in this war, which I have already described"—referring to the Veneti's strong naval power. "Still, there were many reasons urging Cæsar toward this campaign: the wrongs done to those Roman knights who had been detained, the rebellion stirred after a surrender had supposedly been agreed upon" (though there's no indication in the text of any formal surrender, only that Crassus had taken hostages); "the breach of alliance after hostages were given; the conspiracy among so many tribes; and, most importantly, that if this part of the region were left unchecked, others might feel emboldened to do the same." Furthermore, since the Gauls were naturally inclined to revolt and were quick to be stirred into war, and since all men, he noted, are drawn to freedom and hate subjugation, he decided it would be wise to station his army more widely rather than risk a mass conspiracy in Gaul.

Treating Gaul as if it were a grand chessboard, he made plans to secure every area: he would keep the Treviri subdued in their territory (as readers may recall, Treves is far from Brittany). The Belgians needed to be watched, in case they rose up to assist others. The Germans had to be prevented from crossing the Rhine. Cæsar's most trusted general during the Gallic wars, Labienus, was given this responsibility. Crassus was to return to Aquitania and keep the south stable. Titurius Sabinus, who would later meet a tragic end, was sent with three legions, totaling about eighteen thousand men, to the neighboring tribes in Northern Brittany and Normandy. And young Decimus Brutus—whom Cæsar mentions with a fondness reflected in his choice of the word "young," though this Brutus would later play a part in Cæsar's assassination— was given command of the fleet, tasked with defeating these rebellious maritime tribes. Cæsar himself took command of his legions on-site.

All of this was conveyed by Cæsar in fewer words than have been used here to retell it. The reader feels the force of an extraordinary leader whose vision seemed limitless, making any ordinary enemy likely to think, "Surely this is no man, but a god."

Cæsar recounts the powerful effect his presence on the shore had during the battle at sea, even though young Brutus was leading the combat. Describing the action, he states, "What remained of the conflict depended on valor, in which our men were far superior; and this was especially true because the engagement took place so openly within sight of Cæsar and the whole army that no brave act could go unnoticed." The entire hillside and high ground overlooking the sea were crowded with his troops, who were able to watch the battle unfold below, allowing them to witness firsthand the bravery of their comrades.

Of course, Cæsar triumphs over the Veneti and the other seafaring tribes, defeating them even on their own waters. In the end, the Veneti surrender themselves, along with all their possessions, to Cæsar. Wanting to make an example of them and to ensure that the rights of ambassadors would be respected by other "barbarian" tribes in the future, he decided that a particularly harsh punishment was necessary. "Gravius vindicandum statuit," he says—"he resolved that the offense should be punished with exceptional severity." He thus orders the execution of the entire senate and sells the remaining men of the tribe into slavery. The striking brevity and unapologetic forcefulness of this sentence, both in the way he delivered it and in how he recounts it, is as shocking as it is fascinating to read from such a distance in time. "Itaque, omni senatu necato, reliquos sub coronâ vendidit"—"Therefore, having slaughtered the entire senate, he sold the rest of the men with chaplets on their heads," following the Roman custom of marking captives meant for sale with these garlands. We can almost picture him, with a commanding gesture, moving on from the scene. Surely, he appears not merely as a conqueror but as a figure larger than life, almost divine.

His generals were just as successful in their own campaigns. One Gallic leader, Viridovix, based in what is now the Normandy region— perhaps near Avranches or St. Lo—was lured into a trap and defeated along with his army. Meanwhile, in Aquitania, Crassus faced resistance but ultimately forced the region into submission, with the inhabitants relinquishing their arms.

At this point, Cæsar considers that two tribes—the Morini and the Menapii—have yet to submit to him. The Morini lived in the region now known as Boulogne and Calais, while the Menapii were farther away, scattered across the Low Countries, up near the mouths of the Scheldt and the Rhine. These tribes were a challenging group to subdue; they had no permanent towns or structures that could be easily destroyed. Instead, they roamed through dense forests and marshlands, taking refuge in them whenever they faced defeat. By now, summer was almost over, and the journey from Vannes in Brittany to regions as far north as Breda or even Antwerp was no small feat, especially given the vast wilderness of the land and the size of Cæsar's army. Yet he had a few weeks left before winter and was motivated to finally claim that all of Gaul was "pacified." For the moment, though, there was this stubborn northern corner that still defied him: "Omni Galliâ pacatâ, Morini Menapiique supererant"—"all Gaul having been pacified, the Morini and Menapii remained." He also likely started to contemplate that, from the Morini's territory, he could launch the shortest journey to the mysterious land beyond—the island of Britannia.

Seeing an opportunity, Cæsar launches an assault on these evasive tribes. When they retreat into the woods, he orders his men to cut down the forests. Despite felling large stretches of woodland, however, the tribes only retreat further into denser and deeper woods. Bad weather sets in, and his soldiers, accustomed to the warmer climate of Italy, struggle to endure the harsh conditions in their simple tents made of animal hides. Picture these Italian soldiers, unprotected by solid walls or roofs, battling through the raw, damp winters of undrained Flanders, ordered to chop down seemingly endless forests. If a contemporary report like the Times had been available then, instead of Cæsar's Commentaries, we might have heard a lot more about their suffering. Instead, Cæsar simply notes that he was forced to abandon the campaign for that year.

Before leaving, though, he makes sure to leave a lasting mark on the land. He sets fire to all the villages, devastates the fields, and finally withdraws his army to a more hospitable area south of the Seine. There, he places his troops in winter quarters, though probably to the considerable discomfort of the local population who would have to host his soldiers for the season.

Chapter V.

FOURTH BOOK OF THE WAR IN GAUL.— CÆSAR CROSSES THE RHINE, SLAUGHTERS THE GERMANS, AND GOES INTO BRITAIN.—B.C. 55.

In the following year, certain German tribes, including the Usipetes, crossed over the Rhine into Gaul, near where it meets the sea, as Cæsar tells us. He also notes that when he forced these Germans back across the river, it was close to the confluence of the Meuse and the Rhine. Considering the limited information available to Cæsar, it's impressive how accurate his geographical knowledge was regarding the Rhine's flow to the sea and the junction of the Rhine and the Meuse through the Waal. The spot he describes, where the Germans were driven into the river, seems to be close to modern-day Bommel in the Netherlands, where the Waal and Meuse rivers converge at the head of Bommel Island, where Fort St. André now stands or once stood.

The Suevi, those remarkable people of whom he writes, have customs that stand out starkly even by today's standards. Among these Suevi, the men alternate each year between fighting and farming, though they seem to value their cattle more than their crops. They practice a form of communal land ownership, with no private property for their fields. From a young age, Suevi men follow their own will, each living as he pleases. They are tall, strong men, accustomed to a harsh climate, wearing only minimal coverings made of animal skins, even in the cold. They regularly bathe in rivers throughout the year, and they only trade with others to sell the spoils of war. Unconcerned with luxury, they care little for their horses and, when they do ride, prefer to do so without saddles, feeling contempt for men who rely on such "delicate" additions. Wine is foreign to them, and they maintain a strict distance from neighboring tribes, unwilling to live near anyone.

It is these fierce Suevi who have driven other German tribes over the Rhine and into Gaul. Cæsar, upon hearing this, grows deeply concerned. He is keenly aware of his Gaulish allies' weaknesses—how easily they become unsettled, their fondness for rumors, and their tendency toward restlessness. These Germanic tribes have now begun to settle in the lands of the Menapii, the very tribe with whom Cæsar had left some unfinished business in the previous year. With Germans encroaching on Gallic territory, Cæsar realizes that if he allows these newcomers to become comfortable on the Roman side of the river, they could pose serious trouble. Without delay, he sets out to aid the Menapii and put a stop to the German advance.

Naturally, the Germans send ambassadors to negotiate. They explain that they have been forced out of their own lands by their own kin, the Suevi, who, they admit, are stronger than they are. They declare that, in matters of combat, only the Suevi are superior to them—not even the immortal gods could withstand the Suevi. But they insist they are also Germans and are certainly not afraid of the Romans. Yet, in the proposal they present, they show a hint of caution. They ask if Cæsar would permit them to stay where they are or perhaps assign them a different region on the Roman side of the Rhine.

Cæsar responds with an offer of his own: they are welcome to settle among the Ubii, another German tribe living along the Rhine, possibly around where Cologne now stands, or slightly farther north. Some of the Ubii appear to have already been pushed across the Rhine by the

Suevi and have managed to secure a place in the region where Charlemagne would later establish his famous chapel, now known as Aix-la-Chapelle. Here, though they are Germans, they have survived because they successfully defended their ground. The Ubii, too, face trouble with the Suevi, so if these newcomers are willing to go and join the Ubii, Cæsar will see to it that things are arranged fairly for all parties.

The German tribes hesitate but ultimately decide not to relocate, and eventually, they launch an attack on Cæsar's cavalry, achieving some success. In this encounter, there is treachery on both sides—first by the Germans, then by Cæsar—a double deception that later sparked intense criticism against Cæsar in Rome. Because of the deceitful actions in this engagement, some of Cæsar's enemies in the Senate proposed that he should be handed over to the Germans by the Republic itself. But, had such a decree been passed, carrying it out would have been nearly impossible—Cæsar's hold on the army and his influence were far too great.

As expected, the Germans are defeated, and they are driven back toward the river, fleeing into the low, marshy land where the Rhine, Meuse, and Waal intertwine, creating a landscape that was as confusing for armies as for travelers. This may have taken place here in the vast river delta or, perhaps, much farther upstream near Coblentz. The reader may recall the potential location mentioned at the start of this chapter. Cæsar describes the aftermath as if nearly all of the Germans—men, women, and children—were swept away. They had brought their families with them, and when the tide turned against them, the whole group, desperate to escape, fled en masse toward the river. Pursued closely by the Romans, they threw themselves over the banks. Overwhelmed by fear, exhaustion, and the strong currents, they perished in large numbers. The estimated count was 180,000 Germans who were destroyed, while the Roman army emerged from the conflict unharmed to the last man.

Cæsar then decided to cross the Rhine. While it's clear he didn't intend to permanently expand the Republic's control into what he termed Germany, he felt it necessary to show the Germans his strength. The cavalry of the intruding Usipetes had been on the other side of the river foraging, and Cæsar seized the opportunity to demand that the Sigambri, a tribe with whom the cavalry had taken refuge, surrender these horsemen to him. However, the Sigambri refused to comply. The Germans appeared to accept that Cæsar controlled Gaul and could manage it as he wished, but they fiercely opposed his interference beyond the Rhine. Yet, Cæsar, as he often did, managed to maintain allies even among potential foes. Just as he had the support of the Ædui in central Gaul and the Remi in the north, he had the Ubii as his German friends. This tribe, which likely occupied areas on both sides of the Rhine at that time, encouraged him to cross the river and demonstrate his power to intimidate their neighboring rivals. Cæsar agreed to their request. However, crossing the river in boats wouldn't suit either his sense of security or his sense of pride, so he decided that he would build a bridge.

Is there a student in England, or one who has attended any school where Cæsar's writings are taught, who doesn't recall the famous phrase "Tigna bina sesquipedalia"? With these words, Cæsar begins his vivid account of constructing the bridge. Considering the Rhine's width, swift current, and the limited availability of tools and building materials in such a wild and remote region, the construction of this bridge astonishes us. It reveals the brilliance of Cæsar's planning and his remarkable ability to execute ambitious projects. He drove paired piles into the riverbed, positioning them to counter the flow of the river, with each pair slanting against the current. In our time, we might accomplish this as well, but we would rely on coffer-dams, steam-pumps, mechanical rammers, and a team of engineers. Cæsar explains that he designed the supports in such a way that the current's force only served to further stabilize them. In an astounding ten days, the bridge was complete, and the entire army, including the cavalry, was led across.

Cæsar doesn't delve into the hardships involved or mention if any soldiers were lost during the process. This simplicity in his writing is a striking feature of his Commentaries. We're familiar with the construction challenges faced by modern armies, as well as projects that today's armies would find nearly impossible. We can think of the infamous road up from Balaclava, or the railway that was sent from England during another campaign. With all the advantages of modern technology, such feats require an immense amount of time and resources. Yet, for Cæsar, the obstacles seem minimal, barely worthy of mention. He simply built his bridge, crossed with his entire army in ten days, and said nothing of the inevitable difficulties, harsh conditions, or potential casualties involved.

Once the bridge was completed, German ambassadors arrived without delay. From the moment construction began, the Sigambri fled and concealed themselves in the woods. Cæsar responded by burning their villages, destroying their crops, and advancing into Ubii territory. Once there, he reassured the Ubii, solidifying their alliance. News of his approach soon reached the formidable Suevi, who immediately began preparations for large-scale combat. However, Cæsar, noting that he hadn't crossed the Rhine to wage war against the Suevi specifically, decided that he had already achieved enough in terms of demonstrating the might of Rome and intimidating the Germans. After spending eighteen days across the river, he led his troops back and dismantled the bridge, erasing this remarkable feat as efficiently as he had created it.

Then follows a section that stirs mixed feelings in a Briton's heart—feelings of embarrassment over our remote ancestors' supposed insignificance and irritation at what seems like Cæsar's clear misunderstanding of our ancient character. After returning across the Rhine, he found only a few weeks of the fighting season remaining. What better way to spend this leftover time, Cæsar thinks, than to cross the sea and conquer Britannia? This first record of an invasion of our island is mentioned almost as an afterthought, as if Cæsar intended it merely to make productive use of the remaining days of summer. Though the island seems distant and mysterious, Cæsar claims that British warriors had been aiding the Gauls throughout his campaigns. This sense of interference from across the water sparks his interest in a reconnaissance mission.

Before embarking with his army, he sends over a reliable messenger to scope out the coasts and harbors of Britain. This envoy, however, doesn't muster the courage to actually land. He returns to Cæsar with a limited report—essentially a brief summary of what he glimpsed from the safety of his ship. Meanwhile, Cæsar, ever efficient in his planning, assembles a substantial fleet in the region of Boulogne and Calais, mobilizing it for his daring voyage across the Channel. Word of his intended invasion has evidently spread, as he receives messages from Britain—at least according to his account—pledging submission to the Roman Republic. Whether we take this account at face value or not is another question, but it's clear that Cæsar at least implies a slight acknowledgment of Britain's willingness to submit, a hint of respect for the land that even the people of Boulogne and Calais didn't quite receive.

As Cæsar recounts, these Gallic people—known as the Morini—approach him asking for pardon for their past resistance. They come with offers of hostages and excuses, claiming they were misguided by poor counsel. Cæsar graciously extends them some measure of clemency. He admits that he was inclined to accept their submission and move forward, not wishing to let these minor affairs in Gaul interfere with his new purpose. "Nor did he consider that such trifling affairs as these should stand in the way of his expedition to Britain," he explains. One hopes the Boulogne and Calais people still remember and appreciate Cæsar's choice of words—dismissing them as "trifling matters" when his sights were set on Britain.

With ample hostages taken to secure peace on the mainland, Cæsar turns his focus to preparing for the crossing. He organizes his fleet, and they set out around the third watch, roughly around midnight. As often happens on this particular crossing even in modern times, the cavalry detachment faced delays, no doubt made worse by the fact that they were leading horses along with them. Cæsar himself, however, crosses successfully and arrives near the British coast around the fourth hour—roughly eight or nine in the morning. Approaching the white cliffs of Kent, he sees Britons lined up along the heights, braced for his arrival and ready for resistance.

He anchors offshore and waits for his full fleet to assemble, holding his position until around two in the afternoon. The cavalry unit is delayed further and doesn't manage to cross until four days later. Once his forces are in place and he has surveyed the coast, Cæsar gives the command to land. Seizing the right moment and finding an appropriate stretch of shore, he orders his vessels toward the beach and initiates the landing, a historic moment marking the beginning of Rome's encounters with the people of Britain.

Cæsar admits he faced significant challenges in landing his troops on British shores. Knowing the difficulties we face today in making a similar crossing to the Kent coast, even with modern technology, one can appreciate Cæsar's struggle. His large ships, loaded with heavily armed Roman soldiers, could not come in close to shore because of the shallow water. This forced the soldiers to jump overboard, fully equipped, and wade through the waves to reach land—all while battling not only the rough seas but also the fierce Britons waiting to confront them. The British fighters, unencumbered by heavy armor and far more agile, knew the shallows well. They maneuvered easily, attacking from the shore and darting into the surf to hinder the Roman troops. Cæsar observes that his men, unsteady in the water, were less surefooted and less effective in combat than they typically were on dry land—something he explains without surprise.

Cæsar had two types of ships at his disposal: "naves longæ," or long ships, designed for carrying soldiers, and "naves onerariæ," larger ships meant to transport supplies. The long ships were more maneuverable and versatile than the transports, though they were not the dedicated war vessels Romans typically used in naval battles. To gain an advantage, Cæsar brought his long ships broadside to the shore, allowing his men to launch stones and arrows at the Britons, unsettling the defenders and buying time for his troops to make their way onto land.

In a moment of intense bravery, the eagle-bearer of the tenth legion jumped into the sea, shouting to his comrades that he would fulfill his duty and challenging them to follow if they did not wish to see their standard—their sacred eagle—fall into enemy hands. "Jump down, my fellow soldiers," he called, "unless you wish to betray your eagle to the enemy. I, for one, will do my duty to the Republic and to our General!" Inspired by his courage, the rest of the soldiers plunged into the water, leaving the safety of their ships. A fierce battle ensued, with the Britons doing their best to drive the Romans back into the sea. Cæsar describes the clash as sharp and intense—"Pugnatum est ab utrisque acriter," he says, which roughly means "Both sides fought fiercely." Yet, despite the resistance, the Romans pushed forward, and the Britons eventually retreated.

The only thing missing from Cæsar's customary fortune, he notes, was a strong cavalry force to pursue the fleeing Britons and fully secure the island. Considering his short stay, though, this complaint seems a bit exaggerated; Cæsar wasn't planning to remain in Britain for long. Still, he could claim victory: the Britons offered a general surrender and handed over hostages. However, a sudden storm disrupted his plans, damaging his fleet and leaving him unsure if he could even make it back to Gaul. He was further confounded by unusually high tides, which he had not anticipated. Since he had only prepared for a brief incursion rather than a prolonged campaign, he lacked sufficient food supplies and urgently needed to return to the mainland. Observing his difficulties, the Britons regained their courage, believing they could perhaps overpower him. They launched an attack, putting the seventh legion at risk, which had ventured out to forage. Cæsar managed to rescue them, but his damaged fleet was still a major concern.

Realizing the necessity of repairs, Cæsar decided to dismantle some of the most severely damaged ships to use their parts to fix the others. It's astonishing to think of the speed and efficiency with which he managed this, especially given that they had no access to the sort of facilities—dry docks, tools, or even stable work environments—that we rely on for similar repairs today. Despite these challenges, he succeeded in getting his ships seaworthy again. During this time, he also faced another assault from the Britons but was able to repel them, inflicting damage and destroying their resources to quell resistance. Once again, British leaders approached Cæsar to sue for peace, and this time, he demanded twice as many hostages as before. Due to the lateness of the season and the damage to his ships, he arranged for these hostages to be sent to him later in Gaul rather than taking them with him.

With his fleet now repaired, Cæsar prepared for the return journey. Amazingly, only two of his transports went missing, drifting down the coast with about three hundred men aboard. These soldiers soon found themselves threatened by the Morini, who demanded their surrender. But Cæsar quickly dispatched reinforcements, rescuing them from a dangerous predicament. Following this minor skirmish, he continued with his signature tactics—burning villages, destroying fields, and leaving a desolate landscape behind to deter any further defiance.

One can only wonder what might have changed in the world's history if the Britons had seized this opportunity to destroy Cæsar's fleet and end his incursion, leaving not a single Roman ship to carry word back to Gaul. But instead, Cæsar was able to report his "victory" to Rome, securing his desired outcome: a formal public thanksgiving, decreed to last a full twenty days, in recognition of his conquests and achievements.

Chapter VI.

FIFTH BOOK OF THE WAR IN GAUL.— CÆSAR'S SECOND INVASION OF BRITAIN.—THE GAULS RISE AGAINST HIM.—B.C. 54.

Upon his return from Britain, Cæsar, as was his custom, crossed over the Alps to oversee his other provinces and manage affairs in Italy. Yet he was resolved to undertake another expedition to the island. He could not yet claim to have truly "conquered" it, so he left detailed orders with his generals for constructing new ships and repairing the damaged ones. He sent requests to Spain for various supplies and materials to fully equip his fleet. Remarkably, there's never any mention of financial obstacles. Though he received substantial funds from Rome to support his legions, Cæsar made no hesitation in letting the spoils of war fund further military endeavors whenever possible. In fact, Cæsar had started his campaigns heavily in debt; he had borrowed an immense sum—over 830 talents, or about £200,000—from Crassus, Rome's wealthiest man at the time, just to take on his Spanish province. When the wars concluded, however, Cæsar returned to Rome with immense wealth, having collected a considerable fortune. Like Clive in India centuries later, who came across hoards of treasure among the locals, Cæsar likely took his share from the barbarians he defeated— though unlike Clive, Cæsar probably took all he found.

Once he'd secured his ship orders, Cæsar turned his attention to a brief matter in Illyricum, where he managed to raise additional tribute. He notes this winter activity in no more than a dozen lines, showing his preference for brevity when recording the less remarkable episodes. With his affairs quickly handled, he made haste to rejoin his army and fleet. By the time he returned, his instructions had been followed to such precision that he found a fleet of the newly-designed ships awaiting him—these were lighter, faster vessels, each fitted with just one bank of oars. He counted six hundred of these ships and an additional twenty-eight of the larger kind. Cæsar acknowledged the efforts of his soldiers, commending their hard work and efficiency. He promptly ordered his fleet to sail for the Portus Itius, which historians believe lay somewhere between modern Boulogne and Calais, likely near Wissant.

With his second British expedition nearly prepared, Cæsar quickly diverted his attention to a separate matter brewing in the land of the Treveri. Two rival chieftains were locked in a dispute, and Cæsar thought it best to intervene before their quarrel destabilized the region. With four legions and eight hundred cavalry—totaling around 25,000 men—he marched into the Treveri lands. In typical fashion, he resolved their conflict swiftly, in a manner not unlike the clever monkey settling the dispute over the oyster. Satisfied with his intervention, Cæsar wrapped up the affair almost as quickly as he'd begun it, returning to his fleet at the Portus Itius in little more than a page and a half of his account.

Cæsar decides to take five of his legions to Britain along with two thousand mounted Gaulish allies. In total, he has gathered around four thousand horsemen from various parts of Gaul, many of them chieftains and nobles. These allies serve a dual purpose: they will provide additional military support, but their presence also helps ensure that the tribes in Gaul remain loyal while he is absent, as their chieftains are effectively held as hostages. Cæsar divides this cavalry force, taking half with him to Britain and leaving the other half behind with three of his legions under Labienus, stationed in the Boulogne area. This contingent would serve as a base, maintaining provisions and guarding against any disturbances in his absence.

However, a complication arises with Dumnorix, a prominent Æduan chieftain, who was supposed to be one of Cæsar's staunchest allies. Instead, Dumnorix tries to flee with all the Æduan horsemen, apparently unwilling to join the campaign. Cæsar, resolute in his discipline, orders a pursuit, resulting in Dumnorix's capture and death. With this matter resolved, Cæsar is ready for departure. He sets sail with a fleet of over 800 ships at sunset, benefiting from a favorable south-west wind. By noon the next day, he reaches the coast of Britain, but the cliffs are deserted, with no Britons in sight. He suspects that the sheer number of his ships has intimidated the locals into hiding. Wasting no time, he establishes a secure camp near the shore.

That very night, Cæsar advances roughly twelve miles inland—about eleven Roman miles, as their measurements were slightly shorter than ours today. There, he encounters the Britons, who have gathered their forces for resistance. A skirmish ensues, after which Cæsar returns to fortify his camp on the coast. Shortly thereafter, a fierce storm hits, wreaking havoc on his fleet despite his efforts to secure them in a sheltered spot. The tempest tears the ships from their anchors, tossing them onto the shore and smashing them against one another. The damage is extensive, forcing Cæsar to send a message to Labienus, instructing him to construct additional ships to replace the wrecked ones.

Determined to salvage what's left, Cæsar orders his men to haul the damaged ships onto land, closer to the camp. This task is grueling, requiring around ten days of continuous labor, day and night. His soldiers endure incredible strain to complete the task, but with the fleet finally secured, Cæsar advances once more into the heart of Britain to confront the assembled tribes.

At this point, the Britons, who had often been at odds with one another, have united under a single leader: Cassivellaunus, a powerful chieftain from across the Thames, likely in what we now know as Middlesex or Hertfordshire. The internal conflicts of Britain have been set aside temporarily, as the tribes rally together to resist the Roman invasion under Cassivellaunus's command.

Cæsar's description of the island and its people is fascinating. He notes that the interior is inhabited by "aborigines" or native Britons, while the coastal areas are dominated by immigrants from Belgium, who have retained the names of their continental tribes. The population is dense, with houses that are numerous and closely grouped, much like those in Gaul. The Britons possess an abundance of cattle and use currency, either in the form of copper coins or iron rings, which are quite heavy. Tin, he observes, is plentiful in the center of the island, while iron is only found near the coast and in limited quantities. Brass is an imported metal. Their timber is similar to that in Gaul, except that Britain lacks beech and fir trees.

Interestingly, he notes cultural practices that strike him as peculiar. The Britons keep hares, chickens, and geese not for food but as pets, believing it wrong to eat them. The climate is milder than in Gaul, and Cæsar provides a rough description of the island's shape, which he describes as a triangle. He estimates the southern side (the Kentish coast) to be 500 miles long, overshooting the real distance by about 150 miles. His geographical knowledge becomes a bit less precise when describing the western side, which he suggests is oriented toward Spain and where Ireland lies. He speculates that Ireland is roughly half the size of Britain and situated about the same distance from Britain as Britain is from Gaul. He also mentions an island named Mona (likely the Isle of Man) and suggests the existence of other islands where, he claims, thirty days of continuous darkness occur at midwinter—a notion that veers into myth.

Moving on to describe the British people, he praises the men of Kent as the most "civilised" among the Britons, stating they are nearly as advanced as the Gauls. Those further inland, however, lead simpler lives, subsisting on milk and meat rather than corn, and they wear garments made of animal skins. They stain their skin with woad, which gives them a blue tint, and sport long hair, though they shave everything but the head and upper lip. A rather shocking detail is that it's customary for groups of ten or twelve men to share wives. Cæsar's observations, colored by Roman attitudes, provide an intriguing glimpse into what he perceived as both the peculiarities and barbarism of the Britons.

In his detailed account, Cæsar provides a fascinating and even somewhat admiring description of the impressive skill and agility with which the ancient Britons maneuvered their war chariots in battle. "This," he explains, "is the nature of their chariot-fighting." He tells us that they begin by speeding across the battlefield "per omnes partes"— in all directions—causing confusion in their enemies' ranks through the sheer terror induced by the powerful sight of their horses and the thunderous clatter of the chariot wheels. As they race forward, they skillfully hurl darts, disrupting and disordering the enemy ranks by both the weapons and the intensity of their approach. Once they have created an opening, these Britons leap from the chariots, abandoning their initial positions, and join the fight on foot, facing their enemies as infantry soldiers.

The charioteers, meanwhile, maintain a clever strategy: they drive just far enough away from the active battle to stay clear of immediate danger but remain close enough to provide rapid support when needed. The chariots are positioned in such a way that, if their comrades on foot are overwhelmed, they can quickly and efficiently rejoin the fray to either support a retreat or bolster an offensive. In this way, the Britons ingeniously combine "the speed of cavalry" with "the endurance and stability of infantry." Their continual practice has made them extremely adept at managing this dual approach, so much so that they can keep their highly energized horses steady even on rugged, sloped, or otherwise treacherous terrain. The Britons' skill extends to remarkable feats, such as maneuvering the horses at a full gallop, running along the chariot pole, balancing on the yoke that binds the horses, and then, as swiftly as they departed, leaping back into the chariot—all while in motion. "All of which is very wonderful," Cæsar remarks, highlighting his genuine amazement at their skill and technique.

Naturally, there is a considerable amount of fighting throughout this campaign. As Cæsar's legions make headway, the Britons, gradually becoming familiar with the Romans' strategies, adapt their tactics, avoiding large-scale confrontations in favor of smaller, guerrilla-style skirmishes. This shift to more evasive and sporadic attacks slows Cæsar's progress, yet he presses onward, making his way deeper into the heart of Britain and reaching the banks of the Thames. Here he encounters yet another significant challenge: crossing the river. The passage is treacherous, and Cæsar can only ford the river at one particular spot—and even then, with great difficulty. While he doesn't specify the exact location, historians later speculated that this ford might have been near what we now call Sunbury. The crossing was perilous, with the Roman soldiers nearly submerged, their heads barely above the water, but even in these conditions, their advance was so fierce that the Britons, seeing the determination of the Romans, abandoned their defensive positions on the opposite bank and fled.

Once across, Cæsar soon compels the Britons to yield, leading to a series of unconditional surrenders, hostages taken in his favor, and promises of tribute to Rome. Cassivellaunus, the British leader, recognizing that his position is becoming increasingly precarious, seeks refuge in what he considers a fortified settlement, believed to have been located near the modern site of St. Albans. Cæsar, however, points out that the British concept of a town, or "oppidum," is somewhat rudimentary by Roman standards, consisting simply of an area where they have surrounded dense woods with a ditch and a rampart. Despite this fortification, Cæsar's legions force their way into the stronghold, driving out the Britons and effectively dismantling their defensive position.

With their defenses breached, the Britons have little choice but to surrender once again. Cæsar secures further hostages and reaffirms the demand for tribute. He leaves behind strict orders as he departs, speaking with the authority of one who expects immediate and absolute compliance. Cassivellaunus, the British leader, is now required to relinquish his authority in favor of Mandubratius, whom Cæsar installs as the new ruler of the Trinobantes—the tribe inhabiting what we know today as Middlesex and Hertfordshire. He specifies the annual tribute that the Britons are to send to Rome as a token of their subjugation and, notably, orders that Cassivellaunus must not interfere with Mandubratius's rule.

Once these arrangements are in place, Cæsar prepares to leave Britain. His fleet is insufficient to carry the entire army in one crossing, so he divides his forces, sending half of his soldiers across the Channel and instructing the ships to return for the remaining troops. He observes, almost with a sense of pious gratitude, that although he lost many ships when they were empty, during the return voyage—when they were filled with soldiers—hardly any were damaged.

Cæsar's second expedition to Britain marked the end of his attempts to conquer the island. Though he could claim certain accomplishments—landing twice on British shores, establishing some measure of dominance, and returning his army safely—he was far from subduing Britain as he had done with Gaul. His achievements were by no means the complete victory that Cicero's brother had reported back home with the word "confecta"—implying that Britain was "finished." Indeed, Cæsar's incursions into Britain felt more like probes into an uncharted land than decisive campaigns for conquest. The insurmountable natural barrier posed by the English Channel was an unyielding ally to the Britons, one that made it difficult for the Romans to establish a true foothold. Both landings had been challenging, and Cæsar found his army's very survival often hanging in the balance. In each attempt, the struggle against the channel's treacherous waters was nearly as daunting as the battles against the Britons themselves.

One might conclude that Cæsar's primary motive for invading Britain was to demonstrate his reach rather than to permanently extend Roman control across the channel. His objective may have been more psychological and strategic—showing the Gauls that no land, not even distant islands, was safe from Rome's influence, thus reinforcing his authority. Since Britons had supported the Gauls against him in previous battles, it was crucial for Cæsar to discourage them and anyone else who might think of assisting Rome's enemies. Whether his orders to the British chiefs after his departure were actually obeyed is uncertain. It seems unlikely, however, that the tribute he demanded would be delivered with consistency or enthusiasm. Ultimately, Cæsar returned to Gaul without achieving full subjugation, marking his invasions as symbolic more than substantive.

Upon his return to Gaul in the late summer, Cæsar encountered a significant problem: a severe shortage of provisions due to an unyielding drought that had left the crops in poor condition. To feed his army, he was forced to split his forces and disperse them across various tribes, stationing each legion in a different area. He assigned one legion and a half under his generals L. Titurius Sabinus and L. Aurunculeius Cotta to the Eburones, a tribe living near the Meuse in what is now the region of Liège and Namur. The Eburones were known for their strong resistance to Roman control, and placing his men among such a tenacious people was a calculated risk. Cæsar hoped that dispersing his legions this way would alleviate the strain of food scarcity, though he understood the dangers of dividing his forces in such a contentious land. Taking care to position most of his legions within a hundred miles of each other for mutual support, he stationed one particularly isolated legion in a more subdued region—the territory of the Essui, near modern-day Alençon. But despite this attempt at prudence, the decision to spread his army would soon lead to one of the greatest disasters Cæsar would face in his entire career.

Throughout Cæsar's campaigns in Gaul, the spirit of the Gauls to reclaim their autonomy never wavered. Their longing for freedom from Roman subjugation simmered just beneath the surface, with each tribe harboring a deep resentment toward the occupying force. To the Gauls, Cæsar was nothing short of a monstrous curse—a figure of incomprehensible power whose presence was as inescapable as it was destructive. Though some tribes aligned with him temporarily, he had no true allies among the Gauls. Even the Ædui, who had enjoyed a privileged alliance with Rome, chafed under his authority. Dumnorix, the Æduan chieftain who defected with his horsemen during Cæsar's second invasion of Britain, had resisted fiercely before his death, protesting his right to freedom as a member of a free state. His resistance was a tragic illustration of the Gauls' struggle against Rome's harsh demands. To Cæsar, who wielded authority with "godlike simplicity," this opposition was little more than an inconvenience. He expressed no remorse for the countless lives lost or villages burned under his command, viewing these acts as mere steps in a grand design. His power was exercised with the impassive detachment of a deity who believed such matters inconsequential—a means to an end. If brutality was required to maintain order, he considered it justifiable, his actions calculated for their effect on both the Gauls and his Italian supporters. The display of might was intended to reinforce the invincible image of Rome, making it clear that resistance to Cæsar was futile.

Yet, as the reader witnesses the unyielding spirit of the tribes crushed under Roman might, the narrative evokes a profound empathy for the Gauls. Figures like Dumnorix, asserting his freedom to the last breath, resonate as symbols of defiance. Even tribes like the Carnutes, who were nominally under Cæsar's control, refused to fully submit. When Cæsar installed his own puppet king, Tasgetius, among the Carnutes, they promptly revolted during his absence in Britain and killed Tasgetius, rejecting his rule as an affront to their sovereignty. Now, the Eburones—strongly independent and led by their two kings, Ambiorix and Cativolcus—recognized an opportunity in the scarcity and division of Cæsar's forces. They saw their chance to break free from the grip of Rome and dared to strike at the legion under Titurius and Cotta, igniting a revolt that would soon reveal the vulnerabilities in Cæsar's formidable empire.

Ambiorix, the crafty and cunning chieftain of the Eburones, hatches a plan that reveals his deep understanding of both diplomacy and deception. With smooth words and clever maneuvering, he convinces the Roman generals to meet with him under a flag of peace, where he begins his tale with apparent sincerity. Ambiorix professes admiration and gratitude toward Cæsar, expressing the highest regard for the Roman leader who has shown him kindness in the past. He assures them that he harbors no personal ill will against Cæsar or his soldiers. However, he explains, the situation has escalated beyond his control: an immense force of Germans has crossed the Rhine and is rushing toward the Roman camp with overwhelming numbers. There is no possibility, he says, of the Romans withstanding such a force if they remain where they are; destruction is inevitable.

Ambiorix suggests, with feigned concern, that the best course of action would be for the Romans to abandon their camp and join their allies, either the legion stationed under Quintus Cicero, the orator's brother, among the Nervii to the east, or Labienus's legion on the southern borders, near the Remi and Treviri. As a token of his supposed allegiance to Cæsar, Ambiorix offers to personally guide the Romans safely through Eburone territory, allowing them to escape while they still have the chance. It is an offer he presents as one of goodwill, a gesture of reverence for Cæsar himself. Ambiorix even pleads with Titurius and Cotta to take his advice, pressing them to make a swift decision.

Faced with this proposal, the two generals are divided. Titurius, convinced by Ambiorix's seemingly heartfelt warning, is in favor of taking the advice and evacuating the camp. But Cotta, along with several tribunes and experienced centurions, remains skeptical. He argues that it is foolish to place trust in the words of an enemy and warns against acting without orders from Cæsar. Cotta points out the risk of basing their strategy on the suggestions of a potential adversary and urges that they stand their ground and await further instructions. However, Titurius, undeterred by the caution of his colleague, insists upon immediate action. After heated debate, and likely weary from Titurius's persistence, Cotta reluctantly agrees.

At the break of dawn, the Roman forces, carrying all their baggage and supplies, set out from the camp with an air of misguided confidence, as though they were marching through friendly lands. They assume, in their naïveté, that Ambiorix's offer of safe passage was sincere. Yet no sooner do they leave the relative safety of their encampment than Ambiorix's true intentions reveal themselves. The Eburones had, as expected, prepared a deadly ambush. With the Romans caught off guard, an assault is launched on both their rear and front, throwing the legion into a state of complete disarray and panic.

The battle unfolds in a series of tragic events. Outmaneuvered and overwhelmed, the Roman soldiers are struck down, their formation shattered by the surprise attack. Titurius, in a desperate bid for peace, steps forward to plead for mercy. He is met with a demand to lay down his arms—a request that, to a Roman, represents the ultimate dishonor. Nevertheless, Titurius, consumed by a flicker of hope, complies, casting aside his weapons. But Ambiorix's apparent mercy is merely a ploy. As Titurius stands weaponless and vulnerable, Ambiorix distracts him with a speech, drawing out the moments until, finally, the Roman general is surrounded and mercilessly slain. Cotta, unwilling to surrender, dies fighting, refusing to abandon his men or his honor in the face of overwhelming odds. More than half the soldiers fall in battle; the remainder, horrified and desperate, retreat to the camp under the cover of night.

The survivors, once within the camp's confines, realize the gravity of their predicament. With no hope of rescue and burdened by the shame of their defeat, they decide to end their own lives rather than face the dishonor of capture. In the end, only a handful of soldiers manage to slip away, escaping through the chaos and eventually bringing word of the disaster to the camp of Labienus.

Despite the usual sympathy that the reader might feel toward the Gauls' fight for freedom, the fate of the Roman legion stirs a particular sense of tragedy. One can't help but feel that the ambush was an unnecessary cruelty, and that Titurius, though tragically flawed, should not have led so many men to their deaths. The story is especially poignant when we hear of the gallant eagle-bearer, Petrosidius, who, in the throes of battle, hurls the eagle standard over the camp's fortifications to protect it from capture, and then dies defending it. It is a moment of Roman honor in the midst of a doomed struggle, making us wish, if only for a moment, that Ambiorix's treachery had not met with such success.

However, there is a sense of ominous certainty as well. Knowing Cæsar's relentless determination and his unwavering sense of retribution, one can be sure that Ambiorix's betrayal will not go unpunished for long.

Having achieved such a devastating blow against the Romans, Ambiorix and the Eburones press on, seizing the moment when Cæsar's forces are still scattered and the Romans are grappling with their recent disgrace. It's clear to the Gauls that if they are to prevail against Roman domination, now is the time. Ambiorix, emboldened by his success, leads his forces toward the camp of Quintus Cicero, who is stationed with his legion among the Nervii. The Nervii, fierce opponents of Rome, are eager to join the fight, and together with the Eburones, they lay siege to Cicero's encampment.

The assault is brutal. The Romans, outnumbered and caught off guard, find themselves struggling to hold their defenses. The barbarians unleash red-hot balls of clay and fiery arrows into the camp, igniting fires and creating chaos. Cicero's situation grows more desperate with each passing day. Several attempts to send messengers to Cæsar for reinforcements end in tragedy, as the couriers are intercepted and slain before they can reach him. Hope dwindles among the Romans, who begin to despair of any escape. They know, with a kind of fatalistic certainty, that without Cæsar, their defenses may not hold. The might, the renown, and the very essence of Roman invincibility seem to reside solely in their general. Cicero, though both a courageous and prudent leader, is aware that he and his men are in dire straits. Eventually, he manages to send a Gaulish slave, who cleverly conceals a message in a hollowed-out dart, hoping it will find its way to Cæsar.

In the midst of this tense standoff, Cæsar offers a brief but memorable episode featuring two Roman centurions, Pulfius and Varenus, who are constantly arguing about who is the braver man. When Pulfius, in a fit of bravado, charges out alone against the enemy, Varenus, not to be outdone, follows him into the fray. Pulfius soon finds himself in danger, and Varenus rushes to his rescue, fighting off the attackers. Just as Varenus begins to extricate Pulfius, he too is surrounded by enemies, only to have Pulfius come to his aid in turn. Against all odds, both centurions manage to return to camp, unharmed. It's a rare moment of levity amid the grim reality of war, and it leaves the question of their rivalry unresolved — to this day, no one can say who was truly the better man.

Meanwhile, Cæsar, upon receiving the concealed message, wastes no time. He prepares a relief force and sends word back to Cicero, attaching a reassuring letter to another dart. Though the dart barely reaches Cicero before Cæsar himself arrives, the distant smoke and fires that mark the advancing legions' line of march give the beleaguered Romans the first glimmer of hope. Soon after, Cæsar's forces engage the Gauls. The fighting is fierce, but Cæsar, as always, prevails, rescuing Cicero and his legion from what had seemed an inevitable defeat.

Labienus, stationed on the borders of the Treviri, also faces his own challenges. The Treviri, another tribe with a deep-seated enmity toward Rome, prepare to launch an assault on his position. However, word of Cæsar's victory over the Eburones and Nervii spreads swiftly, instilling fear in the Treviri, who decide to abandon their plans rather than risk a battle against a freshly reinforced Roman force.

Yet, despite these successes, Cæsar is no longer under the illusion that Gaul is pacified. He realizes that, although he has repeatedly claimed to have subdued the region, Gaul as a whole is still seething with resistance, prepared to rise against Roman rule whenever the opportunity arises. It is during this winter that Cæsar comes to an important understanding: the Gauls have no desire to submit quietly to his authority. His presence is unwelcome, and his work in Gaul is far from over. The opposition against him has grown not only in strength but in unity, and the resistance is now so widespread that he decides to remain in Gaul for the winter, foregoing his usual return to Italy.

In the meantime, Labienus takes action against Indutiomarus, the chief of the Treviri, killing him in an effort to quell the unrest in that area. However, even with this victory, Cæsar can only report that Gaul is now "a little quieter" — a small step toward submission, but still far from the subjugation he seeks. The land remains turbulent, with Roman control tenuous at best. These events underscore for Cæsar the monumental challenge he faces in taming the Gaulish spirit.

Notably, it is during this turbulent winter that Cæsar's authority as proconsul is extended for another five years, granting him additional time to realize his ambitions in Gaul and beyond. Though he has achieved much, Cæsar knows that his work is not yet complete. His empire-building efforts will demand even greater resolve, cunning, and strength in the campaigns to come.

Chapter VII.
SIXTH BOOK OF THE WAR IN GAUL.— CÆSAR PURSUES AMBIORIX.—THE MANNERS OF THE GAULS AND OF THE GERMANS ARE CONTRASTED.—B.C. 53.

Cæsar wastes no time in launching the next campaign, even before winter has released its grip. The previous campaign had extended far beyond the usual season, with the cold creeping in while battles still raged across Gaul. The situation had grown increasingly dire: the Gauls were learning the power of unity, and their resistance was more determined than ever. Cæsar had already suffered severe losses—an entire Roman force of likely ten thousand men had been wiped out along with its generals, Titurius Sabinus and Aurunculeius Cotta. Another legion, led by Quintus Cicero, was only saved from the same fate by Cæsar's timely intervention. Labienus's troops had also been engaged in fierce conflict. It seemed as though all of Gaul was preparing for war, and although Cæsar had managed to claim at the end of the last campaign that the region was a little quieter, he understood full well that his work was far from over.

At the start of the new campaign, Cæsar had formidable resources: eight legions, comprising 48,000 soldiers, all recruited from the Italian side of the Alps. Alongside these were substantial contingents of Gaulish cavalry and light infantry, supplementing the core of his army. Yet he had also experienced losses. An entire legion and a half had been obliterated, and further gaps had been made during his campaigns in Britain and in the battles with the Nervii under Cicero. But Cæsar intended to demonstrate to the Gauls that Rome's power would not falter—even after such setbacks. In fact, he would show them that Rome's strength could grow even greater in response to opposition. He would astonish them with a display of Rome's might, aiming to instill a lasting impression on Gaul's people that Rome could rebound swiftly and with even greater force after any defeat. To this end, he not only raised new troops but also borrowed a legion from Pompey, stationed outside Rome's walls.

Cæsar tells us that Pompey lent the legion out of "Friendship and for the Republic." Though Pompey and Cæsar were partners in the Triumvirate, Pompey likely felt he had no real choice. Replenished and reinforced, Cæsar reestablished the annihilated legion, filled the ranks of the others, and, with two new legions, now commanded an army probably numbering as many as 80,000 men.

His first strike was directed at the Nervii—an old and persistent foe, who had come close to defeating Cicero's forces before Christmas and were now conspiring again with various Germanic and Belgic tribes. The reader may remember that, in a previous book, Cæsar claimed to have nearly wiped out the Nervii, leaving hardly a trace of them. But evidently, enough of them survived to threaten the Romans once more. After quelling this latest resistance, Cæsar moved toward Paris, known in his writings as Lutetia Parisiorum—a city that now appears for the first time in recorded history. With the support of his allies, the Ædui and the Remi, he negotiated a peace with the tribes of the central region, including the Senones and the Carnutes.

With this accomplished, Cæsar focused his full attention on Ambiorix. The memory of his lost legion, his fallen generals, and the heavy blow Ambiorix had dealt to Roman pride drove him to a personal vendetta against the chieftain. According to legend, Cæsar vowed not to cut his hair or shave until he had avenged their deaths. However, he knew that before he could punish Ambiorix directly, he would need to deal with his allies. One of these was the Menapii, a tribe that had eluded Cæsar's control in previous campaigns. The Menapii lived along the southern banks of the Meuse near the sea and had yet to send any emissaries to Cæsar to plead for peace. He responded by devastating their villages, seizing their cattle, enslaving their people, and taking hostages, compelling them to forswear any alliance with Ambiorix.

Meanwhile, Labienus, Cæsar's trusted lieutenant, achieved a decisive victory over the powerful Treviri, a prominent tribe in the northeastern region. By skillfully luring the Treviri into a confrontation just before they were to receive reinforcements from the Germans, Labienus effectively crushed their hopes of mounting a successful resistance. The ancient adage, Quem Deus vult perdere prius dementat—"Whom the gods wish to destroy, they first make mad"—seems almost tailor-made for the unfortunate Gauls and Germans, who repeatedly fall into Roman traps. Cæsar provides a memorable recounting of Labienus's speech to his troops, urging them to take advantage of the moment. "Now," Labienus said, "you have your opportunity. You have your enemy thoroughly at a disadvantage. Show now the valour that you have displayed so often before the Imperator, Cæsar. Imagine that he is here, watching you." The respect and reverence with which Labienus invokes Cæsar's name speaks volumes about how Cæsar was regarded by his officers and men. Indeed, Cæsar describes this moment as though it were perfectly natural that Labienus and the soldiers should view him with almost divine reverence.

Through his relentless tactics and remarkable tenacity, Cæsar was determined not only to reclaim any ground lost to the rebellious Gauls but to ensure that Rome's dominance would be unshakable.

After this battle, in which the Treviri are, predictably, thoroughly defeated and slaughtered, Cæsar decides to construct a second bridge over the Rhine, a little upstream from the location where he had previously crossed. He explains that he undertakes this for two main reasons: first, because the Germans had sent aid to the Nervii, and second, because he wants to prevent his formidable enemy, Ambiorix, from finding refuge among the Suevi on the German side of the Rhine. This bridge-building feat also gives him an occasion to share some insights on the distinct customs of Gaul and Germany.

Cæsar observes that, among the Gauls, there are always two factions within each tribe, village, and even family, ensuring that one group can always check the other, preventing either from gaining absolute power. He provides this explanation here to clarify his original choice to ally with the Ædui and intervene against the Germans—especially in driving Ariovistus back across the Rhine. In eastern Gaul, a longstanding rivalry existed between two powerful tribes, the Ædui and the Sequani, each vying for dominance. The Sequani, seeking an advantage, had invited the Germans to assist them, leaving the Ædui in a dire situation. Desperate, the Ædui had appealed to Rome, citing their previous alliance with the Republic. Divitiacus, the high-ranking magistrate of the Ædui and brother of Dumnorix (whom Cæsar later had executed for his defection with the Æduan cavalry before Cæsar's second British invasion), had spent time in Rome and enjoyed influential friendships there, including that of Cicero.

Initially, there had been some debate in Rome about whether to support the Ædui, but Cæsar ultimately decided in their favor, thus setting the course for the confrontations that ensued. As we know, he succeeded in expelling Ariovistus back into Germany, and Ariovistus's family—his wives and daughters—were lost in the process. Thus, Cæsar explains, the Ædui were recognized as the preeminent allies of Rome among the Gauls, while the Remi, who had quickly joined Cæsar's cause when the Belgians rose against him, were given the status of Rome's second most honored allies.

Cæsar delves deeper into the social structure of the Gauls, highlighting that two classes of men are held in particular esteem: the Druids and the knights. This implies that for the Gaulish elite, there are essentially two noble professions—priesthood and the military. Meanwhile, the ordinary populace, he says, lives in a condition barely better than servitude. When burdened by debt, high taxes, or fear of powerful foes, common people often surrender their freedom, willingly entering a form of servitude to gain protection. Among the Gauls, the Druids wield the greatest influence, possessing supreme authority not only in religious matters but in civil life as well. They enforce this power through the dreaded sentence of excommunication, rendering any man who disobeys them an outcast, deprived of all civil rights.

The Druids are led by a single chief Druid who, upon death, is succeeded through a general election among the other Druids—unless one member is so clearly preeminent that no election is necessary. Their most sacred site is in the territory of the Carnutes, located at the heart of Gaul, and their spiritual and disciplinary teachings originate in Britain. Whenever faced with complex issues, they make pilgrimages to Britain to consult with their British counterparts. The Druids are exempt from military service and from paying taxes, a privilege that makes their role highly desirable among the Gauls. However, the path to becoming a Druid is arduous; training can last twenty years, as everything must be committed to memory. All Druidic knowledge is passed down orally, for their laws and doctrines are never to be written. Their core belief is in the transmigration of souls, so that people are taught that death is merely a transition rather than an end, removing much of the fear associated with it. Beyond this, they are esteemed for their knowledge of astronomy, geography, natural science, and, naturally, theology.

Through these explanations, Cæsar offers a fascinating window into Gaulish life, illustrating not only the complex social structure but also the impressive and revered position held by the Druids. Their influence, coupled with the loyalty of the knights and the submission of the general populace, shaped a society that, while diverse in customs, was unified by powerful, controlling forces.

The knights, or nobles of Gaul, according to Cæsar, had no calling or pursuit other than that of war. Before the so-called "benefits" of Roman order and control, they found themselves in a rather unpleasant predicament of perpetual warfare with each other, year upon year, driven by necessity to fight among their own. Of all peoples, Cæsar observes, the Gauls are steeped most deeply in superstition. So fervent is their belief that, in times of great peril or crisis, they frequently resort to human sacrifices, with the Druids, their spiritual leaders, officiating as the grim mediators between man and their fierce gods. These sacrifices are conducted by fire, where victims are burned alive to appease the deities. They have a particular preference for burning criminals—thieves and murderers—believing that the gods take special delight in such tainted offerings. However, when such morally compromised individuals are not available, they will even sacrifice the innocent.

In terms of their gods, Cæsar tells us that the Gauls chiefly worship Mercury, whom they revere as the most clever and versatile of all gods. Beyond Mercury, they also honor Apollo, Mars, Jove, and Minerva, assigning them the familiar attributes recognized by other nations. While Cæsar uses the Roman names for these deities, he doesn't imply that the Gauls themselves used these terms. Rather, they had their own names and mythologies, adapted from their native beliefs. How precisely the Roman gods merged with Druidic practices is left unexplained; Cæsar himself expresses no particular surprise at this amalgamation. Among the Gauls, trophies captured in war are consecrated to Mars, and some states even maintain vast reserves of these sacred spoils. Few Gauls would dare to appropriate these sacred items for their own use, but if anyone commits this sacrilege, they face a terrible punishment—death by torture.

In family life, the Gauls hold fathers in the highest veneration. Sons do not dare to approach or even stand publicly in the presence of their fathers until they are mature enough to bear arms, a rule that underscores the respect accorded to paternal authority. Marital property arrangements are also unique: a husband's fortune must be made to equal his wife's dowry, and afterward, their wealth is held in common. This system of shared assets would likely appeal to many British wives today, Cæsar notes approvingly. However, the next custom he describes would be met with quite a different reception. Among the Gauls, husbands have the power of life and death over their wives and children. When a man of importance dies and there is suspicion of foul play, his wives are questioned under torture. Should any incriminating confession be extracted, the guilty party is put to death by torture. This practice reveals that polygamy was not uncommon among the Gauls.

The Gauls are also known for their grand funeral rites. Objects and creatures that were cherished by the deceased are committed to flames as part of the ceremony. In Cæsar's time, this included animals, but in earlier days, it extended even to slaves and other close dependants who had been especially beloved by the departed. In matters of governance, Cæsar notes that the best-organized Gaulish states are scrupulously careful about public discussions of state affairs. It is forbidden to spread rumors or debate matters of public importance outside of the formal council. Instead, any news or intelligence must be relayed directly to a magistrate, ensuring that discussions on critical matters are limited to official gatherings. Thus, Cæsar provides a fascinating insight into Gaulish society, highlighting both their superstitious devotion and their structured approach to public order.

Turning his attention to the Germans, Cæsar explains that they diverge significantly from the Gauls in customs and beliefs. They do not have Druids, nor do they care much for sacrifices or ritualistic practices. Instead, their worship is directed solely toward the natural elements that they can observe and derive benefit from—principally the sun, fire, and the moon. The Germans live with a single focus on hunting and warfare, caring little for agriculture or cultivation of the land. Their diet consists mainly of milk, cheese, and meat, and they treat land communally, moving on after a year rather than establishing permanent homesteads. This way of life is deliberately maintained to discourage any attachment to the land that might detract from their warlike spirit. They avoid fixed settlements to prevent the emergence of social divisions, where the wealthy might gain dominance over the poor, and to forestall a dependence on comfort that could erode their resilience to cold and heat. By resisting these trappings of civilization, they aim to stave off the allure of wealth, so that no one individual can aspire to be higher or more powerful than another.

In this account, Cæsar presents the Germans as a society with an almost modern-sounding grasp of political philosophy, favoring equality, communal property, and a rugged lifestyle that keeps them ready for war and free from the corrupting influence of wealth and social hierarchy. Through these contrasts, Cæsar paints a portrait of two cultures—one marked by its spiritual and familial rituals, the other by its stern simplicity and communal ethos—each with unique customs that defined their societies.

The Germans, as Cæsar observes, take great pride in having no close neighbors. For them, an ideal arrangement is to have a broad, empty buffer zone surrounding their territory, enhancing both their security and their independence. Each tribe, therefore, cultivates this wide margin of separation, holding it as a matter of honor and protection. In times of war, the chieftains wield absolute authority over life and death, a reflection of the Germans' rigorous approach to leadership in battle. In times of peace, however, they have no appointed magistrates or formal legal systems. Justice is instead a matter for the chiefs, who strive to mediate and resolve disputes as best they can within each canton. Interestingly, among the Germans, theft within one's own tribe is punishable, but theft from a neighboring state is considered honorable. In fact, they organize expeditions specifically for this purpose, allowing individuals to join voluntarily. However, should anyone join and then back out, serious consequences await. Despite this penchant for thieving expeditions, they are notably hospitable to foreign travelers passing through.

Cæsar reflects on the evolving power dynamics between the Gauls and the Germans, noting that there was once a time when the Gauls were the stronger people, capable of invading and conquering German lands. In fact, even in his own time, some Gaulish tribes were still living across the Rhine, having adopted German customs and lifestyle. However, Cæsar suggests that the Gauls' proximity to the Roman Province has softened them, introducing them to luxuries that have made them less capable in battle. Thus, as Roman civilization advanced and introduced refinement, the Gauls have gradually lost some of the fierce resilience they once possessed. In contemplating these accounts of the customs and beliefs of various tribes, one gains insight into what was considered beneficial or harmful by different European peoples long before the rise of Christianity.

Cæsar goes on to describe the Hercynian Forest, an immense, dense woodland stretching from what is now northern Switzerland across the Danube. This vast forest was formidable in its size: it would take nine days for a traveler to cross it in width, while its length was seemingly endless, requiring sixty days to reach the farthest point. This

Hercynian expanse, likely including the Black Forest region, was home to several strange and fascinating animals. Among them were bisons with a single horn and elks that resembled large stags but lacked joints in their legs, meaning they could neither lie down nor get back up if they fell. These elks, Cæsar tells us, sleep leaning against trees, though they sometimes topple when a tree breaks, leaving them helpless. Another extraordinary creature in the forest is the "urus," a fearsome beast nearly the size of an elephant, which is aggressive toward both humans and animals. Killing a urus is a significant feat for any German, and its horns are prized, often mounted in silver to be used as drinking vessels.

Though Cæsar ventures into the German lands briefly, he does not linger long. He crosses back over the Rhine, partially dismantles the bridge, and resumes his pursuit of Ambiorix, the elusive chieftain who has continually evaded him. Cæsar's lieutenant, Basilus, nearly captures Ambiorix, but the crafty king escapes once again, leading Cæsar to reflect philosophically on the capriciousness of fortune. Ambiorix, as we may remember, shared his kingship over the Eburones with an elder named Cativolcus. However, Cativolcus, worn down by the relentless pressure on his people, curses Ambiorix for bringing these misfortunes upon their nation and ultimately takes his own life by poisoning himself with yew-juice.

The Belgic tribes—comprising both Gaulish and Germanic peoples—were now under intense pressure. Many had assisted, or might have assisted, Ambiorix and the Eburones, or, if left unchecked, could potentially aid them in the future. To deal with this widespread unrest, Cæsar decides to split his forces, yet he remains committed to tracking down Ambiorix himself, pushing deep into the damp, challenging landscapes near the mouths of the Scheldt and Meuse rivers. Here, Cæsar faces a difficult dilemma: he is driven by an unyielding determination to annihilate the entire tribe that dared to strike down his army—a crime, in his eyes, so grave that it demands nothing less than their total eradication. Yet he is also wary of the toll that such a campaign in these inhospitable regions might take on his own troops. He resolves this by inviting neighboring Gaulish tribes to assist in his mission, thus ensuring that Gauls, rather than his Roman legionaries, would suffer the brunt of hardship in this hostile terrain.

Cæsar's objective, however, is crystal clear and unbending: the Eburones must be obliterated, so that their very name will be erased from history. "Pro tali facinore, stirps ac nomen civitatis tollatur" — "For such a crime, the very lineage and name of their state must be wiped out."

In dividing his forces, Cæsar had stationed Quintus Cicero, with a single legion and a considerable amount of the army's heavier baggage and spoils, in a fortress strategically located precisely where the previous tragedy had occurred—the place from which the unfortunate Titurius Sabinus had been drawn out and killed due to the deceit of Ambiorix. Cæsar had made it known that the wealth of the Eburones was fair game for any who could claim it, hoping to encourage the complete decimation of that rebellious tribe by turning them into prey for other tribes. Learning of this opportunity for plunder, a group of Germans, known as the Sigambri, crossed the Rhine to gather the spoils left by the Eburones.

However, their focus soon shifted when they were tipped off about a potentially much richer target: the fortress of Quintus Cicero, where Cæsar's stores and wealth lay heavily guarded. Encouraged by this suggestion, the Germans seized the moment, launching an attack on Cicero's camp just as much of his force was away, searching for provisions. For the Romans, this position in the heart of the Eburones' territory once again proved nearly disastrous, with Cicero's legion narrowly escaping annihilation. Yet, while the Germans gained some success in the initial assault, they lacked the skill and experience to press their advantage fully. Satisfied with the spoils they had gathered, they chose to retreat and crossed back over the Rhine, leaving Cicero's force battered but alive.

As before, Cæsar arrives on the scene with divine-like timing, but Ambiorix, that relentlessly elusive leader, still manages to evade capture. Cæsar expresses bitter frustration that the Sigambri, rather than helping to harm Ambiorix as intended, had instead indirectly aided him, allowing the Eburones to slip through Cæsar's grasp once again.

Determined to capture Ambiorix, Cæsar spares no effort, offering substantial rewards to any who can help bring him in. He even persuades his soldiers to endure unimaginable hardships in their relentless search. Despite this, Ambiorix, accompanied by a small band of trusted companions, always manages to stay just a few steps ahead, eluding Cæsar with daring and skill at every turn. Nevertheless, Cæsar exacts his revenge in other ways. He methodically burns every village of the Eburones, laying waste to their land so thoroughly that even after his army withdraws, no one will be able to live there. Only when he has accomplished this complete devastation does he likely feel content enough to end his vow and shave, having finally satisfied his need for retribution.

Ambiorix continues to be spotted here and there, appearing briefly before slipping away again. In the meantime, Cæsar moves southward as winter approaches, settling in Rheims—then known as Durocortorum. Briefly, almost as an afterthought, he mentions his treatment of Acco, a leader among the Carnutes and Senones who had incited a conspiracy within central Gaul. With typical severity, Cæsar has Acco tortured to death and ruthlessly punishes others involved in the plot, exiling or outlawing those who managed to escape his grasp. Having quelled this rebellion and secured his legions in their winter quarters, Cæsar once again turns back to Italy to hold court, tending to his personal and political matters amid the complex affairs of the Republic.

So, with his vengeance taken against the Eburones and his dominion in Gaul once more firmly established, Cæsar concludes another campaign season, retreating momentarily from the constant demands of war to focus on the wider ambitions of his burgeoning empire.

Chapter VIII.
SEVENTH BOOK OF THE WAR IN GAUL.— THE REVOLT OF VERCINGETORIX.—B.C. 52.

In the opening of his account of this seventh campaign, Cæsar makes one of the rare references to events in Rome that appears in these Commentaries. Clodius, the notorious political agitator, had been assassinated, an incident that had caused great upheaval in the city. By this time, Crassus had also perished in his ill-fated campaign in the East, meeting his end at the hands of the Parthians. In the aftermath of Clodius's death, Pompey had been appointed sole Consul, effectively granting him dictatorial powers. Yet Cæsar only briefly mentions Clodius's murder, quickly pivoting back to events in Gaul. He notes that the Gaulish tribes, aware of the volatile state of affairs in Rome and sensing the gravity of Cæsar's involvement there, believed that he would be unable to leave Italy. They saw an opportunity to rise against Roman rule, hoping to cast off the Roman yoke while they assumed Cæsar's attention was entirely on the troubles in his homeland.

Indeed, the events in Rome must have weighed heavily on Cæsar. He likely saw in these developments the looming clash for supremacy within the Republic. Clodius, a political figure with whom Cæsar had maintained an uneasy but strategic alliance, was now gone. Crassus, once a wealthy and influential member of the Triumvirate, was also gone, leaving only Pompey to share power with Cæsar. Pompey, who just a year prior had sent a legion to aid Cæsar "for the sake of the Republic—and of friendship," was now firmly positioned in Rome with unprecedented authority. By now, Cæsar undoubtedly foresaw the inevitable showdown between himself and Pompey. The Republic was already shedding its traditional forms, and both Cæsar and Pompey must have realized that a new power structure would soon emerge. It was clear that the strength required to seize control of such a force would need to be formidable, and Cæsar knew that time was not yet ripe. Having dedicated six years to subduing Gaul, he would not forfeit the prestige, strength, and resources that such a conquest offered him. Though Rome's affairs were urgent, his most prudent course was still to return to Gaul and complete his campaign. News reached him that the tribes of Gaul were conspiring, assuming that the emergency in Rome would prevent Cæsar from leaving Italy to suppress them.

In this final book of the Commentaries, Cæsar recounts the extraordinary story of Vercingetorix, the brave leader from the Arverni (a region known today as Auvergne), whose father, Celtillus, had once sought to be the supreme leader of Gaul but was executed by his own people for his ambition. Vercingetorix stands out as the foremost hero of the Gaulish resistance, though we hear of him for the first time in this seventh campaign. The conspiracy against Rome began with the Carnutes, whose chief city, Genabum (modern-day Orleans), was the starting point of the revolt. Vercingetorix attempted to rally his own people, but they expelled him from their town of Gergovia, fearing the wrath of Rome. However, he continued to gather support, attracting followers from all over the region, including from as far north as Paris and from the western shores by the Atlantic.

Assuming command, Vercingetorix implemented harsh laws to maintain discipline. For severe offenses, he would burn the offender alive after subjecting them to excruciating tortures. For minor infractions, he would cut off a man's ears, gouge out one of his eyes, and send him back home as a stark, visible warning to others. With these ruthless methods, he managed to rally a significant force, threatening extreme punishment to any who resisted his call to arms and meting out punishment to those who wavered in their loyalty or showed even a hint of cowardice. Hearing of these escalating threats, Cæsar—still in Italy—realized that he could not delay any longer. He settled his affairs with Pompey as best as he could under the circumstances, then rushed back into Gaul.

Cæsar recounts the difficulties he faced just in reaching his forces, underscoring the urgency of protecting even the Roman Province itself from possible invasion. In the depth of winter, he forced his way through the Cevennes, a mountain range considered impassable at that time of year due to the heavy snows. His daring passage over these snow-clad peaks astonished even his allies and inspired fear among his enemies. Forced into early battle due to the tenuous loyalty of certain tribes (such as the Ædui, who could easily be swayed to join the revolt if not convinced of Roman strength), Cæsar had to balance the risks of a winter campaign with the very real threat of a Gaulish uprising.

Cæsar acknowledges the difficulty of his decision, recognizing that he would have preferred to wait for spring. But seeing that hesitation would allow the tribes to rally further support, he resolved to act at once. Thus began his seventh and most decisive campaign, in which he would face not only the bravery and skill of a single Gaulish hero but a widespread and deeply rooted Gaulish insurrection determined to restore their independence.

With remarkable swiftness, Cæsar maneuvers his forces across central Gaul, capturing three towns in quick succession, beginning with Genabum (modern-day Orleans), thus securing essential provisions for his army. This development unsettles Vercingetorix deeply. He realizes that, with the Romans gaining access to the very food and supplies of Gaul, his forces face a critical threat. Vercingetorix, therefore, proposes a drastic strategy to his followers: they must destroy their own towns and resources, leaving Cæsar with no way to sustain his army off the land. He addresses his people, urging them to endure the destruction of their homes and possessions, arguing that it would be far more devastating to suffer the capture of their wives and children as slaves under Roman rule. Convinced by his words, they act upon his order and burn twenty cities within a single tribe's territory, reducing them all to ashes. Neighboring states follow suit, embracing this scorched-earth tactic as their last defense.

However, one city stands out: Avaricum, known today as Bourges. Its beauty and strategic value as the pride of the surrounding region make it difficult for the Gauls to consider destroying it. They insist that Avaricum's strong natural defenses would make it a valuable asset rather than a risk. Vercingetorix initially insists that Avaricum should be burned just like the others, but eventually, he yields to his people's pleas, allowing the city to remain standing—for now.

Cæsar, determined to capture Avaricum, soon finds that his task will be challenging. The Gauls have systematically removed all sources of food and livestock from the area, leaving his army with no easy means of sustenance. Even the Ædui, who were supposed to be Cæsar's allies, do little to support him, and their neighbors, the Boii, a smaller and less capable tribe, are equally unhelpful. For days, Cæsar's soldiers endure grueling hunger, with the army at times entirely without food. Yet, Cæsar notes with pride that despite the suffering, his soldiers maintain their discipline and morale. "No word of complaint is heard unworthy of the majesty and former victories of the Roman people," he writes, underscoring their unwavering resolve. When Cæsar offers to lift the siege, seeing the difficulties they face, his men adamantly refuse. They declare their readiness to endure any hardship rather than abandon a siege once begun. They remind Cæsar of their unbroken record of success under his leadership and insist on finishing what they've started, to avenge the Roman citizens killed by the Gauls at Genabum. Cæsar describes this in a way that convinces the reader of the soldiers' loyalty and commitment. By now, Cæsar's legionaries have grown into seasoned warriors who no longer flinch in the face of adversity.

Meanwhile, Vercingetorix faces dissent among his own people. As the Romans close in on Avaricum, doubts and suspicions start to plague the Gauls. Fearing betrayal, they accuse Vercingetorix of conspiring to hand them over to Cæsar. The situation grows tense until

Vercingetorix gathers his followers and delivers a speech to reassure them. To back up his words, he brings forth Roman prisoners and presents them as proof of the Romans' struggling condition. Vercingetorix insists that these men are Roman soldiers, claiming that their presence shows the dire state of Cæsar's army. This demonstration temporarily quells the unrest among his forces.

In response, Cæsar defends his legionaries against Vercingetorix's claims, asserting that the prisoners paraded before the Gauls were merely slaves, not soldiers. As the siege continues, the contrast between the two leaders becomes more pronounced—Vercingetorix relies on persuasion and unity among the Gauls, while Cæsar depends on the discipline, loyalty, and resilience of his legionaries, determined to see through the siege of Avaricum despite the mounting difficulties.

While Vercingetorix holds his position in a camp some distance from Avaricum, Cæsar is resolute in his determination to capture the city. The account of the siege is vivid and sharply drawn, capturing the intensity of the struggle on both sides. Cæsar describes the city's walls and how skillfully the Gauls defended against his troops. They proved adept in mining and countermining, constantly countering the Romans' advances with a relentless energy that included flinging hot pitch and boiling grease upon the invading soldiers. As each Gaul fell in the defense, another took his place, stepping forward undeterred to continue the fight. When a plan emerged among the defenders to abandon the city at night and escape to the safety of Vercingetorix's camp, their own women, in fear of Roman retribution, begged them to stay. Ultimately, however, the Gauls could not hold out, and the city fell to Cæsar's forces.

The fate of Avaricum's people is chilling. Cæsar recounts with cool detachment the massacre that followed, sparing neither the elderly, the women, nor the children. Of the forty thousand Gauls within Avaricum's walls, Cæsar states that only around eight hundred managed to reach Vercingetorix, who awaited them outside. While the exact number might be debated, there is no doubt that the Romans left almost no survivors, slaughtering the entire population with ruthless efficiency. Cæsar rationalizes the carnage as retaliation for the earlier murder of Roman traders in Genabum—traders, who, it should be noted, were primarily usurers exploiting the local population. According to Cæsar, this incident alone justified the massacre of Avaricum's innocents. One might concede that Gaul, if it were to be conquered, required decisive action of this kind; but it is difficult not to recoil from Cæsar's calm acceptance of such a brutal method.

Remarkably, Vercingetorix does not falter after this staggering loss. Displaying resilience, he reminds his followers that had they listened to his initial advice, Avaricum would have been burned by their own hands, sparing them the bloodshed that followed its defense. He maintains that, despite this setback, Gaul's many tribes are now prepared to rally to their cause. Vercingetorix then sets about fortifying his camp in a style influenced by the Roman methods he has observed, signaling a new determination and a tactical shift in the conflict. Until now, the Gauls had relied either on the defenses of walled cities or on the natural cover of forests and hills when they fought in open terrain.

Meanwhile, Cæsar faces yet another problem with his allies, the Ædui, whose internal divisions threaten to disrupt his campaign. A dispute has arisen over who should serve as their chief magistrate: an elderly contender or a younger rival. The Ædui appeal to Cæsar to settle the matter, despite the fact that he is fully occupied with the war effort. Recognizing the necessity of maintaining order among his allies, Cæsar goes to one of their towns in person to make a decision. He appoints the younger man as magistrate but seizes the opportunity to request reinforcements from the Ædui, asking for ten thousand infantry and all their cavalry to assist him against Vercingetorix. Bound to comply, the Ædui send their forces—but the arrangement is far from amicable.

As it turns out, the dismissed elder magistrate conspires with the Æduan general, leading their army to side not with Cæsar but with Vercingetorix instead. Treachery and deceit abound among the Ædui, and their schemes inevitably reach Cæsar's ears. Time and again, they deceive him, working covertly to undermine his efforts, yet Cæsar continually chooses to overlook their betrayals, or at least he pretends to. It is part of his calculated approach to demonstrate to the Gauls the benefits of Roman friendship and the generosity of his own character. One might wish that he had directed his wrath toward the disloyal Ædui instead of the defenseless citizens of Avaricum, but then, if he had acted differently, he would not have been the Cæsar history knows—the Cæsar whose combination of ruthlessness, clemency, and political acumen kept him advancing inexorably toward his objectives.

While dealing with the fickle loyalties of his supposed allies, Cæsar also faces the mounting threat posed by his enemies. After the brutal loss at Avaricum (modern Bourges), Vercingetorix retreats with his followers to the heart of his homeland in Auvergne, where he strategically positions his forces on the hill of Gergovia. This hill, topped with a flat surface, is a natural stronghold, well-known to those who have visited Clermont, as it dominates the landscape. There, Vercingetorix sets up three camps, securing the approach with a river between him and Cæsar. Confident in his advantage, Vercingetorix anticipates that this river, difficult to ford, will keep the Romans at bay.

Cæsar, however, is undeterred. He builds a bridge and positions his legions before Gergovia, determined to seize the town. Though we cannot delve deeply into each maneuver, this siege of Gergovia stands out as one of Cæsar's most dramatic encounters. Against all odds, he captures the three Gaulish camps. The women of Gergovia, fearing the worst, lean over the walls, pleading for mercy from the Romans, begging not to suffer the fate of the women of Avaricum. Driven by courage or desperation, some Roman soldiers even climb into the town, as if victory is within reach. Readers, familiar with Cæsar's unbroken string of successes, expect him to prevail as he usually does. Yet, this time, Cæsar faces a surprising defeat and is forced to withdraw. Vercingetorix emerges victorious, masterfully defending Gergovia.

Cæsar explains the setback with a rationale that resonates with readers inclined to trust his account, even when disliking his methods.

He attributes the loss to the over-eager bravery of his soldiers rather than any strategic misstep on his part. It's plausible, given Cæsar's track record and the unwavering confidence he inspires in his men. Nevertheless, after suffering a loss of 700 men and 46 officers, he retreats, crossing the Allier River back into the territory of his unreliable Æduan allies. Here, Cæsar narrowly avoids disaster, as his position grows increasingly precarious. Had Vercingetorix capitalized on his victory and blocked Cæsar's retreat over the Allier, the Roman general might have faced total defeat. But, as Cæsar suggests, the Gauls lack the tactical awareness and experience the Romans possess.

The Ædui, predictably, betray him once more. His stores, treasure, and essential supplies, safeguarded at Noviodunum (modern Nevers), are seized by these disloyal allies. The Ædui destroy what they can't carry off, leaving Cæsar's army at risk of starvation. The land around him is stripped bare, and with no bridges or fords available, the Loire River stands as an additional barrier between his troops and the food they desperately need. Still, Cæsar's resourcefulness prevails: he identifies a shallow stretch and orders his men to cross with water nearly up to their shoulders. Despite the risks, they manage the ford and secure much-needed provisions.

Meanwhile, Cæsar's lieutenant Labienus, stationed with four legions near modern Paris, is also feeling the strain. Hearing of Cæsar's defeat at Gergovia, Labienus recognizes the urgency of rejoining his commander. He fights his own battle, securing a hard-won victory, which Cæsar recounts with as much fervor as if he himself had led the charge. With this victory achieved, Labienus brings his troops south to reunite with Cæsar.

But the Gauls are far from conceding. They assemble a grand council at Bibracte, the Ædui's principal city (modern Autun), to further their resolve in ousting the Romans. The Ædui, confident of their stature as Cæsar's longest-standing allies in Gaul, insist on leading the fight against Rome, believing themselves entitled to command. However, the assembled tribes instead elect Vercingetorix as their leader, recognizing his skill and commitment to their cause. The Æduan leaders, disappointed at being overlooked, nurse their grievances.

Undeterred, Vercingetorix takes advantage of Cæsar's apparent retreat southward to the Roman Province. Declaring that Cæsar's forces are retreating, he rallies his troops to launch an offensive. Although Cæsar may indeed be falling back to regroup, he soon turns to meet the Gauls head-on, dealing them a heavy defeat and killing around three thousand in the ensuing skirmish. Once again, Vercingetorix is forced to retreat, this time barricading himself within the fortified town of Alesia. With his enemy entrenched, Cæsar prepares for yet another intense siege, signaling that the struggle for Gaul is far from over.

The siege of Alesia marks the final, brutal episode of Cæsar's Commentary on the Gallic War, and it stands out as perhaps the most harrowing of all. Here, civilization advances, but in the most ruthless manner imaginable. Besieged in the town with his entire army, Vercingetorix finds himself trapped as Cæsar constructs extensive fortifications, ditches, ramparts, and lines surrounding the town, cutting off every possible route of escape. Yet, before the Roman works are fully completed, Vercingetorix sends out a group of his horsemen, desperate for reinforcements. Their mission is to rally Gaul's tribes, urging them to bring all available fighting men to lift the siege and drive away the Romans.

The urgency is clear: Vercingetorix warns them that he has only thirty days' worth of provisions for the town. Though they may find ways to stretch the food supply slightly, beyond that, if no help arrives, he and the eighty thousand souls with him will be doomed. Cæsar's account portrays Vercingetorix's plea as heartfelt and desperate, aware that their fate lies entirely with the resolve and speed of their Gaulish kin. These horsemen successfully escape, while the chief and his people inside prepare to wait out the harrowing days ahead.

The challenges in uniting Gaul for a concerted effort seem daunting, especially given the distance and fragmented loyalties of the tribes. Yet Cæsar, with characteristic matter-of-factness, tells us that nearly all Gaul responds, each tribe sending the number of men requested, with the only exception being the Bellovaci, the people of Beauvais. They declare that they prefer to wage war independently, but in a show of solidarity still lend two thousand men for the cause. Even Cæsar's Gaulish allies, including Commius—whom he had raised to kingship over the Atrebates and who had aided him in Britain—join this national uprising, motivated by a fervent desire to free Gaul from Roman domination. So deep runs this yearning for liberty that memories of Cæsar's friendship and past favors prove no deterrent. An immense force of eight thousand cavalry and two hundred and forty thousand foot soldiers assembles in the lands of the Ædui, ready to march on Alesia and liberate Vercingetorix.

Inside Alesia, however, hope is fading fast. The days of waiting drag beyond the promised thirty, with no word reaching them of any coming relief. As food supplies dwindle, desperation rises among the trapped men and women. Some argue for unconditional surrender, while others propose a daring escape attempt, cutting their way through the Roman lines. In this grim moment, one figure, Critognatus, takes the floor to offer his own horrifying solution, and Cæsar chooses to recount his speech in vivid detail.

Critognatus disregards those speaking of surrender, finding their proposal so disgraceful that he barely acknowledges it. As for those advocating a suicidal breakout, he argues that enduring suffering is nobler than seeking a quick end. "Many a man can die," he insists, "but only the bravest can suffer and survive." Rather than rushing to die, he urges them to hold out a little longer and trust in the loyalty of the Gaulish tribes.

Then he makes a shocking suggestion: let those who can fight survive by consuming those who cannot—the weak and the sick. By rationing in this way, he argues, the defenders can hold out until the promised relief arrives. It's a proposition so dreadful that even the leaders of Alesia, though desperate, cannot bring themselves to adopt it fully. Yet they implement an equally tragic measure: all the women, the elderly, and the infirm are forced to leave the town, a last attempt to stretch their meager rations. If this act of brutal self-preservation proves insufficient, they are ready to resort to even more unimaginable actions.

Alesia itself belongs not to Vercingetorix's tribe but to the Mandubii, who are now the most pitiful of victims in this grim episode. Pushed out of the gates with their children, these helpless civilians find themselves caught between the Romans and their own people, no longer welcome inside the besieged town, yet facing certain death or enslavement if they try to pass the Roman fortifications.

Memory updated

But where would they go? Cæsar has told us that there was a strip of ground between his lines and the city wall—an enclosed space from which there was no escape except into Cæsar's camp or back to the besieged town. The weak ones—elderly men, women, and children—stand here and beg Cæsar to let them enter his camp so they could make their way into the open country. There they stood, pleading for mercy, on that narrow strip of land between the two armies. Their own people, without enough food, had driven them from their homes. Would Cæsar show mercy? With a wave of his hand, Cæsar showed he would not. He tells us his decision in just eight words: "At Cæsar, depositis in vallo custodiis, recipi prohibebat." "But Cæsar, placing guards along the wall, forbade that they should be allowed in." We hear no more about them, but we know that they perished.

The gathered forces of Gaul do finally arrive to try to rescue Vercingetorix—and they arrive just in time; but was their arrival enough to change anything? They attack Cæsar in his camp, and a huge battle takes place, watched closely by those inside Alesia. Cæsar, however, is very careful to ensure that the people now trapped in the town don't manage to join up with the Gauls who were scattered around him in the countryside. We read how, during the battle, Cæsar himself appears, recognized by the color of his cloak. As we read his account of the fighting, we again feel that the Gauls nearly win, and that they should win. But in the end, they are pushed back in a chaotic retreat—all the gathered forces of all the tribes. The Romans kill many, and if the task of killing were not so difficult, they might have killed everyone. However, a huge crowd does manage to escape, scattering back into their tribes.

The next day, Vercingetorix surrenders himself and the city to Cæsar. During the battle, he and his men, shut up inside the walls, had only watched the fighting. Cæsar sits in his lines before his camp; and there, the chieftains, led by Vercingetorix, are brought to him. Plutarch tells us a story about the chieftain riding up in front of Cæsar to surrender himself, wearing gilded armor, on a grand horse, circling and prancing. It's hard to imagine any horse from inside Alesia being fit for such a display after the siege. The horses from Vercingetorix's stables had probably been eaten many days before. Then, once more, Cæsar forgives the Ædui; but Vercingetorix is taken as a prisoner to Rome, where he is kept for six years. He is then displayed in Cæsar's Triumph, and after these six years, he is killed as a sacrifice to add to Cæsar's glory, so honor can be brought to Cæsar! Cæsar places his army in winter quarters and decides to stay in Gaul through the winter. When the news of these events reaches Rome, a "thanksgiving" of twenty days is declared in his honor.

This is the end of Cæsar's Commentary on the "Gallic War." The conflict continued for two more years, and an account of Cæsar's actions during these years—51 and 50 B.C.—was written in Cæsar's style by Aulus Hirtius. Hirtius makes no claim that this was Cæsar's own work, as he includes a brief introduction where he apologizes for daring to continue what Cæsar had started. The most notable event in these two campaigns is the capture of Uxellodunum, a town in southwestern France, though its exact location is unknown today.

Cæsar took the town by cutting off the water supply, and then he horrifically mutilated the inhabitants who had dared to defend their homes. "Cæsar," says the historian, "knowing well that his clemency was acknowledged by all, and feeling secure that no punishment he inflicted would be blamed on cruelty, realized that he could never know where his plans might lead if such rebellions continued. He decided that other Gauls should be deterred by the fear of punishment." So he cut off the hands of all those who had fought at Uxellodunum and turned the helpless victims loose in the world. His defender then adds that Cæsar spared their lives so that the punishment of these rebels—who had only fought for their freedom—would serve as an example to all! This was perhaps the height of Cæsar's cruelty, justified, as we see, by the reputation he had built for mercy!

Soon after this, Gaul was truly conquered, and we begin to hear the first hints of the coming civil war. At Rome, attempts were made to ruin Cæsar in his absence. One of the consuls in 51 B.C. tried to cut short his term as proconsul and prevent him from running for the consulship in his absence. He was also ordered to return two of his legions. Cæsar complied, though he hadn't yet decided to cross the Rubicon. The official demand was for one legion from Cæsar and one from Pompey, but as the reader may recall, Cæsar had with him a legion borrowed from Pompey—meaning, in effect, Cæsar was required to give up two legions. And he surrendered them, not yet fully prepared to make his decisive move.

Chapter IX.
FIRST BOOK OF THE CIVIL WAR.—CÆSAR CROSSES THE RUBICON.—FOLLOWS

POMPEY TO BRUNDUSIUM.—AND CONQUERS AFRANIUS IN SPAIN.—B.C. 49.

Cæsar now begins his account of the civil war in which he and Pompey struggled for control over Rome and the Republic. In his first Commentary, he recorded his campaigns in Gaul—campaigns where he subdued tribes that, even if not exactly hostile, were at least foreign. Through his success, he carried forward the strength, traditions, and mission of the Roman Republic. Romans aimed to rule the known world, and to them, only those lands that had become Roman were truly "known." Any expansion of this world could happen only by adding so-called barbarian tribes to the number of Roman subjects. By conquering Gaul, fighting the Germans, and even crossing into Britain, Cæsar was doing what all loyal Romans hoped to see done, matching in the West the great accomplishments of Pompey for the Republic in the East. But in this second Commentary, he has to address a topic less pleasant for Roman readers: he describes the victories he won with Roman legions over other equally Roman legions, which led him to dismantle the Republic's freedom.

In fairness to Cæsar, liberty in Rome had already decayed before his time. Power had led to wealth, and wealth to corruption. Roman tribes were bought and sold during elections, while a few powerful oligarchs, from either faction, shared the top roles of trust, honor, and authority—always reaching for public wealth. An honest man with clean hands, principles, and love of country had little place in public office. In these times, Cato seemed almost laughable, and even Cicero, though he tried to adapt to changing circumstances, was too honest for the era. Laws were twisted from their purpose, and even the Tribunes, meant to protect the people, had become tyrants. Perhaps a master was needed—and Cæsar thought so, at least. Undoubtedly, he recognized this need throughout his years of fighting in Gaul and resolved to be no less than First in the new order. So he crossed the Rubicon.

Readers may find this second Commentary less captivating than the first. It has fewer elements of adventure, less of the new and unfamiliar, and lacks the healthy, exuberant sense that Cæsar felt while fighting in Gaul—that, by crushing the Gauls, he was achieving something unquestionably good. To us today, his actions in Gaul seem cruel, but to him and the Romans, they were no stain on his character. How other Roman conquerors treated the defeated can be judged by the fact that Cæsar was considered merciful for his restraint in Gaul. He writes as if free from any guilt, as he describes the punishments he felt policy required. Yet, in recounting the civil wars, there is no such tone of complete self-satisfaction, and he is, in fact, much less cruel.

He could witness or order the deaths of countless Gauls—men, women, or children—without hesitation, whether they were burned, drowned, starved, mutilated, or tortured. He gave such commands without more regret than one might have ordering the removal of a litter of unwanted puppies. But he could not bring himself to kill Roman soldiers, even in fair combat, with any sense of ease. Either he was more compassionate or he had a deeper patriotism than many who have fought in civil wars since. In the Wars of the Roses or Cromwell's battles, we see no such restraint. American generals did not show it either. But Cæsar seems to have valued a single Roman legionary above an entire tribe of Gauls.

Cæsar, however, crossed the Rubicon. We've all heard of this famous crossing, yet Cæsar himself says nothing about it. The Rubicon was a small river, now almost unknown, flowing into the Adriatic between Ravenna and Ariminum—modern-day Rimini—and marking the boundary between Cisalpine Gaul and territory directly under the authority of Rome's magistrates. North of the Rubicon, Cæsar was effectively within his own province, where he held complete command. But according to the law, he was strictly forbidden from even entering Rome's territory while in command of a Roman province. Thus, by crossing the Rubicon, Cæsar directly broke the law and challenged the authority of the city's governing officials.

However, it doesn't appear that this specific act was viewed as especially significant at the time, nor was the crossing itself seen as an unmistakable sign of Cæsar's intentions or as an irrevocable action. Many stories describe Cæsar hesitating at the river's edge, debating whether he should take a step that would plunge the world into civil war. These tales recount how a mysterious spirit appeared to him, leading him across the river to the sounds of martial music, and how Cæsar, declaring "the die is cast," crossed over the fateful stream. But all this was myth, later invented by Romans who wanted to add drama to Cæsar's life. In reality, Cæsar's intention was likely well known when he brought one of his legions down to that part of his province, but offers to negotiate were still made by Pompey and his allies after Cæsar had entered the Roman side of the river.

When the civil war began, Cæsar still had two and a half years remaining in his assigned period of governance over the three provinces; but his victories and increasing power had been carefully monitored with great concern from Rome, and the Senate had attempted to order his recall. By now, Pompey was no longer Cæsar's ally, nor did Cæsar expect Pompey's friendship. Pompey, who had recently made a series of strategic mistakes and must have felt their weight, was now free from any alliance with Cæsar due to the deaths of Crassus, their fellow triumvir, and Julia, Cæsar's daughter, along with the changing political climate in Rome. This alliance had been a calculated arrangement created by Cæsar, mainly to curb the influence of his rival. Pompey's earlier successes had always made him seem almost godlike to the Romans.

While still a young man, Pompey had led armies and won decisive victories. Women adored him, soldiers idolized him, and even Sulla had given him the title of "the Great," raising his hat in respect. Pompey had been granted the honor of a Triumph while still a youth, celebrated a second Triumph before reaching middle age, and went on to earn a third Triumph—each one symbolizing a conquest in a different quarter of the world. In all his undertakings, he had known nothing but success and widespread admiration. He had driven pirates out of Mediterranean harbors, securing Rome's food supply by ensuring a steady flow of grain. He returned victorious with his legions from the East, then dared to disband his forces in order to live again as an ordinary citizen. Later, when the city faced internal disorder, he was appointed sole consul to restore stability.

Today, we better understand Pompey's character than we do the special position his consistent success had won him in the minds of both Rome's aristocracy and its people. Even after Cæsar's successful campaigns in Gaul, Pompey retained a certain aura of divine power that inspired trust among Romans. Pompey was proud, controlled, and self-possessed, permitting no equal, yet enforcing his status with a calm restraint. He was grand, handsome, and generous when necessary; ruthless when required; cunning, heartless, intensely loyal to Rome, and fiercely brave.

However, Pompey possessed one fatal flaw: when the time came for the final conflict, he was uncertain about his own intentions. He hadn't formed a clear vision of his future. The challenges he faced were immense, and he was left undecided when certainty was crucial. In contrast, Cæsar fully understood the situation and harbored no doubts. The story of Cæsar standing on the bridge over the Rubicon, torn between obedience and rebellion, may be captivating, but in truth, there was no hesitation and no inner conflict. Cæsar knew precisely what he intended and exactly what he wanted.

Cæsar begins his second account with a focus on the wrongs he feels have been done to him. He describes how his own supporters are silenced both in the Senate and throughout the city, while his enemies—Scipio, Cato, and Lentulus the consul—dominate the discussions, leaving no one able to speak on his behalf. "Pompey himself," he claims, "urged on by Cæsar's opponents and unwilling to share his honor with anyone else, has completely broken off their friendship and returned to the company of the very enemies he had made for Cæsar during their alliance." Additionally, Pompey, troubled by the "scandal" surrounding the two legions he had kept from going to Asia and Syria, is eager to see the matter resolved by force. Those two legions weigh heavily on Cæsar's mind. One of these legions, as we recall, had been lent by Pompey "for the sake of friendship—and the Republic." At the start of the power struggle between them, the Senate had sought to reduce both leaders' forces by demanding one legion from each. Pompey had then asked Cæsar to return the one he had lent in good faith, and Cæsar, too proud to refuse, sent it along with another legion as ordered. These legions were supposedly meant for service in the East, but now they were under the control of Pompey, once his friend and now his foe. It's little wonder that Cæsar speaks with anger about the "scandal" of these two legions. His frustration about them comes up repeatedly.

In January, Cæsar was in Ravenna, just north of the Rubicon, still within his province. Messages were exchanged between him and the Senate, where he made his demands, and the Senate made theirs. They insisted that he must lay down his arms or else be deemed an enemy of the Republic. The city of Rome was in turmoil. While this account is Cæsar's, it seems clear that Rome truly was in an uproar. "Soldiers are recruited all over Italy; weapons are gathered, taxes are imposed on the municipalities, and funds are taken from sacred shrines; all divine and human laws are disregarded." Cæsar then gathers his soldiers and tells them of his grievances and Pompey's crimes. He reminds them of their shared victories and of how, under his leadership, they have "pacified" all of Gaul and Germany. He calls on them to defend the leader who made these achievements possible. He has only one legion with him, but that legion pledges its loyalty—to him and to the tribunes of the people, some of whom have joined him in Ravenna from Rome in support of his cause. We can sense Cæsar's aim in mentioning the tribunes: it's a move to suggest that there remains some connection between himself and the governing authorities. With his soldiers' support assured, Cæsar heads to Ariminum, and in doing so, he crosses the Rubicon.

More messages follow, and Cæsar says he feels deeply saddened by being forced to wait in such suspense. Yet, for the good of the Republic, he is prepared to endure everything—"omnia pati reipublicæ causâ." All he asks is that Pompey go to his province, the legions stationed around Rome be disbanded, the old forms of free government be restored, and that panic be put to rest. If all that is done, then any remaining issues can be settled in a short conversation. In response, the consuls and Pompey reply that if Cæsar returns to Gaul and disbands his army, then Pompey will go to Spain. However, Pompey and the consuls refuse to budge with their troops until Cæsar provides assurances that he will leave first. Essentially, each side insists that the other move first. These messages, of course, lead nowhere.

Bitterly denouncing the injustice he faces, Cæsar sends part of his small force deeper into Roman territory. Marc Antony leads five cohorts to Arezzo, while Cæsar stations a cohort in three other towns. The real wonder is that Pompey didn't attack him and push him back. We can assume that Pompey's troops weren't particularly trustworthy when it came to opposing Cæsar, likely because these soldiers had served under him before. Cæsar misses his two legions, and it's likely those two legions miss him as well. Regardless, the consuls and Pompey, along with their forces and many senators, retreat southward to Brundusium—Brindisi—planning to depart Italy from the same port we all now use to travel eastward. During this retreat, the first blood of the civil war is spilled at Corfinium, a town that would now be found in the Abruzzi, if it still stood. Cæsar achieves a small victory there and captures the town. He spares the captured Pompeian officers, even allowing them to take money which, he believes, they had seized from the public treasury.

As he moves south, Pompey's soldiers—many of whom had once served Cæsar—rejoin him along the way. Pompey and the consuls keep retreating, and Cæsar keeps pursuing them, despite Pompey's previous boast that he only had to stamp his foot on Italian soil and legions would rise up ready to obey him. Pompey is fully aware, however, that beyond Italy, in Rome's provinces like Macedonia, Achaia, Asia, Cilicia, Sicily, Sardinia, Africa, Mauritania, and the two Spains, there are legions that remain loyal to Rome and are yet untouched by Cæsar. Perhaps it would be wiser for Pompey to stamp his foot somewhere outside of Italy. He sends the consuls and attending senators along with part of his army across the sea to Dyrrachium in Illyria, and he follows with the rest as Cæsar closes in. Cæsar tries to intercept Pompey's fleet but fails. And so, Pompey leaves Italy and Rome—never to see the imperial city or its beautiful lands again.

Cæsar explains his decision not to follow Pompey immediately to finish the fight. Pompey has ships, and he does not, and Cæsar knows that Rome's power lies in her provinces. Moreover, Rome could be starved by Pompey if Cæsar doesn't ensure that the grain-producing lands, which serve as Rome's granaries, are kept accessible for the city's needs. He must secure Gaul, Sardinia, Sicily, and even Africa if he can. He also needs to win over the two Spains, especially the northern region, which currently leans toward Pompey. He sends one lieutenant to Sardinia with a legion, another to Sicily with three legions—and from there, on to Africa. These regions were controlled by Pompey's supporters, but Cæsar quickly gains the upper hand. Cato, known for his uprightness, had been assigned to govern Sicily, but without an army, he finds himself defenseless. Bitterly complaining that he has been abandoned and betrayed by the head of his faction, Cato flees, leaving the province to Cæsar's officers. Cæsar then resolves to take the war to Spain himself.

However, before heading to Spain, Cæsar found it necessary to stop in Rome. His account of what he did there, though, may not be entirely candid. We believe him when he explains that, gathering what senators he could—since Pompey had already taken those he could persuade to join him—he proposed to this diminished Senate the idea of sending ambassadors to negotiate with Pompey. The Senate accepted the idea, but no one was willing to take on such a dangerous task, especially after Pompey had already declared that those who stayed in Rome were his enemies. It's likely true, as Cæsar claims, that he found a particular tribune in Rome who opposed all his actions, though we doubt the resistance was very strong. Still, his real motive in coming to Rome was to seize the Republic's treasury—the sacred funds, the sanctius ærarium, stored in the Temple of Saturn for the state's direst emergencies. It's not surprising he would take this treasure, but it is surprising that he tries to claim he did not. He insists he was so obstructed by this pesky tribune that he couldn't complete the plans he came for. Yet, it's clear he did take the money, and there's little doubt he came to Rome specifically to secure it.

En route to Spain, Cæsar stops in Marseilles, known in ancient times as Massilia. Like today, it was then a major Mediterranean port, full of thriving commerce. Although located in the province of Further Gaul, Massilia was actually a Greek colony and quite prosperous. Now, however, Cæsar needs control of the city. When the local magistrates are called upon for their support, they give a very diplomatic reply: they assure him that they hold both him and Pompey in high regard, that they are troubled by this dispute between two such worthy men, and that they prefer to keep to their own affairs. Cæsar takes this decision as an affront and uses it to justify a siege. He lays siege to the city by both land and sea, appoints officers to continue the blockade, and proceeds to Spain.

At that time, all of Spain was under the command of three generals loyal to Pompey. However, judging by his earlier comments, Cæsar seems less concerned about resistance in the south. Afranius commands in the north and east, holding key passes in the Pyrenees. Petreius, stationed in Lusitania in the southwest, quickly marches north to support Afranius as soon as Cæsar approaches. The two armies soon face off near Ilerda (modern-day Lérida), by the small river Sicoris (now the Segre), which flows into the Ebro. The proximity of the mountains, the swift rivers, and the rugged terrain all shape the course of the campaign. Cæsar gives an extremely detailed account of this campaign, making it thrilling by the clarity and intensity of his narrative.

Afranius and Petreius occupy Ilerda, well-stocked with provisions, while Cæsar's army suffers from shortages. The crops and grass are not yet grown, and last year's harvest is nearly gone. The situation becomes so dire that reports reach Rome suggesting Afranius has already defeated Cæsar, leading many still undecided in Rome to choose Pompey's side.

Despite these difficulties, Cæsar eventually forces Afranius and Petreius to abandon Ilerda. Using techniques he learned in Britain, he ferries his men across a river on coracles, diverts another river, fords a third by breaking up its flow with his horses, and even builds a bridge over a fourth. Realizing they can no longer hold their ground, Afranius and Petreius try to escape south across the Ebro and seek refuge among the more primitive tribes there, hoping to reach the Celtiberians farther south in what would later be called Castile. Cæsar notes that while these tribes know Pompey's name, his own reputation has not yet spread to these distant peoples. But Afranius cannot cross the Ebro without Cæsar's consent, and Cæsar has no intention of giving it. He cuts off their path, using that severe tactic of deprivation that he himself had endured. Now he drives the Pompeians across the land, keeping them north of the Ebro and denying them access to water, until they are ultimately forced to surrender.

In the final days of this conflict, the soldiers under Afranius—known as the Afranians, who are, after all, Roman legionaries just like those under Cæsar—start to fraternize with the troops in Cæsar's camp. Soon enough, there's a sort of informal communication happening between the two armies. Eventually, the soldiers serving Afranius come to a decision: they resolve to surrender to Cæsar, but they insist on a condition—that their own generals be kept safe. Afranius is agreeable to the idea; however, his fellow commander, Petreius, is staunchly opposed. With a heart firmly loyal to Roman pride, Petreius is horrified at the thought of surrender. As we'll see later, Petreius meets a rather unusual fate in his own right. For now, he crushes the brewing plot with vigorous resolve and even forces an oath against surrender from his men and from Afranius himself. He issues a strict order that any of Cæsar's soldiers found mingling in their camp are to be killed. As Cæsar recounts, Petreius effectively "restores the affair to the old form of war." But ultimately, even Petreius's fervor cannot alter their dire situation. The lack of water becomes so desperate for the Afranians that their generals have no choice but to capitulate and formally surrender their arms.

Cæsar's account of these moments demonstrates his remarkable skill with concise language, and the flexibility of Latin itself. In describing the Afranians' distress, he uses just five Latin words: Premebantur Afraniani pabulatione, aquabantur ægre. This translates roughly to, "The soldiers of Afranius were much distressed in the matter of forage, and could obtain water only with great difficulty." Translating Cæsar's five words into English requires about twenty words to capture the same sense accurately, and likely more than twenty in any English historical retelling.

Upon winning, Cæsar displays extraordinary generosity toward his fellow Romans. Had his defeated foes been Gauls, he would have likely sold them into slavery, executed their leaders, cut off their hands, or driven them down to the river, letting them die in the waters. But here, his enemies are Roman soldiers. Cæsar's only condition is that Afranius's army be disbanded and its leaders free to go wherever they choose. He delivers a speech in which he explains how unfairly they have treated him, yet assures them he will not harm anyone. He tells them that he has borne these wrongs and will continue to bear them with patience. His only requirement is that the generals leave the Province and that the army they commanded disband immediately. Cæsar even assures the soldiers that he won't keep anyone who doesn't wish to stay with him, and he promises to pay those who haven't yet received compensation from Afranius, using his own funds. Those who own homes and lands in Spain are free to remain; those who have nothing, he will first feed and then escort—if not back to Italy itself, then at least to the edge of Italian territory. As for any belongings taken from them by his own soldiers during the battle, he promises that those items will be returned, and he will personally make up any losses. Keeping his word, Cæsar leads those unwilling to stay under his command to the banks of the Var River, which marks the boundary between Italy and the Province, releasing them there. Surely, they left filled with gratitude toward their merciful conqueror. This was mercy indeed—or, perhaps, the most strategic foresight imaginable! Cæsar had completed his entire campaign in Spain within just forty days.

Meanwhile, Decimus Brutus—whom Cæsar had appointed over the ships prepared against the Veneti in western Gaul, and who would later become one of his assassins in the Senate—secures a naval victory against the much larger fleet of the Massilians. The Massilians had prepared seventeen large ships—referred to by Cæsar as naves longæ—but Brutus either captures or destroys nine of them. In his next account, Cæsar will continue describing the siege of Marseilles, detailing the events both at sea and on land after this decisive battle.

Chapter X.

SECOND BOOK OF THE CIVIL WAR.—THE TAKING OF MARSEILLES.—VARRO IN THE SOUTH OF SPAIN.—THE FATE OF CURIO BEFORE UTICA.—B.C. 49.

In his account of the Gallic war, Cæsar structured each book to tell the story of a full year's campaign. When describing the civil war, however, he uses the first two books to recount just one year. The second book narrates three major events from that year's campaign: the siege and capture of Marseilles, the submission of southern Spain—which, though it surrendered quite easily, is described as being subjugated— and the defeat of a Roman army in Africa by a barbarian king. This section is perhaps the least compelling of Cæsar's writings, as it shares little of Cæsar's personal actions, instead focusing on the deeds of his lieutenants both on land and at sea.

Cæsar begins by recounting the immense efforts made by both the besieging forces and the defenders at Marseilles, which was being held for Pompey by Domitius. To strengthen their naval defense, Pompey sent a fleet under Nasidius. Brutus the Younger, who, as we recall, was leading Cæsar's forces in the harbor, had already won a victory over the Massilians even before Nasidius arrived; meanwhile, Trebonius was conducting the siege from the land side for Cæsar. Interestingly, Decimus Brutus, one of the commanders here, would later become one of the conspirators who ultimately turned against and killed Cæsar, along with Trebonius, who would also join that plot.

The sensible Greeks of the city had explained to Cæsar, when he initially asked for their support, that they genuinely cared for both Pompey and Cæsar equally. However, they had felt compelled to take Pompey's side because Domitius, Pompey's general, was the first to enter their city. Now, out of necessity, they found themselves fighting as Pompeians, not only to defend their wealth but also to protect their homes. So, by circumstance, they became staunch defenders of the Republic against the autocracy, as it was during the siege of Marseilles that Cæsar was appointed Dictator—a decree passed in Rome, where such decisions were easily made in the absence of Pompey, the consuls, and most senators who sided with him.

Now fully committed to their chosen side, the people of Marseilles fought with everything they had. We learn that Cæsar's troops, from their elevated camp positioned by Trebonius, could look directly down into the city and see "how all the youth left in the city, along with the elders, their children, wives, and the guards, either stretched their hands to the heavens from the city walls or entered the temples of the immortal gods and cast themselves down before the statues, praying for divine assistance in winning this battle." None of them, Cæsar tells us, doubted that the outcome would determine all they held dear— their liberty, property, and lives. It's clear that the Massilians knew well of the fates of Avaricum, Alesia, and Uxellodunum. "When the battle began," Cæsar writes, "the Massilians showed no lack of courage. Remembering the recent speeches made to them by their own people, they fought as if this battle was their one hope of survival. For those who fell in combat, it was only an early end to what the rest would face if the city were captured."

As he wrote this, Cæsar must have recalled the harsh actions he had taken in Gaul, where his policies sometimes demanded severe measures. Here, however, he skillfully emphasizes his own mercy, as he is about to describe his lenient treatment of Marseilles. He knew that depopulating a wealthy city would be unwise, as the trade it generated benefited both Rome and the Province. Thus, Cæsar carefully highlights how little mercy the besieged expected from him, making his ultimate decision seem all the more generous. Reading his words, we sense that each line has been thoughtfully crafted, even though Cæsar must have had little time for such careful composition given his constant state of action and the many demands on his attention.

Nasidius, whom we may call Pompey's admiral, proved to be of no help at all. The Massilians, emboldened by his arrival, launch a bold attack on the ship carrying young Brutus's flag; but Brutus is too swift and skillful for them. The desperate Massilians end up crashing two of their largest ships into each other as they try to trap Brutus's flagship between them. In the end, the Massilian fleet is completely scattered. Five ships are sunk, four are captured, and one manages to escape with Nasidius, who flees without even attempting to fight. According to Cæsar, Pompey may have sent Nasidius merely to give an appearance of help, not to truly engage in the battle. One lone ship makes it back to the harbor with the grim news, and the Massilians—though briefly disheartened—resolve to continue defending their walls.

The town of Marseilles was well prepared for a defense, the people being resourceful, well-trained, and equipped with necessary materials. They had strong twelve-foot poles with iron tips that could be hurled from their wall-mounted engines with such force that they pierced through four layers of the wicker screens and stationary shields that Cæsar's forces had set up for their protection, thinking nothing could penetrate them. This part of the description inevitably brings to mind modern artillery, with our cannons, armor plating, granite forts, and earthen defenses. These dreadful missiles, launched from the "balistae," were hard on Cæsar's troops, so they came up with the idea to build an enormous tower, constructed so high that it could not be reached by enemy weapons and reinforced so that nothing flammable was exposed. They built this tower one level at a time, each level reinforced against fire and the enemy's projectiles.

As we read about this careful engineering feat, it's easy to think Cæsar himself might have been trained as an engineer, especially given his attention to detail. Yet, in truth, Cæsar was not even at this siege himself and didn't oversee the tower's construction. He must have received a written description of this effort from his officer on site— just as he likely did earlier when constructing the famous bridge over the Rhine. Once the tower was completed, his forces created a covered passage or "muscle," as Cæsar calls it. This structure extended from the massive tower to a strategic point in the town's walls. The muscle's sloped roof was so solid that nothing hurled at it could penetrate or set it aflame. The Massilians tried to stop it with flaming tubs of pitch and large stones, but these simply slid off and were cleared away with poles and prongs. Cæsar's troops, from the height of their impressive tower, gained a deadly advantage, making it nearly impossible for the Massilians to defend their walls, and a breach was nearly made.

At last, the Massilians had nothing left to give. The very gods seemed against them. So, in the humble garb of supplicants, they went to meet the conquerors, offering to surrender the city to Cæsar. They requested Trebonius to wait for Cæsar himself to arrive. Trebonius understood well enough that if his soldiers broke through into the city before Cæsar's arrival, there would be dire consequences. A slight delay would do no harm. No action would be taken until Cæsar came.

Fortunately, Cæsar had previously ordered that the city be spared, and a truce was arranged until he arrived to accept the surrender. Trebonius struggled to keep his soldiers from plundering the town, but he managed to hold them back. The two sides, attackers and defenders alike, waited together for Cæsar's arrival.

But these Massilians were clever and cunning. The Cæsarean soldiers, having agreed to wait for Cæsar's arrival, let their guard down and passed the time in idle amusement. Seeing this, and with a strong wind to aid them, the Massilians suddenly rushed out and managed to set fire to the tower, the covered passage, the rampart, the sheds, and all of Cæsar's siege equipment. Though the tower was made of brick, it burned easily in the fierce wind. Trebonius, however, set to work again and rebuilt everything. Since no more wood was available near the camp, he created a new kind of rampart—one built from bricks, something unheard of before. The Cæsarean soldiers likely had to make these bricks themselves, and we can imagine their growing resentment toward the Massilians. Still, they worked with such diligence and determination that the Massilians soon saw their recent victory was useless. They had nothing left. Neither trickery nor courage would save them now, and once again, they surrendered—this time, intending no further deceit. "Sese dedere sine fraude constituunt," Cæsar writes, which means, "They resolved to surrender themselves without treachery."

Domitius, the general for Pompey, managed to escape on a ship. He set out with three ships, but only the one he was on managed to avoid capture by "young" Brutus. Surely now Marseilles would face harsh punishment, similar to what befell the Gaulish cities. But Cæsar had other plans. He took their public treasury and ships, and reminded them that he spared them more for the city's reputation and ancient standing than for any loyalty shown to him. He left two legions stationed there and departed for Rome.

At Avaricum, where the Gauls had fought to protect their freedom, he had ordered the destruction of everyone. At Alesia, he had condemned every inhabitant when they had merely requested permission to pass through his camp. At Uxellodunum, he had cut off the hands and gouged out the eyes of Gauls who had dared to fight for their homeland. But these Gauls were barbarians, whom Cæsar believed needed to be pacified. The Massilians, on the other hand, were Greeks—a cultured and civilised people who might still serve a useful purpose.

Before turning his attention to Marseilles, Cæsar still had some business to finish in Spain. As mentioned in the previous chapter, he had already forced Afranius and Petreius to surrender their arms and disband their legions. Among those aligned with these generals was a third Pompeian leader named Varro—a respected figure, though not necessarily a skilled military strategist. Cæsar describes how Varro, trying to navigate the political currents of Rome, initially wavered between supporting Pompey and Cæsar. However, once Varro heard that Afranius was successful around Lerida, he ultimately chose to support Pompey—a decision that did not work in his favor.

Varro, stationed further south in Spain, in the region known then as Bætica (present-day Andalusia), found that Cæsar's cause was significantly more popular in that part of the country than Pompey's. Consequently, Cæsar encountered minimal resistance. The legions under Varro's command soon deserted him, and Varro, seeing little chance for victory, quickly surrendered. Although Cæsar does not delve into the specifics of how he handled Varro, history records that he extended his usual courtesy and respect toward this fellow Roman. Varro was a highly learned man, a friend of Cicero, and a prolific author, credited with writing 490 volumes. He was considered a true scholar— a source of pride for Rome due to his literary contributions, if not his military prowess. Remarkably, Varro lived to the age of eighty-eight, a rare feat for a Roman involved in political affairs during these tumultuous times.

Cæsar swiftly restored order in southern Spain, returning the money and valuables Varro had seized from the towns and expressing his gratitude to the local people for their support. With matters in Spain settled, he then crossed over the Pyrenees and proceeded to Marseilles, where he again restored stability to the region.

In the meantime, however, matters were far from calm in Africa. At this time, "Africa" referred to a small province under the Republic's control, lying to the east of Numidia, where the ancient city of Carthage had once stood. This province included the promontory that extends toward Sicily, with Utica serving as its Roman administrative center. Earlier, when Cæsar had decided to secure certain provinces of the Republic before pursuing Pompey across the Adriatic, he had sent a lieutenant to Sicily with three legions, instructing him to advance to Africa as soon as things were settled on the island in favor of Cæsar's cause. In Sicily, there was little resistance, as Cato, the upstanding man to whom Pompey had entrusted the island's governance, chose to depart when Cæsar's legions arrived. He left with a strong sense of grievance, bitterly criticizing Pompey's management.

Afterwards, Cæsar's lieutenant sailed to Africa with two legions, tasked with driving out one Attius Varus. According to Cæsar, Varus had taken control of the province without proper authority and was holding it for Pompey, blocking the rightful governor from even setting foot on its shores. This lieutenant was a favorite of Cæsar's, a young man named Curio. Curio had been elected tribune of the people around the time the Senate was attempting to recall Cæsar from his command in Gaul. At that critical moment, Curio, as tribune, had come to Cæsar's aid, and Cæsar, in turn, held a deep affection for him. Curio belonged to a class of men who, despite noble birth, had thrown themselves into popular causes, much like Catiline and Clodius had done. He was unpredictable, turbulent, unprincipled, prone to vices, reckless with money, indulgent in pleasure, greedy, yet also well-educated, brave, and smart. Cæsar himself had been somewhat like this in his youth and could overlook such flaws in a man who, along with these traits, possessed the even greater virtue of loyalty to Cæsar. Cæsar trusted Curio completely and expected significant accomplishments from him.

Curio, with a sizable fleet and his two legions, landed in Africa, preparing to capture the province on Cæsar's behalf. He gained some initial success and was even hailed as "Imperator" by his troops—a title reserved for a general after a victorious battle. However, Cæsar's account suggests that Curio's officers and soldiers had little confidence in him, uncertain whether to continue following him, take over the ships and return to Sicily, or perhaps switch sides to Attius Varus, who had previously commanded them in Italy before they defected from Pompey to Cæsar. A war council was held, full of uncertainty and debate. Their concern lay not only with Varus, their Roman opponent, but also with Juba, the Numidian king, who would surely join Varus and fight against Curio. Juba was a declared ally of Pompey and an equally declared enemy of Cæsar, harboring a particular grudge against Curio. If Juba arrived personally with his full forces, Curio would find himself in dire straits, especially if caught away from his camp. Driven by the council's hesitation, Curio, wanting to secure his soldiers' support for a battle, addressed his legionaries with a rousing speech. And, of course, we must remember that this speech, as recorded by Cæsar, was likely crafted by Cæsar himself.

The speech begins with Curio speaking in the third person, referring to himself indirectly as he reminds the soldiers of how helpful they were to Cæsar at Corfinium, the town where they had switched allegiance from Pompey to Cæsar. Then, Curio shifts into the first person, putting direct words in his own mouth. "For it was you and your actions," he says, "that set an example for every town; and it's no surprise that Cæsar thinks kindly of you, while the Pompeians bear you no love. For Pompey, though he hadn't yet lost a single battle, fled from Italy simply because of what you accomplished. And now, Cæsar—who holds me in highest regard and who relies on Sicily and Africa to secure Rome and Italy—has entrusted these territories to your honor. Some suggest that you desert me—what could be more satisfying to such people than trapping me and staining your reputation with betrayal? But tell me, haven't you heard about what Cæsar achieved in Spain? Two armies defeated, two generals subdued, and two provinces taken—all in the span of just forty days from the moment Cæsar first set eyes on his enemy. How can those who couldn't resist him before even losing, hope to stand against him now in defeat? And you—who followed Cæsar even when his victory was uncertain—would you now switch sides, aligning with the defeated just as you're about to reap the rewards of your loyalty?

"But perhaps you love Cæsar yet still distrust me. I won't boast about my own services to you—they may be less than I hoped to achieve or than you expected of me." Though he claims not to speak of himself, Curio does indeed take a moment to address his own efforts. "But why should I skip over my own accomplishments, the progress we've made so far, or the good fortune I've had in battle? Does it not matter to you that I brought our entire army here safely, losing not a single ship? That, upon my arrival, I scattered the enemy's fleet at my first strike? That, within two days, I had won twice with our cavalry; that I seized two hundred transport ships from the enemy's harbor; that I weakened them to the point that neither by land nor sea could they gather enough food to sustain themselves? Do you really wish to turn your backs on such fortune, such leadership, to align yourselves instead with the disgrace of Corfinium, the flight from Italy"— referring to Pompey's escape to Dyrrachium—"the surrender of Spain, and all the misfortunes of this African campaign?

"I have wanted nothing more than to be known as Cæsar's soldier, and you yourselves have called me your commander. But if you regret calling me so, I gladly return the title to you. Restore to me my name if you feel it was in mockery that you ever honored me with that title."

This account is filled with energy, and Cæsar's rhetorical description of Curio's speech to his troops is fascinating in itself, as it reflects how Roman commanders were expected to inspire and interact with their soldiers. It also gives insight into the unique challenges of civil war, where loyalty to either side could waver, as soldiers faced the prospect of fighting for one Roman leader they respected against another. Both sides of the conflict were led by Roman Imperators whom the soldiers had come to admire. Curio, we know, was a man capable of persuasive words in moments like these. However, it's unlikely he actually spoke the precise words that Cæsar attributes to him. Cæsar was eager to offer a tribute to his gallant young friend, who had given his life for Cæsar's cause, memorializing him for all time with a speech crafted to glorify his legacy.

Yet, before his ultimate fall, the young commander experiences a brief period of success, one that, had he truly spoken Cæsar's words, would have seemed to justify his confidence. Curio launches a bold attack on the army of his fellow Roman, Varus, and achieves a victory, pushing Varus and his men back to the town of Utica. Curio then resolves to lay siege to the town, and Cæsar hints that the outcome could have been in his favor, due to the sympathies of some townspeople for Cæsar's cause—if not for the advancing threat of the dreaded Juba, king of Numidia. News reaches Curio that Juba has swiftly resolved another matter and is now free to confront the Roman forces in Africa. Varus, too, hears the rumor inside the town. Craftily, Juba sends ahead only a small contingent under his lieutenant, Sabura, giving Curio the false impression that the approaching force is limited. Confident, Curio believes he can handle Sabura and his band of Numidian cavalry with ease.

From this moment, however, we sense that Curio is doomed. Cæsar, in a few poignant lines, offers his apology for his friend's ill-fated decision: "Youth itself was to blame, as well as his high spirits; his earlier successes and trust in his fortune also misled him." There is no trace of reproach in Cæsar's words. Curio makes another speech, rallying his men with, "Hasten to your reward, hasten to your glory!" And hasten they do—but not as Curio had hoped. His troops advance with such speed that the front lines are far ahead of the rest, scattered along the road. When they reach Sabura's force, they find themselves hopelessly outmatched and are swiftly defeated by Juba's soldiers.

As the battle takes its toll, one of Curio's officers urges him to retreat back to camp. But Cæsar records Curio's tragic response, his last words, declaring he would never face Cæsar again after losing the army that had been entrusted to him. These words, reported to Cæsar by that officer, likely bear some truth. "So, fighting, he was slain," Cæsar concludes, and with this, the life of the man Cæsar loved comes to an end.

What happened next was deeply tragic for a Roman army. Many soldiers rushed down to the ships by the sea, hoping to escape, but the scene was one of utter panic and confusion. Things were so chaotic that only a few managed to reach Sicily safely. The others tried to surrender to Varus, and if they had succeeded, their situation might not have been so terrible. A Roman surrendering to another Roman, after all, would likely face little worse than a forced change of allegiance. But Juba, the Numidian king, arrived and claimed the defeated soldiers as his prize, and Varus did not dare to stand against this powerful ally.

Juba ordered most of the captives to be killed but spared a few whom he thought could serve his purposes and add to his renown. In doing so, Juba behaved no worse than Cæsar had often acted in Gaul; yet Cæsar always wrote as though not only Romans but the entire world should view a Roman as something more than an ordinary human. By demanding such respect and making these assertions of superiority, the Romans were often indeed viewed that way. We are then told that the barbarian king of Numidia rode into Utica in triumph, with captured Roman senators trailing behind him—a symbol of his victory. Cæsar makes sure to record the names of two particular senators in this humiliating procession, marking them for posterity. Wherever possible, we'll let them rest in peace.

As for King Juba and his eventual fate, we will hear of him again.

Chapter XI.

THIRD BOOK OF THE CIVIL WAR.—CÆSAR FOLLOWS POMPEY INTO ILLYRIA.—THE LINES OF PETRA AND THE BATTLE OF PHARSALIA.—B.C. 48.

Cæsar begins the final book of his last Commentary by stating that this was the year in which he, Cæsar, had the legal authority to appoint a consul. He selects Publius Servilius to serve alongside him. This means that, since Cæsar had been made Dictator and Pompey had taken the previous year's consuls with him to Illyria, Cæsar was now the sole magistrate with the power to elect a consul. Although he certainly chose the man himself, the election was conducted in a way that maintained the appearance of following the Republic's established procedures. He stayed in Rome as Dictator for only eleven days, during which time he passed several laws aimed at reducing the instability caused by the breakdown of usual governance. Then he departed for Brindisi, following Pompey's path.

Cæsar had twelve legions with him, but lacked sufficient ships to transport them, and he admits that his soldiers were suffering from poor health after enduring a harsh autumn in southern Italy—a climate much tougher than the healthy air of Gaul and northern Spain, to which they were accustomed. He tells us that Pompey had had an entire year to prepare his forces, a year without active warfare, during which he gathered soldiers, ships, and funding, as well as support from many places—Asia, the Cyclades, Corcyra, Athens, Bithynia, Cilicia, Phœnicia, Egypt, and the free states of Achaia. Pompey had nine Roman legions and was awaiting two more with his father-in-law, Scipio, coming from Syria. He had assembled three thousand archers from Crete, Sparta, and Pontus, as well as twelve hundred slingers and seven thousand cavalry from Galatia, Cappadocia, and Thrace. A bold prince from Macedonia had brought him two hundred mounted men, and five hundred Galatian and German cavalry—who had been stationed in Egypt to secure Ptolemy's loyalty—were sent to Pompey by his son Cnæus, who had also brought along eight hundred armed members of their own retainers.

Antiochus of Commagena contributed two hundred mounted archers as mercenaries, with a promise of significant pay. Warriors from the regions of Dardania (from the lands of ancient Troy), the Bessi (from the banks of the Hebrus), Thessaly, and Macedonia had all flocked to Pompey's side. We sense that Cæsar lists these forces with a degree of anticipation, savoring the impressive strength of Pompey's assembled forces even as he prepares us for the outcome—Cæsar will soon reveal how he, with his smaller force of Roman legionaries, would scatter these armies to the winds after successfully landing on the shores of Illyria.

Pompey has also gathered an impressive stock of grain—"frumenti vim maximam," as Cæsar phrases it. If literally translated, it would be "a great power of corn," like an expression from an old Irish tale. Pompey's forces have filled the seas with ships to block Cæsar's exit from Italy. Eight vice-admirals command these fleets, each named by Cæsar, while the overall commander is Bibulus, who was once Cæsar's co-consul before the Gallic campaigns. Bibulus had been so overwhelmed by Cæsar's influence during that time that he secluded himself in his house, leaving Cæsar to act as if he were sole consul. Now, Bibulus is bent on revenge, but Cæsar seems to imply that Bibulus's efforts to retaliate will be just as ineffective as before.

With his legions at Brindisi, Cæsar makes a speech to his troops, displaying an audacity that surpasses most of his actions. He tells them that since they've nearly completed all his "business" for him—the last task being to bring down the Republic itself, with Pompey, his legions, and all the forces loyal to the Republic, not to mention King Ptolemy in Egypt, King Pharnaces in Asia, and King Juba in Numidia—they should leave behind their belongings from previous wars. Doing so will allow them to pack more tightly in the boats he intends to use to get them across to Illyria. There's no promise of recovering their possessions later; Cæsar simply expects his soldiers to rely on his goodwill for their future gains. They respond with one unified cheer, showing their readiness to follow him without hesitation. With seven legions, he makes the crossing, skirting those dreaded "rocks of evil fame," the Acroceraunia, known to us from Horace, and manages to avoid Bibulus, who, it seems, has retreated to his ship as he once withdrew into his house.

Cæsar appears to have taken on this dangerous voyage fully aware that a run-in with Bibulus could spell disaster. Indeed, with a bit of vigilance and effort, Bibulus could have turned the situation in his favor. Yet Cæsar still tries his luck, relying on "Fortune," and succeeds, landing at a site he calls Palæste on the Epirus coast, considerably south of Dyrrachium in Illyria, where Pompey had landed the year before. There, Pompey has stored the vast provisions Cæsar mentions.

Finally, Bibulus decides to take action and attacks the ships Cæsar sends back to bring the rest of his army. Coming across thirty empty vessels, Bibulus vents his frustration by burning them all, as well as killing their sailors and captains, supposedly to discourage others from making the trip. Cæsar tells us this, adding that Bibulus acts "with all the wrath caused by his own negligence and regret." It's not hard to feel a sense of grim satisfaction when we learn that, although Bibulus continues to roam the seas, seemingly tireless, he achieves little and eventually dies—possibly of sheer frustration.

Bibulus does manage to capture another ship later, but this time it's not a military vessel. Instead, it carries the non-combatant followers of Cæsar's camp—families, servants, and others traveling for personal reasons. Bibulus, showing no mercy, slaughters everyone on board, down to the youngest child. However, we should remember that this account is from Cæsar's perspective, and he was not known to speak kindly of Bibulus.

Mark Antony remains at Brindisi, commanding the legions that Cæsar couldn't transport on his initial trip due to limited ship capacity. Cæsar presses Antony urgently to make the crossing. Meanwhile, negotiations for peace begin, though Cæsar appears to use them primarily to buy time until Antony and the remaining legions can arrive. We learn that by now, Cæsar and Pompey's camps are positioned very close, separated only by the river Apsus, as Cæsar has advanced northward toward Pompey's stronghold. Soldiers from both sides talk across the river, agreeing not to throw any weapons as they converse.

Cæsar seizes this opportunity and sends Vatinius to the riverbank to discuss peace. Vatinius shouts across, questioning whether "citizens should be allowed to send ambassadors to fellow citizens to discuss peace," adding that even deserters and brigands had been permitted to negotiate, especially when the aim was to prevent citizens from fighting one another. This logic seems compelling, and a date for further talks is set. Labienus, who had once been loyal to Cæsar but has since joined Pompey's side, arrives at the river to negotiate on one side, while Vatinius stands on the opposite bank.

But then, according to Cæsar's account, Cæsar's own soldiers suddenly hurl their weapons at Labienus, likely unable to tolerate the sight or sound of a man they now consider a traitor. Labienus manages to escape, shielded by his men, but leaves seething with anger. "From now on," he declares, "let us speak no more of peace. There will be no peace until Cæsar's head is brought to us." Despite this turn, these riverside talks likely serve Cæsar's purpose by stalling for time.

Eager to get his troops across from Italy, Cæsar grows frustrated with Antony for the delays. A famous story—one Cæsar doesn't tell himself—circulates that Cæsar, in his impatience, attempted to cross the sea back to Brindisi himself. Boarding a small boat in the midst of a storm, he reportedly encouraged the fearful boatmaster by declaring, "You carry Cæsar and his fortunes." They attempted the crossing but were ultimately forced back by the fierce winds.

At last, a southwest wind rises, giving Antony the chance to set sail with his fleet, despite Pompey's warships still patrolling the waters and guarding the Illyrian coast. But fortune is on Antony's side, and the second half of Cæsar's army catches favorable winds and is carried northward toward the shore, right in view of Pompey and his soldiers stationed at Dyrrachium. However, two ships fall behind and are captured by Otacilius, a Pompeian officer. One ship is filled with recruits, the other with seasoned veterans. Both groups are asked to surrender, and Otacilius swears not to harm them if they comply.

Cæsar then remarks on the importance of presence of mind in securing safety. The recruits, trusting Otacilius's oath, surrender, only to be killed when he goes back on his word, ignoring his promise. But the veterans are not so easily deceived. They refuse to surrender, well aware of how little they can trust Otacilius. Instead, they run their ship ashore in the night, fighting fiercely and ultimately making it safely to Antony. Cæsar wryly notes that the recruits might have done the same had they not been weakened by seasickness, but even the storm and the ship's foul conditions couldn't shake the courage of the old soldiers, who endured it all without faltering.

Then, we hear of Metellus Scipio, who, on his journey from Syria to join Pompey in Macedonia, nearly robs the temple of Diana at Ephesus. Scipio gathers a group of senators to act as witnesses to ensure that he fairly counts the money as he removes it from the temple. But just as he's about to complete this profitable task, letters from Pompey arrive, urging him onward. Scipio decides not to delay his journey further, even though he misses the chance to complete the theft. He hurries to meet Pompey, eager to share in the command in the coming decisive battle.

Meanwhile, Cæsar sends his lieutenants into Thessaly, Aetolia, and Macedonia to secure allies, capture cities, and gather supplies. Although this territory is thought to be loyal to Pompey, many have heard of Cæsar's successes, and the Greeks are keen to align themselves with the strongest Roman of the moment. They must decide whom to support based on who is likely to win, and the decision is not easy. Soon, we'll see Cæsar's way of clarifying matters for the citizens of Gomphi, who waver in their support.

In the meantime, Cæsar unites his forces with those Antony has brought from Italy. Now, he is determined to force Pompey into a decisive confrontation.

We can divide the rest of this final book of Cæsar's second Commentary into two main episodes. The first is the account of what happened within the lines at Petra, where Pompey emerged victorious. However, despite the scale of his success, this victory has received little recognition in history. The second episode, which the whole world knows, is the battle of Pharsalia, where Cæsar emerged triumphant and assumed ultimate control. Ironically, the events at Petra should have made Pharsalia unnecessary, as Pompey's complete success there could have halted further conflict. Yet two factors worked against this outcome: the fact that the Commentary was written by Cæsar rather than Pompey, and that, unfortunately for Pompey, the battle of Pharsalia came after Petra.

Cæsar's description of the movements and strategies employed by both armies at Petra is complex and difficult to untangle. Even if it were simpler, our purpose here wouldn't allow us to present the full narrative in detail. By now, Cæsar had successfully combined his own legions, which he brought over from Italy, with those that had arrived later with Antony, and was eager to force a battle. His soldiers, although fewer than Pompey's in number, were battle-hardened and experienced in the arts of war. Pompey's soldiers, on the other hand, were mostly new to fighting; yet they were steadily learning, and each week they spent in preparation worked in Pompey's favor.

Hoping to compel a confrontation, Cæsar managed to position his forces between Dyrrachium, where Pompey kept his military supplies and stores, and Pompey's army itself, effectively cutting Pompey off from his base by land. Yet the sea remained open to Pompey. His fleet was well-established along the coast, whereas Cæsar's forces had not a single ship capable of challenging Pompey's naval forces.

North of Dyrrachium lay a rugged, rocky promontory, known as Petra, which had direct access to the sea. Here, Pompey positioned his army, taking advantage of a broad strip of pastureland at the base of the rock. He fortified this position with impressive Roman defenses— a continuous trench, bank, and wall stretching across fifteen Roman miles, or just over thirteen English miles, from sea to sea. His fortifications included twenty-four towers and numerous earthworks, creating a line so secure it seemed nearly impregnable. Within this perimeter, Pompey secured ample grazing land for his horses, while the open sea allowed him access to supplies and reinforcements. From the vast stores he had amassed at Dyrrachium, all along the coasts of Greece, Asia, and Egypt, Pompey could freely draw provisions. His only limitations were adequate grass for his horses and access to fresh water. In contrast, Cæsar faced extreme shortages of nearly everything but grass and water, as he was backed against the harsh, mountainous lands of Illyria. The local inhabitants, who typically relied on imported corn to survive, were already struggling due to Pompey's strategic foresight in emptying the storehouses and leaving nearby towns desolate.

Yet, undeterred, Cæsar resolved to confine his opponent. He began constructing lines around Pompey's position, effectively trapping him at Petra. Small garrisons and towers were set up on hills surrounding Pompey's encampment, gradually connecting these posts with continuous fortifications from one sea to the other. This strategy was aimed at blocking Pompey's horsemen from venturing out for forage and weakening the horses trapped within. Furthermore, Cæsar believed that news of Pompey being besieged would diminish Pompey's reputation—his auctoritas—in the eyes of foreign nations and make it seem that Pompey dared not engage Cæsar in direct combat.

In modern retellings of history, Cæsar is often depicted as an unstoppable force, with Pompey almost overshadowed. But in passages like these, we see that this was far from the case. Up to this point, Pompey was the more accomplished man; he had achieved great deeds and commanded immense respect. On his side were Rome's wealthiest and most respectable citizens. Pompey was, in essence, the leader of the Conservative faction, confident that he simply had to hold his position until Cæsar's rebellion exhausted itself. To Pompey, Cæsar and his followers were like the fringe revolutionary forces of France before they proved their strength, or the Reform Bill and Catholic Emancipation to figures like George IV and Lord Eldon—an unwanted upheaval that might still be quashed.

Pompey's confidence is evident in a boast he reportedly made to his men, which Cæsar recounts: Pompey would consider himself a failed general if Cæsar's legions could escape the precarious position they had recklessly created for themselves without "very great loss"— maximo detrimento—a loss so significant it would approach ruin. And Pompey's assessment was nearly correct.

There was a lot of fighting over the grassy areas and the good spots to take cover. Most of this fighting happened right between the two opposing lines. Cæsar faced a disadvantage because his fortifications, being much longer, required a larger number of men to build, extend, and maintain them. On the other hand, Pompey, with the inner line, needed fewer men for his works, so he had more soldiers free to fight. Although Cæsar's men, being experienced, had the upper hand in actual combat, Pompey's inexperienced soldiers were gaining the practice they needed. Even so, Pompey was struggling a lot. They couldn't find water on the rocky ground, and whenever he tried to dig wells, Cæsar would divert the water sources, leaving Pompey's wells dry. Cæsar says he even blocked off streams to create small lakes, preventing the water from flowing underground to where Pompey's men could reach it. However, it seems that any reservoirs like this would eventually overflow and become useless.

Meanwhile, Cæsar's soldiers had no bread except what they made from a wild cabbage called "chara" that grew there. They mixed it with milk, eating it without complaint, even though it didn't taste very good. To show Pompey's men the kind of food seasoned soldiers could make do with, they tossed loaves made from this mix across the lines, since they were close enough to talk and taunt each other. Pompey's men mocked Cæsar's troops for their lack of food, but Cæsar's forces had plenty of water and meat, and they assured him they would rather eat tree bark than let Pompey escape.

Cæsar always had one big concern: that Pompey might land troops behind him and attack from the rear. To prevent this, Cæsar built another trench and bank running from the shore at a right angle to his main line, intending to connect this new line to his main fortifications along the coast between his two positions. But then, just as he was working on these defenses, disaster struck, nearly leading to his defeat. While his men were digging trenches and building towers, the fighting was so intense that, according to Cæsar, there were six battles in a single day. Pompey lost two thousand soldiers, while Cæsar lost only twenty. However, every Cæsarean soldier defending a certain tower was wounded, and four officers lost their eyesight. Cæsar estimated that thirty thousand arrows were shot at the men guarding that tower and mentions an officer named Scæva who had two hundred and thirty arrow holes in his shield. It must have been a large shield, and counting all the holes would have taken a lot of time. Cæsar was so impressed that he rewarded Scæva with a large sum of money—over £500—and promoted him six ranks up to become the first centurion, or Primipilus, of the legion. We know of no other instance of such rapid promotion in a true account, though there is a story in verse about a brave sailor who was made first-lieutenant on the spot, but that sailor was actually a woman.

Two perfidious Gauls to whom Cæsar had Cæsar had some Gallic soldiers who had once been loyal to him but whom he had to discipline for some serious thefts they committed. Though he didn't have time to punish them, they went over to Pompey and revealed all of Cæsar's plans—details about his ditches, forts, and walls, whether they were completed or still under construction. Before this, Cæsar assures us that none of his men had defected to the enemy, even though many of the enemy's soldiers had joined him. But these untrustworthy Gauls caused a lot of damage. Hearing from them how far Cæsar was from finishing his defenses along the seashore, Pompey gathered a large fleet of boats and managed to land a large force during the night between Cæsar's two lines, splitting his army and hitting him at his weakest point.

Cæsar admits that his troops panicked and that many were killed. It seems that the sheer size of his own defenses led to his downfall, as the different sections were separated, leaving each group unable to help the others. This event ended in the complete defeat of Cæsar's forces. Cæsar himself had to flee, and if Pompey had pursued him, it might have been the end for Cæsar. He confesses that he lost 960 legionaries, 32 officers, and 32 standards in the two battles fought that day.

Then, Cæsar recounts a story about Labienus, who had been his most trusted lieutenant during the Gallic wars but had now joined Pompey, unwilling to fight against the Republic. Labienus requested the prisoners from Pompey and had them all killed, mocking them and asking if seasoned soldiers like them were used to running away. Cæsar was very angry with Labienus, but Labienus might have argued that executing prisoners was something he learned in Gaul. As for those mocking words, Cæsar couldn't have heard them himself, and it's understandable that he would want to speak harshly of Labienus.

Pompey was immediately declared "Imperator," and he accepted the title, even though his victory had sadly been over fellow Romans. "The effect of this victory on the spirits and confidence of Pompey's followers was so great that they no longer thought about continuing the war, only about the success they had just achieved." Then, Cæsar criticizes the Pompeians, defending himself in the same words. "They didn't consider that it was the small number of our soldiers that led to their victory, or that the uneven ground and narrow passages played a part, or that our men were thrown into confusion by being trapped between two sets of defenses. Nor did they remember that our forces were split in two, so one part couldn't assist the other. They also overlooked how our soldiers, constrained as they were, couldn't fight a fair battle and that their own crowding in the narrow gorges caused more trouble than the enemy did. They forgot the usual risks of war—that small issues, like a baseless fear, a sudden panic, or a superstition, can lead to disaster. They ignored how easily a general's error or an officer's misjudgment can harm an army. Instead, they spread the news of their victory across the world, sending letters and stories as if their success was purely from their own bravery, and they believed there could be no setback for them after this." This was the event at Petra, which nearly reversed Cæsar and Pompey's places in history.

Cæsar now admits that he must change his entire campaign strategy. He addresses his troops, explaining that this defeat, like the one at Gergovia, might still bring success in the future. The victory at Alesia had come after the setback at Gergovia because it encouraged the Gauls to fight, and the losses at Petra might lead to similar fortune—since surely now Pompey's army would no longer shy away from battle. He punishes and demotes a few officers. His remarks about his army after their defeat are very moving. "Such sorrow fell over the whole army from this loss, and such a strong drive to redeem their honor, that no one now wanted the role of tribune or centurion in his legion. All, as a form of self-imposed punishment, took on more work, and every man was eager for battle. Some of the higher-ranking soldiers were so inspired by Cæsar's words that they believed they should stay and fight right where they were." But Cæsar, being a wise general, did not do that. He marched southeast, and while retreating, managed to outmaneuver Pompey, who only half-heartedly pursued him. Soon, Pompey abandoned the chase. His father-in-law, Scipio, had brought a large army from the east and was now in Thessaly. As we read this, we can't help but recall how recently it was that Cæsar had been Pompey's father-in-law and friend, as Pompey, deeply devoted, clung to Julia, his young wife. Now, Pompey moved east to unite his forces with Scipio's army, while Cæsar, taking a more southern path into Thessaly, joined up with troops under his lieutenant, Calvinus, who had been keeping an eye on Scipio and barely avoided capture by Pompey before reaching Cæsar. But wherever fortune or chance could play a role, the gods always favored Cæsar.

Then Cæsar recounts how he dealt with two towns in Thessaly, Gomphi and Metropolis. The situation for Gomphi was unfortunate; Cæsar arrived there first. By now, the news of Pompey's victory at Petra had spread widely, and the people of Gomphi—who, in fairness, would have supported either Cæsar or Pompey depending on who appeared stronger, as they only wished to secure their town's safety—believed that Cæsar was struggling. Seeing him as a losing force, they decided to shut their gates against him and quickly sent messengers to Pompey, hoping he would come to their aid. They believed they could hold out for a short time, confident that Pompey would arrive soon to help defend them.

However, Pompey did not arrive in time, and the Gomphians' ability to withstand Cæsar's forces proved brief. At around three in the afternoon, Cæsar began his siege on the town. By sunset, the walls had fallen, and Cæsar's soldiers poured into Gomphi, plundering it as a punishment for resisting him. News of Gomphi's fate reached the nearby town of Metropolis just as they were preparing to bar their own gates. Realizing what Cæsar's wrath might mean, they quickly changed their minds and opened their gates to him. Cæsar, in turn, rewarded Metropolis with his protection, allowing the townspeople to remain safe. Word of these contrasting fates spread throughout Thessaly, and the towns learned the benefits of staying in Cæsar's good graces.

Meanwhile, Pompey, after merging his forces with those of his father-in-law Scipio, shared his honors and command with him. This gesture hinted at Pompey's difficult position; he was known to be a proud leader who would never share his status unless compelled. Commanding with Scipio by his side and a Senate of Roman officials in his camp was no easy task for Pompey. Although having the Senate with him might have been a mark of his authority, these senators, unused to strict military discipline, were likely more challenging to control than seasoned soldiers. They even accused Pompey of keeping them in Thessaly simply to exercise power over them. Yet, despite these internal disputes, they were all confident that Cæsar's downfall was near. In Pompey's camp, the senators and officers eagerly discussed the rewards they would claim in Rome once their old order was restored by Pompey's victory.

As the anticipated battle drew near, Labienus, Cæsar's former trusted lieutenant, reappeared and delivered a speech that Cæsar retells, clearly intending for readers to measure its words against the battle's outcome. Labienus, who had once served Cæsar faithfully in Gaul and Germany as his second-in-command, now spoke to Pompey with scorn for Cæsar's current army. "Do not think, O Pompey, that this is the same army that conquered Gaul and Germany," he declared, emphasizing his personal experience in those campaigns. "I was there for every battle and know what I speak of. Only a small part of that original army remains. Many have died in countless battles. Disease took many in Italy during the autumn, others have returned home, and many were left behind on the far shore." Labienus went on to remind Pompey of news they'd received from their friends who had remained behind in Italy, mentioning that "these cohorts of Cæsar's were pieced together just recently at Brindisi." He implied that Cæsar's current army had been hastily assembled, filled with recruits from both Gauls, but that its real strength had been lost in previous battles, particularly during the fierce confrontations at Dyrrachium within the defenses of Petra.

As if to seal their confidence, Labienus swore that he would not rest under a tent again until he had claimed victory over Cæsar, and Pompey, along with all the officers around them, joined in the oath, each pledging to share in the imminent triumph. They all departed filled with certainty about their upcoming victory. There was, no doubt, a strong sense of overconfidence. As for the words attributed to Labienus, we can clearly sense Cæsar's resentment toward him and might question whether Labienus truly spoke them. Nonetheless, Cæsar uses this account to emphasize the opposition's bold yet ultimately misplaced confidence before the decisive clash.

Finally, the location of the decisive battle was chosen—near the town of Pharsalus, along the Enipeus River in Thessaly. This battle would later become legendary, known as the Battle of Pharsalia, with "Pharsalia" widely considered the name of the plain where it occurred. However, neither "Pharsalia" nor "Enipeus" are mentioned in Cæsar's Commentaries, and the exact spot of the battle remains somewhat uncertain. The battlefield now lies within Turkish territory, near the mountains that form the border between modern Greece and Turkey, a difficult area for historical researchers to access. Cæsar had been maneuvering his forces close to Pompey's, pressing him until Pompey found himself forced to engage in battle. Labienus had already delivered his boasts and made his oath, and so, at last, the date and place were set. Cæsar, for his part, was fully prepared. At this point, Cæsar was fifty-two years old, and Pompey was fifty-seven.

Cæsar reports that Pompey commanded 110 cohorts, or eleven legions. If these legions were at full strength, Pompey's forces would have numbered 66,000 legionaries. However, Cæsar states that Pompey's army was closer to 45,000 men, meaning about two-thirds of their potential capacity. He doesn't miss the chance to remind us that among these eleven legions were the two he had once turned over to the Senate by their demand. Pompey stationed himself with these very two legions on the left flank, away from the river, alongside all his auxiliary troops—slingers, archers, and cavalry, who were not counted among the legionaries. In the center, he placed Scipio, who had brought legions from Syria, according to Cæsar's account. Additional sources indicate that Lentulus commanded Pompey's right wing by the river, while Domitius, remembered for his attempt to defend Marseilles against young Brutus and Trebonius, commanded the left.

Cæsar's army consisted of 80 cohorts, or eight legions, which, at full strength, should have numbered around 48,000 men. However, as

Cæsar notes, he led only 22,000 legionaries into battle, meaning his forces were short by more than half. Following his usual formation, he placed his elite tenth legion on the right, farthest from the river. His ninth legion, severely weakened by earlier battles at Petra, was joined with the eleventh and positioned on the left wing near the river. Antony commanded the left wing, Domitius Calvinus (whom Cæsar refers to by both names at different times) took charge of the center, and Sulla led the right. Cæsar positioned himself on the right flank with his tenth legion, directly across from Pompey.

From what can be gathered, the battlefield itself offered neither side much advantage in terms of terrain. Thus, with both armies set, the historic confrontation began.

The account Cæsar provides of the actual battle is relatively straightforward and perhaps lacks the drama we might expect. As was customary, he made a speech to his troops beforehand. But if Cæsar truly spoke the words he records, it was one of the most misleading speeches ever given. He began by reminding his soldiers that they themselves had seen his efforts to secure peace. He then referenced past treaties he'd supposedly pursued in good faith, though these had often been little more than strategic delays he used to outmaneuver Pompey. He claimed he had no desire to waste the lives of his soldiers or to harm the Republic by destroying either army—whether it be Pompey's or his own. Both armies were Roman, and he professed that he wished to spare all that belonged to the Republic. It's worth acknowledging that Cæsar was indeed cautious with Roman lives when he could be, yet he was also quick to sacrifice them without hesitation if it served his purpose. He was exceptionally strategic, but tender-hearted? That quality was foreign to him—and perhaps to any Roman of his time.

Then there's a story about one soldier, Crastinus, who vowed to Cæsar that, dead or alive, he would bring him honor in the battle. True to his word, Crastinus hurled the first spear at the enemy and fulfilled his promise—but only in death, as he was killed in his effort to please Cæsar.

Pompey's strategy was conservative; he ordered his first line to hold their position and await Cæsar's charge. Cæsar points out this as a flaw in Pompey's approach, as the surge of adrenaline and momentum often give soldiers a distinct edge in the initial rush of battle. Following their orders, Cæsar's soldiers advanced across the open ground, but, being disciplined veterans, they paused to catch their breath before unleashing their spears. They then hurled their javelins, drew their swords, and closed in on Pompey's forces for hand-to-hand combat.

Pompey's main strategy, however, relied less on his legionaries and more on his substantial cavalry and auxiliary troops. He outnumbered Cæsar overall and believed he could overwhelm him with a formidable array of horsemen, archers, and slingers. Pompey counted on this maneuver to crush Cæsar's forces from the flank, effectively winning the battle without exhausting his legionaries. Yet Cæsar had anticipated this move. Arranged in his usual formation of three lines, he had a surprise fourth line—a select group of soldiers positioned just behind and to the right of his third rank. This special reserve force was tasked specifically with countering Pompey's cavalry when they inevitably attacked the right flank.

As expected, Pompey's cavalry, along with the archers and slingers, moved to encircle Cæsar's right side. At first, Cæsar's own limited cavalry began to fall back before the onslaught. Pompey's horsemen and archers moved in what seemed like an unstoppable wave, sweeping around the flank with the apparent goal of shattering Cæsar's forces. But Cæsar's fourth line was ready. At his command, this reserve line surged forward with fierce speed, charging directly into Pompey's cavalry. According to Cæsar, his soldiers advanced with such force that Pompey's cavalry had no choice but to retreat. They were not just forced back but were quickly driven into full-scale panic, fleeing to the safety of the nearby high ground. This retreat left Pompey's archers and slingers completely vulnerable. With no one to defend them, they were left isolated and were swiftly cut down in large numbers.

This was the undoing of Pompey's grand cavalry assault, which he had hoped would decide the battle without requiring much effort from his legionaries. Instead, it turned into a decisive and devastating failure, with his auxiliary forces overrun and his carefully planned strategy collapsing around him.

Cæsar acknowledges that Pompey's legionaries The soldiers of Cæsar drew their swords with courage and joined the battle with great determination. But immediately after beginning his account of this fight, Cæsar shifts to describing the collapse of Pompey's cavalry and the massacre of the vulnerable auxiliary slingers. In his next breath, he gives the impression that the battle's outcome was already decided. Although Pompey's forces far outnumbered Cæsar's, we learn that Cæsar's third line ultimately pushed against Pompey's legionaries when they were already exhausted—"defessi," as Cæsar puts it. The small, elite group of soldiers who had brilliantly routed Pompey's cavalry on the flank now used their momentum to turn the tide, breaking through the lines of Pompey's main legions and securing the victory.

According to Cæsar, the outcome was swift and decisive, with no doubt left about who had won. Pompey, realizing the battle was lost, retreated to his camp, hoping to make a last stand there. But resistance was futile, and Pompey was forced to flee altogether. Mounting a horse with a few loyal companions, he did not stop until he reached the coast. There, he boarded a supply ship, lamenting bitterly that those same men he had relied on for victory had now betrayed him.

Cæsar paints a vivid picture of what his men found upon entering Pompey's camp—a place prepared for victory with every luxury. Hungry, disciplined, and hardened by their hardships, Cæsar's soldiers entered a scene that was more fit for celebration than for a war camp. Lavish couches were set out, silver dishes were arranged, tables were laden with food, and the tents of the Senate's elite were adorned with fresh ivy. These senators, so certain of victory, had either perished in the chaotic retreat or fled to the barren, desolate mountains, abandoning their once-grand camp to Cæsar's men.

The day after the battle, Cæsar continued his pursuit of the fleeing forces, ultimately forcing a large group of them to surrender. He cornered these fugitives on a hilltop, cutting them off from water. With no choice left, they surrendered unconditionally. In a dramatic moment, these former elite warriors of the Roman Republic, the finest representatives of its military strength, lay prostrate on the ground, hands outstretched, begging Cæsar for mercy. Only the day before, they had sworn not to rest until they had conquered. Now, weeping, they implored Cæsar for their lives. Cæsar, giving a brief speech on his famed clemency, granted them mercy, sparing their lives. He handed them over to his soldiers, ordering that they be neither harmed nor looted.

Cæsar claims he lost only 200 soldiers in this decisive battle, including 30 officers—brave men like the gallant Crastinus, who had vowed to honor Cæsar even if it cost him his life. In contrast, Pompey's losses were staggering: 15,000 of his men had been killed, and 24,000 had surrendered. Cæsar's forces captured 180 standards and 9 eagles, a testament to the scale of his victory. These numbers may seem almost unbelievable, whether for the conqueror's minimal losses or the scale of the vanquished, yet Cæsar's account has been widely accepted as accurate, and it stands as the official record of that day.

Thus, the Battle of Pharsalia was won, marking a turning point that signaled the collapse of the Roman Republic as it had been known.

Yet Cæsar by no means believed his task was complete—far from it. His immediate duty now was to pursue Pompey, for if Pompey managed to escape, he could quickly gather a new army from the Republic's distant provinces and loyal allies. Cæsar's focus, as he says, was to chase Pompey "to the neglecting of all other things." Meanwhile, Pompey, seemingly overwhelmed by the disaster of his defeat, fled across the Aegean Sea with a small group of followers. Along the way, he collected his young wife, who was waiting on an island, and together they made their way toward Egypt.

The story of Pompey's tragic death is well-known. In need of refuge and assistance, Pompey appealed to the young King Ptolemy of Egypt, relying on the past friendship between himself and the boy's father. But Ptolemy, controlled by a treacherous group of advisors—eunuchs, mercenaries, and ruthless soldiers—had no real power over the decision. These men, considering Pompey a threat, concluded that it would be better to eliminate him than to offer help. A royal satrap named Achillas and a Roman soldier, Septimius, acting as messengers from Ptolemy, rowed out to Pompey's ship and coaxed him into their small boat. Then, in full view of his wife, Pompey was assassinated, and his head was severed and taken away as evidence of the deed. This was the end of Pompey, who had once been blessed with boundless fortune—until Cæsar appeared on the scene.

The Roman poet Lucan, who wrote an epic centered on the battle of Pharsalia, remarked that Cæsar could tolerate no superior, and Pompey no equal. Perhaps Lucan sought to cast Pompey in a more noble light by comparison. Yet when we look closely at both men, it becomes evident that Cæsar was just as determined as Pompey to dominate the political landscape, though he proved far more adept at removing any who might share the power he so intensely desired. When Pompey held the position of power in the triumvirate, he admitted his younger ally, Cæsar, to what he must have regarded as an equal share. By contrast, Cæsar, also part of the triumvirate, merely used his elder Pompey as a stepping stone. At Thessaly, Pompey was even forced to share the authority of his position with his father-in-law Scipio. But Cæsar never allowed another to carry any portion of his authority or to share in the mantle of his command.

When comparing Pompey's character to that of his formidable rival, one could argue that Pompey, in his battles both on the field and in the political arena, was motivated by a profound love for the Republic and for Rome as the grandest institution the world had ever known. He was guided by a sense of patriotism that Cæsar, perhaps due to his singular ambition, could not fully grasp. Pompey wanted to lead, but he wished to lead the Republic, preserving its traditions and structure. In contrast, Cæsar held little regard for the institutions of the past; he lacked reverence for Rome's established order. He was without that attachment to tradition, that loyalty to the footsteps of predecessors, which makes many of us cling to our beliefs, even when they are proven flawed. Instead, Cæsar sought to create something entirely new from the ashes of the Republic—an order that, shaped by his ambition and genius, might rise as something better and more enduring than the Republic had been.

The final seven chapters of the third book in Cæsar's Commentary mark the beginning of his account of the Alexandrine war—a record he did not continue beyond these chapters. The fact that Cæsar managed to write any Commentary at all during the intense demands of military campaigns, coupled with the urgent needs of his political situation, stands as one of the most astonishing feats of human capability. Now, he recounts how, after a brief pause in Asia, he set out in pursuit of Pompey, first to Cyprus and then to Egypt, accompanied by a mere 3,200 men. "The rest," he explains, "worn out by wounds, battles, exhaustion, and the vastness of the journey, could not follow him." Nonetheless, he commanded that fresh legions be formed from the scattered remnants of Pompey's defeated army, and, with remarkable confidence in the loyalty of his distant allies, continued on his way to Egypt.

Cæsar notes that he was delayed in Alexandria due to the Etesian winds, yet we also know that Cleopatra sought him out in Alexandria, appealing to him for aid in her struggle to secure the throne of Egypt. Knowing what ultimately transpired between them, it seems fair to question how much of the delay was genuinely caused by the winds. Had Cleopatra been an unremarkable, swarthy Nubian, as some have claimed, one might suspect that Cæsar would have left Alexandria, defying even the strongest winds. But for Cæsar, every wind seemed to fill his sails in the direction he desired.

Once in Alexandria, Cæsar gained control over Cleopatra's brother, Ptolemy, who, according to their father's will, was supposed to rule Egypt jointly with Cleopatra. This arrangement provoked an uproar among the Alexandrians, who revolted against Cæsar in great numbers. In response, Cæsar executed Photinus, one of King Ptolemy's key advisors, saw his own ambassador assassinated, and set the Egyptian royal fleet ablaze—an act which, unfortunately, also led to the destruction of a large portion of Egypt's royal library. "These events marked the beginning of the Alexandrine war," he writes, closing the last chapter of his final Commentary with these words.

Chapter XII.
CONCLUSION.

Having completed these ten concise chapters summarizing the ten books of Cæsar's Commentaries, the author of this brief volume now brings his work to a close. Since he wishes to avoid any impression that he intended to write a history, he would not add further remarks, except that three additional Commentaries about Cæsar's later wars were appended to his original works by other authors. There exists a Commentary on the Alexandrine war, likely penned by Hirtius, who wrote the final book of the Gallic war, along with Commentaries on the African and Spanish wars, which critics believe were written by Oppius, a trusted friend of Cæsar. The Alexandrine war stands as a distinct conflict, one into which Cæsar was drawn by his unparalleled boldness in pursuing Pompey into Egypt, and possibly by the allure of Cleopatra herself. This Egyptian campaign subsequently led to an additional war in Asia Minor, detailed within the same Commentary. The African and Spanish wars, aimed at quelling the lingering sparks of Pompeian resistance, were effectively extensions of the civil war, and their accounts could have easily served as further chapters of Cæsar's "De Bello Civili."

When Cæsar landed in Alexandria in pursuit of Pompey, he was greeted with the unsettling tribute of his rival's severed head—a gift offered to him by the Egyptians upon his arrival. Alexandria at this time was nearly as populous and wealthy as Rome, and throughout its thriving lands, a force of Roman soldiers remained to support and oversee the rule of the Ptolemies. Despite arriving with barely half of a full legion, Cæsar entered Alexandria as if Egypt's obedience to him as Roman consul was a foregone conclusion. Almost immediately, he demanded a vast sum of money, claiming it as repayment for services he had rendered to an earlier Ptolemy. He took young King Ptolemy into custody and, in turn, was captivated by Cleopatra, Ptolemy's sister and co-heir to the throne.

In all of Cæsar's career, his actions in Egypt were perhaps his most daring. The Alexandrians—or rather, the Roman soldiers stationed there under the influence of the young king's satraps—rose against him, forcing Cæsar to fortify his position within the city. Still, he managed to burn the entire Egyptian fleet, and, as he previously recounted in his Commentary, much of the royal library was lost in the flames. Eventually, Cæsar released Ptolemy, thinking that the king's return might ease tensions with the Alexandrians. When the young king left, he shed tears, professing that he valued Cæsar's company even above his own kingdom. Yet, the cunning boy quickly turned against Cæsar as soon as he was free.

Cæsar found himself in grave danger, and it becomes nearly impossible to call his actions in Alexandria anything but recklessly audacious—until we recall that Cæsar was, indeed, Cæsar. He had walked into Alexandria, nearly alone, with the casual assumption of his own invincibility. Driven first by the desire for immediate funds, and perhaps swayed by Cleopatra's charm, Cæsar came perilously close to losing everything in Egypt.

In Cæsar's time of need, a barbarian ally named Mithridates of Pergamus—a supposed son of the legendary Mithridates of Pontus—comes to his aid, bringing with him a much-needed army. Mithridates's arrival changes everything; with his support, Cæsar finally has the resources to mount a counterattack. A decisive battle unfolds along the Nile, one that Cæsar could not have fought alone, and the Egyptian forces are thoroughly defeated. In the aftermath, young King Ptolemy is drowned, Cleopatra is restored to her throne under Cæsar's protection, and Egypt falls under his influence.

Cæsar quickly shifts his focus to Asia, where a troublesome local ruler has dared to defeat a Roman general. This new adversary is Pharnaces, the legitimate son of Mithridates of Pontus. Cæsar, renowned for his relentless pursuit of enemies, wastes no time in dealing with Pharnaces. He confronts him at Zela, utterly decimates his forces, and reportedly inscribes the bold words "Veni, vidi, vici" ("I came, I saw, I conquered") upon his banners. By this point, Cæsar had already been declared Dictator of Rome for a year, had enjoyed the luxury of Alexandria alongside Cleopatra, and was beginning to consolidate power in a manner that foreshadowed true monarchy.

These campaigns, all occurring in 47 B.C., are chronicled in the Commentary "De Bello Alexandrino." Yet, while Cæsar's influence spreads abroad, things are far from settled in Italy. Although his allies in Rome have appointed him Dictator, his soldiers are growing restless, mutinying against their commanders and even challenging Cæsar's own authority. Meanwhile, the Republican forces are regrouping across the Mediterranean in the province of Africa, where poor Curio had previously suffered defeat at the hands of King Juba—a defeat marked by the humiliating presence of Roman senators in Juba's retinue and the complete destruction of Cæsar's forces.

This African province, lying just across from Sicily, was enriched by the Roman culture that radiated from the Republic's closest territories. Now, it has become the stronghold of the Republican faction—the last Roman territory where Cæsar has yet to secure a victory. Although Pompey is gone, his cause lives on, with both of his sons rallying here. Joining them is Scipio, Pompey's father-in-law, whom Pompey had elevated to share command at Pharsalus; Labienus, once Cæsar's trusted lieutenant, now a fierce Pompeian; Afranius, whom Cæsar had spared in Spain; and Petreius, along with King Juba himself, each harboring personal scores to settle with Cæsar.

There is also Varus, who defended the province against Curio, and, most notably, Cato—a towering figure, famed for his uncompromising virtue and his unyielding resistance to Cæsar's rise. Cato, though respected, is seen by many as rigid to a fault; his unbending principles often leave him isolated, and he is remembered as much for his fondness for wine as for his tragic end in Utica, where he chose death over submission to Cæsar.

This gathering of Pompey's former allies and loyalists represents a formidable challenge, a final bastion of Republican resistance against the ambitions of Cæsar.

In Utica, the remnants of Pompey's loyalists gather, making the city their temporary Rome. They establish a Senate, seeking to emulate the governance of the Republic, and place Scipio, a man unworthy of his famous name and inept as a general, as their commander-in-chief. Cato, unwavering in his belief in law and order, insists that rank and precedent demand Scipio's appointment, as he once served as consul and had held joint command with Pompey. The same rigid adherence to rank had previously granted Scipio command, and Bibulus the Republican fleet, purely due to their consular status, regardless of actual skill.

Cæsar, in contrast, rarely promotes based on titles alone. His flaw, if any, is trusting people based on personal affection—what we might call favoritism—as seen when he entrusted Curio with a mission in Africa, a decision that led to disaster and, ultimately, the present troubles. Yet, despite questionable leadership, the Pompeians muster a massive force, with ten Roman legions backed by the entire army of

King Juba. Their numbers reportedly match those of Pompey's forces at Pharsalus. But with their ranks come internal strife: disputes over command, disagreements on tactics, resentment toward their reliance on the barbarian Juba, and an underlying sense that this effort is futile.

Meanwhile, Cæsar, undaunted, pacifies a mutiny among his veteran soldiers in Italy with a few decisive words. Facing them without fear, he listens as they demand to be discharged, and he grants it without hesitation. When they demand their promised rewards, he tells them they'll receive their dues—after he has earned the funds in battle with fresh troops. He then addresses them as "citizens" rather than "soldiers"—"Quirites"—a term they cannot tolerate, as it implies they are no longer his battle-hardened legionaries. The effect is immediate; his veterans rally to him, the legions are re-formed, and Cæsar sails for Africa, initially with little more than three thousand men. In the first engagement, he nearly faces disaster, but his fortune holds.

After a few months of relentless campaigning, the inevitable outcome takes shape. In a climactic battle at Thapsus, fought a year and five months after Pharsalia, the Republican forces face total defeat. The battle marks the final end of the Republic's military resistance. On this occasion, the ferocity of Cæsar's veterans knows no bounds; neither orders nor pleas can stem the bloodshed, as his soldiers, driven by their own intensity, continue to cut down the enemy without restraint.

Separate stories recount the tragic fates of each of the defeated leaders. Cato's story is perhaps the most famous. Realizing he must surrender Utica to Cæsar, Cato calmly arranges his affairs, entrusting his children to Lucius Cæsar, his quæstor. Without betraying his intentions, he retires to his room with his sword and, with quiet resolve, takes his own life. Scipio also ends his life, while Afranius is killed by Cæsar's soldiers. Labienus, Pompey's two sons, and Varus manage to flee to Spain.

Then comes the dramatic tale of King Juba and Petreius. Juba, anticipating defeat, gathers his wives, children, wealth, and treasures into the town of Zama, where he constructs a grand funeral pyre. His plan, if conquered, is to perish in the flames with his family, followers, and riches. However, upon returning to Zama after his defeat, he finds that his wives, children, and subjects, unwilling to share his grim fate, have barred him from entering the town. With no other recourse, he seeks out Petreius, an old Roman ally who once refused to let Afranius surrender to Cæsar at Lerida. The two sit down for a final meal together, and afterward, Juba proposes a duel, allowing one of them to die with honor. They fight, and Juba, being the stronger, swiftly kills Petreius. Then, attempting to take his own life, he fails and ultimately orders a servant to finish the task. Thus, with the Battle of Thapsus in 47 B.C., Numidia becomes a Roman province, and Africa is brought under Cæsar's control. The Republic, in a symbolic sense, dies with Cato at Utica.

The Spanish war, which serves as the subject of the last of the Commentaries, is more an effort to extinguish the final embers of resistance. After his success in Africa, Cæsar returns to Rome, where he is detained by "muneribus dandis"—the distribution of rewards—as he fulfills promises to the veterans who had rejoined him in Italy. Meanwhile, Pompey's sons, Cnæus and Sextus, gather a substantial force in Spain to revive their father's cause. The war culminates in the bloody Battle of Munda, where over 30,000 lives are lost. This is the end of the conflict; Labienus and Varus are slain, and the historian notes that they are given a proper funeral. One of the rebel leaders, Scapula, makes a defiant end—he eats a final meal, is anointed, and dies on a funeral pyre. Cnæus, Pompey's elder son, escapes the battle wounded but is later discovered hiding in a cave and killed. Sextus, the younger son, escapes and remains a rebel leader for several years, until eventually he too is killed by one of Antony's officers.

The final Commentary ends abruptly, cutting off in the middle of a speech in which Cæsar chastises the citizens of Hipsala (modern-day

Seville), reminding them of his benevolence and their disloyalty. After the Battle of Munda, Cæsar returns to Rome, where he enjoys a single year of grand authority and splendor. He is appointed Consul for ten years, Dictator for life, and, finally, is even called "King." His achievements in this final year are significant: he passes numerous laws and, perhaps most enduringly, reforms the calendar, establishing the Julian system that orders months and days into a properly divided year.

However, as there is no Commentary on this last year of Cæsar's life, we will not delve further into it here. His assassination—struck down by Brutus, Cassius, and the other conspirators at the base of Pompey's statue—is familiar to all. Cæsar fell with grace, gathering his garments around him, even in death displaying the dignity and resolve that defined his life.

"Then burst his mighty heart; And in his mantle muffling up his face, Even at the base of Pompey's statua, Which all the while ran blood, Great Cæsar fell."

In the end, it was perhaps a stroke of fortune that he died before the unchecked power of the State could corrupt his legacy. His career, unparalleled in success, closed at a moment that spared his name from the consequences of absolute rule.

THE END.

Instructions to His Generals

Frederick the Great

The King of Prussia's Military Instruction to His Generals

Article I.
Regarding Prussian Troops: Their Strengths and Weaknesses

To shape and maintain my troops, commanding officers must exercise the highest degree of diligence and care. Absolute discipline is essential, and attention to their well-being must be a priority. Prussian soldiers deserve a standard of nourishment superior to that of almost any other European army.

Our regiments are half-composed of native soldiers and half of foreign enlistees who join for financial gain. The latter often seek any opportunity to leave a service to which they hold no personal allegiance, making the prevention of desertion a vital concern.

Some of our generals mistakenly assume that one soldier can replace another without consequence, as long as the ranks are filled. But this view fails to recognize the unique conditions of our own army compared to others. If a deserter is replaced by a soldier equally trained and disciplined, the impact may be minimal. However, if a soldier who has two years of training deserts and is replaced by a poorly trained recruit—or left unreplaced—the effect on the regiment can be significant.

Such lapses in officer vigilance have, at times, led to regiments not only losing personnel but also diminishing in reputation. When regiments lose disciplined soldiers, the army itself weakens precisely when full strength is most needed. Without dedicated effort, you risk losing the best of your forces and may find it challenging to restore your ranks.

While Prussia has a healthy population, finding men of the necessary height for service is no simple task. Even if they are available, they cannot be trained immediately. For this reason, preventing desertion becomes one of the essential responsibilities of generals commanding armies or detachments. To achieve this:

1. Avoid encamping too close to forests unless absolutely necessary.
2. Conduct roll calls several times each day.
3. Send hussar patrols frequently to scout the area surrounding the camp.
4. Station chasseurs in crop fields at night and double cavalry posts at dusk to secure the perimeter.
5. Do not allow soldiers to stray and ensure that each unit is led to water and forage by an officer.
6. Enforce strict punishment for marauding, as it breeds disorder.
7. Keep guards stationed in villages until the troops are assembled on marching days.
8. Enforce strict orders prohibiting any soldier from leaving his rank or division while on the march.
9. Avoid night marches unless absolutely necessary.
10. Deploy hussar patrols on both flanks while infantry move through wooded areas.
11. Position officers at both ends of a defile to maintain order in ranks.
12. If a backward march becomes necessary, keep the reason concealed from the troops, or offer a motivating explanation to maintain morale.
13. Ensure regular provision of essential supplies such as bread, meat, beer, brandy, and other necessities for the troops. Maintaining a steady and dependable issue of these is crucial for morale and health.
14. Identify the root causes of desertion if it begins to affect a regiment or company. Investigate whether the soldiers have received their enlistment bonuses and customary benefits, and determine if any misconduct by captains or officers might be a

contributing factor. However, under no circumstances should discipline be relaxed. Some may believe that this is the responsibility of the colonel alone, yet the efforts of one individual cannot suffice to achieve excellence across the entire force. An army must strive collectively for cohesion and unity, giving the impression of being directed by a single, resolute mind.

An army is largely composed of individuals who, if not under consistent direction, may tend toward idleness. Without vigilant oversight from the general, who enforces a strong sense of duty, this carefully assembled force will begin to deteriorate, losing its effectiveness and ultimately becoming little more than the semblance of a disciplined army. For this reason, constant, purposeful activity for the troops is essential. Commanders who maintain such discipline will see the clear benefits, and they will also notice that numerous minor infractions often go unaddressed by those who lack the vigilance to uncover and address them.

Although this level of continuous attention may initially seem burdensome for a general, the substantial rewards make it well worthwhile. With troops of such exceptional bravery, skill, and discipline, the achievements possible are boundless. A general who may appear reckless or overly bold in other nations would, with our troops, be considered merely diligent in adhering to established standards. With a force of well-provisioned soldiers like ours, any undertaking within human capability can be approached with confidence. Furthermore, the soldiers uphold such a high standard that anyone showing signs of cowardice or hesitation would not be tolerated among them, a stance rarely seen in other armies.

I have personally observed officers and soldiers alike who, even when severely wounded, would not abandon their post or retreat to seek medical attention. With troops of this quality, almost any objective becomes attainable. Supplied adequately, they are capable of incredible feats. Whether marching at a rapid pace to gain an advantage over the enemy, storming a forest position, scaling a mountain, or engaging in cavalry charges, they exhibit unshakable courage and resilience. In close combat, they will press on relentlessly, turning resistance into rout and transforming a mere encounter into a decisive victory.

However, the excellence of the troops alone is not enough. The general's expertise is equally vital, as the incompetence or poor judgment of leadership can squander all advantages. Therefore, I will now discuss the essential qualities that a general must possess. I will also outline specific principles and guidelines, whether derived from the wisdom of experienced generals or from hard-won lessons learned through my own experience.

Article II.
On Troop Subsistence and Provisioning

A notable general once remarked that feeding an army should be its foundational priority, as it sustains all operations. This crucial aspect can be divided into two sections: the first addresses where and how to establish supply depots, while the second covers the effective use and transport of these supplies.

The foremost rule is to establish large supply depots securely in the rear of the army whenever possible. During the wars in Silesia and Bohemia, our main depot was located in Breslau, strategically chosen for its access to replenishment via the Oder River. Establishing depots directly at the front lines may seem efficient, but a single setback could force their abandonment, leaving the army without resources. When depots are organized sequentially in the rear, any operational setback will only be a temporary obstacle rather than a full-scale crisis.

On the Electorate's frontiers, the most strategic locations for depots would be Spandau and Magdeburg, with the latter's position on the Elbe particularly suited for offensive campaigns into Saxony. For operations toward Bohemia, Schweidnitz would be an ideal location.

The integrity of commissaries and their deputies is crucial in this regard, as dishonest conduct directly compromises the state. Therefore, officials of reputable character should be appointed to these positions, and they should regularly conduct personal and meticulous inspections to verify accuracy in all records.

There are two primary methods of stocking depots: one is to procure grain by purchasing it from local nobility and peasants at established finance chamber rates; the other method is through requisitioning specified quantities. Commissaries are responsible for coordinating and authorizing these transactions.

Specially constructed vessels should be used to transport grain and forage along rivers and canals. However, purveyors should only be hired under the most pressing circumstances since even Jewish merchants, known for demanding high prices, are typically more reasonable. Purveyors' inflated rates drive up the costs of supplies, which they then resell at extravagant profits.

Supply depots must be prepared well in advance so that the army has everything it needs when setting out on campaign. Delaying their establishment until winter could mean that freezing conditions halt river transport, or that roads become so bogged down that transporting supplies becomes exceedingly difficult.

In addition to the covered wagons assigned to regiments, which carry an eight-day bread supply, the commissary has provisions for transporting a month's worth of supplies. The use of navigable waterways should never be overlooked; without this transport option, no army can be reliably or abundantly supplied.

Wagons used for transporting supplies should be drawn exclusively by horses. Attempts have been made to use oxen, but they proved inadequate. Wagon masters must pay careful attention to the well-being of their animals, as the loss of horses directly reduces the number of wagons, thereby diminishing the army's provisions. The general must also oversee this matter since neglected horses mean fewer wagons and potentially lost supplies on the march. Inadequately fed or exhausted horses will inevitably falter, leading to a breakdown in logistics and possibly derailing well-planned operations. Thus, the general must diligently monitor these essential factors, which are critical to the success of all military maneuvers.

When conducting a campaign against Saxony, using the Elbe River to transport provisions is highly advantageous. In Silesia, the Oder serves this purpose, while in Prussia, access to the sea is invaluable. However, in Bohemia and Moravia, land transport is the sole means of conveyance. Often, a line of depots is created, as in Bohemia in 1742, when magazines were established at Pardubitz, Nienbourg, Podjebrod, and Brandies. This chain enabled us to keep pace with the enemy and pursue him toward Prague if necessary. Similarly, in the recent Bohemian campaign, Breslau supplied Schweidnitz, which in turn supplied Jaromirez, and from there provisions were carried directly to the army.

In addition to the covered wagons carrying provisions, the army transports portable iron ovens, which have recently been increased in number. These ovens are set up during rest days to bake fresh bread. On any expedition, it's essential to carry a ten-day supply of bread or biscuits. While biscuits are an excellent ration, our soldiers are not accustomed to utilizing them efficiently and typically only enjoy them in soup form.

When marching through hostile territory, the meal depot should be kept in a secure, garrisoned town near the army. For instance, in the 1745 campaign, our depots progressed from Neustadt to Jaromirez and eventually to Trautenau. If our advance had extended further, our nearest secure depot would have been at Pardubitz. Each company has been provided with hand mills, which have proven invaluable. These mills are operated by soldiers who grind the meal, exchange it at the depot, and receive bread in return. This setup allows us to conserve larger stores and remain in camp longer than would otherwise be possible, reducing the need for large escorts and frequent convoys.

Regarding convoy security, I must elaborate. The strength of the escort should match the anticipated threat level from the enemy. Infantry detachments are stationed in towns along the convoy route, providing support points. Sometimes, large covering detachments are deployed, as was done in Bohemia. In terrain with significant cover, infantry should primarily compose convoy escorts, supplemented with hussars to scout for hidden enemy positions and survey the route.

Even in open terrain, I favor infantry over cavalry for convoy escorts, as I find them more effective in this role. For details on convoy escort procedures, I direct you to my military regulations. Securing convoys should be a high priority for the general. One reliable strategy is to deploy troops to occupy key defiles before the convoy reaches them and position the escort a league ahead of the convoy toward the enemy's position. This maneuver effectively masks the convoy, allowing it to pass securely through challenging areas.

Article III.
Of Sutlers, Beer, and Brandy.

When planning any operation against the enemy, it is essential to direct the commissary to gather all available beer and brandy to ensure the army has these supplies, at least for the initial days. As soon as the army crosses into enemy territory, all nearby brewers and distillers must be requisitioned at once. Distillers, in particular, should be set to work immediately so that soldiers won't miss out on their rations, which they rely on greatly for morale.

Sutlers must be protected, especially in areas where local inhabitants have fled and where regular provisions cannot be obtained with money. In such instances, we have some leeway to avoid strict adherence to local regulations concerning the peasantry. The sutlers and accompanying women should be sent to search for vegetables and livestock to supplement rations. Attention must be paid to the prices of provisions, ensuring that soldiers can buy supplies at fair prices while allowing sutlers to earn a reasonable profit.

It's worth noting that during a campaign, soldiers receive two pounds of bread daily and two pounds of meat weekly at no charge—a privilege they greatly deserve, particularly in regions like Bohemia, where the terrain is harsh and resources are limited.

Convoys transporting supplies for the army should also include herds of cattle to guarantee soldiers' nourishment and sustain their strength throughout the campaign.

Article IV.
Of Dry and Green Forage.

Dry forage includes items like oats, barley, hay, and chopped straw, which are stored in the magazine. If the oats are spoiled or musty, the horses are likely to develop mange or farcy, rendering them weak and ineffective even at the beginning of a campaign. Although chopped straw is traditionally given, it merely serves to fill the belly without providing substantial nourishment.

The initial aim of gathering and storing forage is to ensure a strategic advantage, either by preparing ahead of the enemy or by stocking up for a distant campaign. However, when horses are limited to dry forage, the army often cannot afford to stray too far from its supply magazines due to the sheer challenge of transporting enough feed; entire regions sometimes lack sufficient carriages to meet the army's needs. Consequently, this approach is usually reserved for situations lacking rivers to facilitate the transportation of forage.

During the Silesian campaign, my cavalry was entirely reliant on dry forage, but we limited our movement from Strehla to Schwiednitz (where there was a magazine) and onward to Cracau, where we were near the Brieg and Oder Rivers. For winter campaigns, cavalry should carry forage sufficient for five days, firmly bound on their mounts—particularly if action is anticipated in regions like Bohemia or Moravia, where inadequate forage would rapidly weaken the horses.

In regions with standing crops or unharvested fields, forage is gathered there first, moving to village stores only when the fields are exhausted. When the army plans to remain in one location, an inventory of available forage should be taken to ensure that rations are distributed evenly according to the intended duration of stay.

For large foraging operations, the escort typically consists of a body of cavalry sized according to proximity to the enemy and the perceived threat level. In some instances, entire wings or even the entire army may engage in foraging activities.

Foragers assemble on their designated routes, positioned on the army's wings, front, or rear as necessary. Hussars lead the advance, followed by cavalry in open terrain; in rougher areas, infantry precedes the cavalry. This advanced guard moves ahead of the main foraging column, which is divided into sections. Each section of foragers is followed by an escort composed of both horse and foot soldiers. This staggered arrangement continues, with successive detachments of foragers and escort troops. The rear guard comprises a final troop of hussars, completing the orderly formation and protecting the column's tail.

It is important to remember that all escorts should have infantry carrying their cannons and foragers equipped with swords and carbines. Upon reaching the designated foraging area, a protective chain must be set up, positioning infantry near villages, behind hedges, or in sunken paths. A reserve unit combining cavalry and infantry should be centrally located, ready to provide support at any vulnerable points where the enemy might attempt to break through. The hussars are to engage in skirmishes with the enemy to create distractions and draw them away from the foragers. Once the area is secured, the foraging ground is divided among regiments, and officers must ensure that foraged bundles are tightly bound and large enough to maximize the load.

When the horses are loaded, the foragers should return to camp in small groups, each protected by an escort. Once the foragers have vacated the area, the chain troops should gather to form the rear guard, with the hussars following behind to provide additional cover.

Foraging in villages follows a similar procedure, with the key difference being that infantry form a defensive perimeter around the village while the cavalry holds a position slightly behind, ready to act if necessary. Each village should be foraged individually to avoid overly dispersing the chain troops.

In mountainous regions, foraging becomes a challenging operation, requiring escorts primarily composed of infantry and hussars due to the rugged terrain. When camped close to the enemy for an extended period, it's essential to secure the forage located between both camps first. Foraging should then extend outward up to two leagues, beginning with the more distant fields and reserving those nearest to camp for later use. If the army doesn't plan to stay long, foraging can focus on the immediate camp area and surroundings.

When gathering a substantial amount of green forage, it's preferable to send out smaller foraging parties twice rather than spread across too wide an area all at once. This strategy keeps the protective chain more compact and the foragers safer, as stretching the chain too thinly weakens it, making it vulnerable to being breached by the enemy.

Article V.
Of the Knowledge of a Country.

Understanding the geography of a country is essential and can be acquired through two primary methods. The first step is to thoroughly study a map of the anticipated war zone, clearly noting the names of significant rivers, towns, and mountains. This preliminary step helps create a general framework of the area. With this groundwork established, the next phase involves a more detailed examination to understand the layout of major roads, the locations of towns, and whether these towns can be fortified for defense or how best to attack them if the enemy occupies them. The defense requirements for these towns should also be assessed.

It's crucial to have accurate plans of fortified towns to understand their defenses and identify the most vulnerable points. Equally important is the knowledge of rivers, including their depth, navigability, and any potential crossing points, along with seasonal changes—whether rivers are impassable in spring or dry up in summer. Marshes, which could hinder movement, should also be identified.

In a flat, open landscape, fertile areas should be distinguished from barren ones, and it's important to know the possible routes connecting major cities and rivers, including how to secure camps along these routes. Flat areas are easily surveyed; however, in mountainous or forested regions, where visibility is limited, reconnaissance is more challenging. To gather essential information in such terrains, it's helpful to climb high points with a map in hand and bring along local villagers, such as hunters or shepherds, who know the area. If a single mountain stands taller than others, it should be ascended to gain a comprehensive view of the area of interest.

Familiarity with roads is critical—not only to plan marching formations but also to strategize alternative routes for reaching or flanking the enemy's camp should they establish nearby positions. Identifying defensive camps, potential battlefields, and enemy-held posts are among the most important reconnaissance goals.

Each reconnaissance should yield a complete understanding of key locations, valleys, defiles, and all advantageous sites. Every possible action should be carefully considered to create well-prepared arrangements, eliminating confusion when action is required. These preparations should be meticulous, revisited and revised as needed, until they are entirely satisfactory.

When choosing camps for either offense or defense, it is generally essential to ensure proximity to wood and water, a well-shielded front, and an open rear. If a thorough personal inspection of the area is not possible, intelligent, resourceful officers should be dispatched, under plausible pretexts or even in disguise if necessary, to gather the necessary intelligence. They must know precisely what to observe, and upon their return, their findings on potential camps and other locations should be added to the map. However, where possible, personal reconnaissance is always preferable over secondhand accounts.

Article VI.
Of the Coup D'Oeil.

Understanding the coup d'oeil in military strategy can be broken down into two primary skills. The first is the ability to accurately assess how many troops a specific area can hold. This skill only develops through practice; after overseeing the layout of several camps, the eye becomes attuned to space, so estimation errors become minimal.

The second, and more critical skill, is the ability to identify immediately all possible advantages of any piece of ground. While some may seem naturally adept at this, it is a skill that can be learned and perfected. Fortification principles are the foundation of this skill, providing a universal framework adaptable to any army's position. With this knowledge, an experienced general can utilize every defile, marsh, hollow path, or slight rise in terrain to their advantage.

In a space of two square leagues, there might be two hundred potential positions to consider, yet an insightful general will quickly identify the most advantageous one. This begins with examining even small elevations to get a comprehensive view of the surroundings. Using the same fortification principles, the general can pinpoint the weaknesses in the enemy's formation. Ideally, if time allows, the general should walk over the ground to become even more familiar with the terrain.

Fortification principles also guide how to occupy heights effectively, ensuring positions are not easily dominated by higher ground nearby. These principles provide insight on how to secure the wings so the flanks are well-covered, and they also aid in distinguishing strong, defensible positions from those that would be difficult and risky to hold, even for a seasoned leader. Through this approach, a general can also recognize weaknesses in the enemy's setup, whether due to a poorly chosen position, an ill-judged distribution of forces, or limited natural defenses.

These considerations naturally lead into how troops should be arranged to maximize the benefits of their environment, which I will outline next.

Article VII.
Of the Distribution of Troops.

While understanding and selecting suitable terrain is crucial, it's equally important to make full use of these advantages so that each unit is positioned where it can be most effective. Cavalry, known for its speed, should be deployed on open ground to maximize maneuverability, while infantry can handle a wider range of terrain, using their firepower for defense and bayonets for offense. Defensive measures are typically established first to ensure a camp's security, particularly in areas where an enemy engagement is possible at any moment.

Current battle formations are often inherited from earlier strategies and don't always consider the unique features of the terrain. This can lead to a misapplication of tactics. The entire army should be arranged according to what each segment of terrain demands. For example, while plains may suit cavalry, if a plain is small or bordered by woods with enemy infantry positioned there, then cavalry may need to be placed at the edges of the infantry wings to benefit from their support.

There are cases where all cavalry might be positioned on one wing or held in reserve. At other times, infantry brigades may close off their wings. Ideal locations for troops include elevated areas, churchyards, sunken roads, or broad ditches. When used wisely, such terrain features can effectively shield against attacks.

However, placing cavalry behind a swamp or marsh limits their usefulness, as they would be unable to charge effectively. Similarly, positioning cavalry too close to wooded areas could allow enemy forces to cause disarray from cover. Infantry faces similar risks when placed on open ground without protected flanks, as the enemy will likely exploit such vulnerabilities by attacking the exposed side.

In mountainous terrain, I would position the cavalry in the second line, deploying only a few squadrons in the first line for support or for flanking any enemy infantry attempting to advance. Generally, well-organized armies form a cavalry reserve on open plains, while in broken or uneven landscapes, this reserve typically consists of infantry with some light cavalry, such as hussars and dragoons.

The art of troop deployment lies in positioning each unit so it can perform optimally and contribute uniformly to the operation. Villeroi's error at the Battle of Ramillies illustrates this: by stationing his left wing behind an impassable swamp, he prevented it from supporting his right wing, thereby losing the utility of a significant portion of his force. This oversight demonstrates how critical it is to ensure that each unit's placement allows for effective maneuvering and support.

Article VIII.
Of Camps.

To ensure your camp is well-chosen, assess whether a minor movement on your part forces the enemy into a more substantial shift, or if, after one of your marches, they are compelled to make additional ones. The side with the fewest necessary maneuvers is generally in the better position.

The responsibility for selecting the camp's location should rest solely with the general, as the chosen spot often becomes the battlefield, and the success of his operations hinges on this decision. Given the importance of this matter, I'll delve into it in detail, focusing solely on factors that directly impact the general and leaving the specific placement of troops within the camp to my military regulation.

Camps serve two primary functions: defense and preparation for attack. The first type includes camps where troops are gathered primarily for rest and convenience, ideally near the magazine but organized so they can quickly form a battle line. These camps should generally be positioned at a distance from the enemy to avoid disturbances. Ignoring this caution, as the King of England did by encamping along the bank of the Main opposite the French army, led to a significant risk of defeat at Dettingen.

The first essential rule when selecting a camp location is proximity to both wood and water. In our custom, camps are fortified, following the Roman example, to guard against possible surprise attacks by enemy light troops and to discourage desertion. I've noticed consistently fewer instances of desertion when the camp's defenses were solid, such as when redans were interconnected by two lines extending around the perimeter, as opposed to camps without this added security. This may seem trivial but has proven to be a substantial factor in maintaining troop integrity.

Camps of rest, intended for provisioning and observation, are another type. These camps are positioned to monitor enemy movements without being actively engaged, allowing us to respond to their maneuvers. Since relaxation is key in such camps, they are often located behind large rivers, marshes, or other natural barriers that make their front impassable. Our camp at Strehla, for instance, was of this type. When streams or rivers at the camp's front are too shallow, they should be dammed to increase their depth.

Even in camps of this nature, where the enemy threat is minimal, the general must remain vigilant. The time granted here should be used to oversee the troops closely and restore discipline. The general should verify that operations proceed according to protocol, ensuring officers on guard understand and fulfill their responsibilities, and confirm that the standards I've established for positioning cavalry and infantry guards are meticulously observed.

The infantry should undergo their drills three times each week, with new recruits practicing daily; at times, whole corps may execute their maneuvers together. The cavalry should also perform their exercises unless they're engaged in foraging, and the general, who is well-aware of each corps' exact numbers, must ensure that both the young soldiers and inexperienced horses are trained thoroughly. Regular visits to the lines are essential, where the general commends officers diligent with their troops and firmly reprimands those who show signs of neglect, as no large army can sustain itself without active supervision. Armies will inevitably be populated with idle or malingering soldiers who require the general's vigilance to stay engaged in their duties.

Camps like these yield great benefit if used as recommended, as the discipline and structure instilled in them lay a solid foundation for the upcoming campaign's success.

When we establish camp for foraging or other purposes, whether near the enemy or farther off, I will focus on the scenarios when we camp close to enemy lines. Here, choosing fertile grounds and strategically advantageous spots, either by natural terrain or fortified by human efforts, is essential.

Foraging camps positioned near the enemy should be difficult to reach, as foraging missions function like combat detachments sent against the opposition. These teams might encompass as much as one-sixth or even half the army, making it imperative that our location protects against any advantage the enemy might seize during these expeditions. A well-chosen camp can prevent these vulnerabilities.

However, even when our camp is well-positioned and appears secure, we cannot overlook further precautions. We must uphold strict secrecy about the timing and location of foraging missions, and not even the general assigned to lead these efforts should know the details until late the night before.

Sending out multiple scout parties is advisable to monitor any movements from the enemy; unless there are significant reasons against it, we might choose to forage on the same day as they do, though we must remain cautious. The enemy, learning of our intentions, might halt their own foraging and redirect their forces to attack our main group.

An example is Prince Charles of Lorraine's camp near Königgrätz, which was naturally fortified and ideal for foraging purposes. Similarly, our camp at Cholm became robust through human intervention, with abatis placed along the right wing and redoubts erected in front of the infantry camp to reinforce our defenses.

We entrench camps when preparing for a siege, defending a challenging passage, or compensating for terrain disadvantages by constructing defensive works to guard against potential enemy aggression.

When establishing entrenchments, a general should use every marsh, river, inundation, and natural or artificial obstruction to limit the width of defensive lines. It's better to construct smaller, manageable entrenchments rather than excessively large ones, as these barriers alone do not stop the enemy; it is the troops stationed behind them that prevent their advancement.

I would avoid constructing entrenchments unless I had sufficient battalions to line them continuously and a reserve of infantry that could be readily moved to any threatened point. Abbatis and other such barriers are useful only when actively defended by infantry.

The main focus should be on properly reinforcing the lines of countervallation, which typically end at a river. In such cases, the trench should extend into the river itself and be deepened enough to prevent fording; neglecting this precaution risks having your flank turned.

Additionally, it's crucial to secure ample provisions before settling behind defensive lines to lay siege.

Entrenchments' flanks demand particular attention, as no segment should allow the enemy to approach without being subjected to crossfire from multiple directions. When defending mountain passes or defiles, entrenchments must be reinforced with extra caution, as support for the flanks is vital. Redoubts are often constructed on both wings, and sometimes the entire entrenchment comprises redoubts, ensuring that the defending troops are shielded from being outflanked.

Experienced generals skillfully direct the enemy to attack the most fortified points, where trenches are widened and deepened, lined with palisades, with chevaux de frise at entry points, and parapets made cannon-resistant. Additionally, pits are dug in vulnerable areas to further complicate enemy advances.

However, when it comes to covering a siege, I would always prefer deploying an army of observation over relying solely on an entrenched camp. This is simply because experience has shown that the old approach cannot be fully trusted. Prince de Condé saw his entrenchments before Arras overcome by Turenne, and if I recall correctly, Condé in turn broke through the entrenchments that Turenne had set up before Valenciennes. Since then, neither of these seasoned commanders relied on entrenched camps to cover sieges but opted instead for armies of observation.

I will now discuss defensive camps, which are naturally strong due to their position and meant solely to withstand enemy attacks. To make these positions serve their purpose effectively, the front and both flanks must be equally fortified, while the rear remains open and accessible. Ideal examples include elevated areas with extensive fronts and flanks protected by marshes, like Prince Charles of Lorraine's camp at Marschwitz, which was shielded by a marshy river in the front and lakes on the flanks, or our encampment at Konopist in 1744.

An alternative defensive measure is positioning near a fortified town, as demonstrated by Marshal de Neipperg after his defeat at Mollwitz when he took a secure position under the walls of Neiss. As long as a general can hold such a position, he remains secure from direct attack. However, if the enemy begins maneuvers to outflank him, he can no longer safely remain there. His preparations should, therefore, include fallback plans so that, if outflanked, he can retreat to another strong defensive position further back.

The geography of Bohemia, filled with naturally fortified spots, often forces us to occupy these camps, sometimes against our preference, due to the varied landscape that makes strategic maneuvering challenging.

I must reiterate the utmost importance of a general maintaining vigilance to avoid being lured into errors due to poorly chosen positions. A misjudgment in selecting posts could lead to situations where retreat is only possible through narrow, vulnerable defiles. If faced with a skillful opponent, a general could find himself so tightly confined and restricted by the terrain that he may have no option but to accept the most humiliating fate for a soldier: laying down arms without a chance to fight back.

In camps meant to defend a region, the priority should not be on the strength of the camp itself but on safeguarding the key points vulnerable to attack through which the enemy could breach. Such points should be secured by the camp's positioning. This doesn't mean occupying every possible approach an enemy might take, but rather the one route that would most likely lead to their objective. Selecting a strategic post allows us to thwart their plans, forcing them into extended detours while enabling us to disrupt their advances with minimal repositioning.

For example, the camp at Neustadt is strategically placed to protect the entirety of Lower Silesia from an army stationed in Moravia. The ideal positioning involves having Neustadt and the river in front.

Should the enemy attempt to move between Ottmachau and Glatz, we only need to shift our position between Neiss and Ziegenhals, where we can secure a favorable post that blocks them from accessing Moravia. Similarly, the enemy would hesitate to move toward Cosel because positioning ourselves between Troppau and Jaegerndorff—areas with numerous excellent strongholds—would sever their connection to supply convoys.

Another essential camp lies between Liebau and Schaemberg, providing Lower Silesia with formidable defense against threats from Bohemia. In all these scenarios, adherence to the principles I've outlined is vital, though, of course, flexibility in applying them to specific circumstances remains necessary. Additionally, when there's a river before our position, it's crucial to ensure that tents remain no farther than half musket-shot from the front of the camp, keeping defensive readiness intact.

As for the Brandenburg frontier, no camp alone can cover this open terrain, which spans six leagues of uninterrupted plains. Protecting it from Saxony demands control over Wittenberg, either by setting up camp there or following the approach taken in the winter expedition of 1745. The camp at Werben, on the other hand, serves effectively to secure the flank facing Hanover.

In offensive camps, it is essential to have both the front and flanks well fortified. If the flanks, typically the weakest points of an army, are not secured, confidence in the troops will falter. Our camp at Czaslaw, before the 1742 battle, suffered due to this very oversight. Additionally, villages positioned on the wings or in the camp's front are generally garrisoned by our troops, except on combat days when these troops are withdrawn. This precaution prevents potential hazards if the enemy sets these nearby wooden buildings—typical of the region—ablaze, risking loss of men. However, an exception to this rule can be made for villages with solid stone buildings or churchyards detached from flammable structures, as these can provide a defensible position without excessive risk.

Our main principle is to always be on the offensive, not defensive. This kind of position should only be held at the front of the army or in front of its wings; in these places, it will provide a lot of cover for our troops during an attack and will also be very troubling for the enemy throughout the fight.

It's also extremely important to check the depth of the small rivers or marshes that are in front of or on the flanks of our camp. Otherwise, if the rivers can be crossed or the marshes can be passed through, you might realize too late that you've trusted a weak point for defense. Villars was defeated at Malplaquet because he thought the marsh on his right couldn't be crossed, only to find it was just a dry meadow that our troops crossed easily to attack him from the side. Every detail should be inspected with our own eyes, and no matter of this kind should ever be ignored or treated as unimportant.

The front of the first line should be protected by infantry regiments, and if there is a river nearby, guards should be stationed on its banks. The back of the camp should be guarded by guards from the second line. These guards should be protected by simple redoubts joined by light earthworks, so the camp will be defended in the Roman style. We should occupy any villages located on the wings or even half a league away if they can help secure other access points.

The cavalry guards should be set up according to the rules I've outlined in my military instructions. We rarely had more than 300 maîtres de garde among 80 squadrons, unless we were very close to the enemy, as when we marched to Schweidnitz after the Battle of Hohenfriedberg, or when we entered Lusatia on our way to Naumbourg. These advance guards should include all types of troops, such as 2,000 hussars, 1,500 dragoons, and 2,000 grenadiers. The general commanding the forward troops should be a person with good judgment, and since his goal is to gather intelligence and not to engage in combat, his camps should be chosen with care, with woods or narrow passes he is familiar with positioned at the front. He should also send out regular patrols to gather information so that he knows at all times what is happening in the enemy's camp.

Meanwhile, if you use the hussars remaining with you to patrol the rear and the sides of the camp, you've taken every possible measure to protect against any hostile actions. If a large enemy force tries to slip between you and your rear guard, you can be sure they intend to attack it, and you should rush to provide support.

To sum up all I have to say on this topic, it's essential to add that if generals who set up their troops in villages want to be safe from danger and disturbance, they should only occupy villages located between the two main lines.

Article X.
In what Manner and for what Reason we are to send out Detachments.

In war, there's an old saying: "He who divides his force will be beaten in detail." This advice has stood the test of time for a reason. If you're about to engage in battle, it's essential to bring together as many troops as you can, using every effort to gather as large a force as possible. When united, these troops can serve the best purpose in the upcoming fight. History has shown repeatedly that generals who overlook this rule usually find themselves with plenty of regret.

For instance, Albemarle's detachment at Oudenarde was defeated, which cost the great Eugene the entire campaign. Similarly, General Stahrenberg was defeated in the Battle of Villa Viciosa in Spain because he was separated from the English forces, unable to coordinate in time. These aren't isolated cases. Detached forces have repeatedly caused disastrous losses, as seen in the Austrian campaigns in Hungary. Prince Hildburghausen's army suffered defeat at Banja Luka, and General Wallis was dealt a setback on the Timok River's banks. The Saxons, too, were beaten at Kesselsdorf due to their failure to unite with Prince Charles, even though circumstances allowed for it. Personally, I nearly faced defeat at Sohr; it was only the quick thinking of my generals and the courageous action of my soldiers that saved me from such a fate. Had they faltered, I would have paid the price for having fragmented forces.

This leads to an important question: should detachments never be sent out under any circumstances? My response is that detaching forces is a sensitive decision and should only be made under the most urgent necessity and for reasons of the highest importance. When conducting an offensive, sending out detachments should generally be avoided. Even in open country where you may control a few locations, only the minimum number of troops should be spared to protect supply convoys, and no more. Keeping your force unified is paramount.

However, there are exceptions, particularly in specific regions such as Bohemia or Moravia. In these areas, the need for provisions can make it necessary to send out detachments to ensure the arrival of supplies. Encampments should be set up along the chain of mountains where supply convoys must pass. These encampments should remain in place until you've gathered enough supplies to sustain the army for several months. Additionally, securing a strong position within the enemy's territory as a supply depot becomes crucial. Once these detachments are deployed, the main army should move into advantageous camps and wait for their safe return.

An advanced guard, however, should not be considered a detachment. The purpose of an advanced guard is to stay in close proximity to the main army. Under no circumstances should it be stationed too close to the enemy, as its function is not to be exposed to undue risk.

In some cases, particularly when on the defensive, there may be no choice but to send out detachments. For instance, when I deployed detachments in Upper Silesia, they were relatively safe because they kept to the areas near fortified places, as I previously advised. This closeness to strongholds provided them with a safe haven if threatened by the enemy.

Officers tasked with leading detachments should be men of sound judgment and strong resolve. Although they receive general orders from their commanding officer, they must be prepared to independently decide when to advance or retreat, based on their specific situation. If the enemy's force is too powerful, they should pull back strategically. Conversely, if they have the upper hand, they must recognize this advantage and seize the moment. Such decisions require an officer to be flexible and responsive to changing circumstances, knowing that each choice could turn the tide of battle.

If the enemy approaches by night, these officers may sometimes find it prudent to feign a retreat. In some cases, while the enemy believes they're in retreat, the detachment can suddenly regroup and launch a surprise attack, catching the enemy off guard. This tactic can be effective in breaking the enemy's formation and morale. Light troops, however, need not be a concern in these maneuvers.

The primary duty of an officer in command of a detachment is to ensure his own safety and that of his men. Once this is achieved, he can turn his focus to planning and executing attacks against the enemy. Keeping his adversary on high alert by frequently taking the offensive will ensure the enemy is unable to rest. If this officer can succeed in two or three such instances, the enemy will eventually be forced onto the defensive, a position that will grant his forces an advantage.

If these detachments are close to the main army, they should establish communication lines using either a nearby town or forest as a conduit. This connection is crucial for relaying information, coordinating movements, and ensuring that both the main force and the detachment can offer support if either comes under attack. Maintaining such a link enhances the detachment's effectiveness, keeping it as an extension of the main force rather than an isolated unit vulnerable to enemy strikes.

In a defensive war, we often find ourselves needing to make detachments. Generals with limited experience tend to worry about preserving everything, while a skilled and daring leader focuses only on the main objective, aiming to strike a significant blow. Such a leader accepts smaller setbacks if they help prevent a larger disaster.

The enemy's army should be our primary focus. We must work to uncover their plans and counter them with as much force as possible. In 1745, we chose to leave Upper Silesia exposed to Hungarian raids so that we could better interfere with the plans of Prince Charles of Lorraine. We refrained from making any detachments until after we defeated his army. Once that victory was secured, General Nassau cleared Upper Silesia of the Hungarians in just fifteen days.

Some generals have a habit of making detachments before launching an attack, intending for these forces to strike the enemy from the rear during the battle. However, this approach is risky because the detachments often lose their way and end up arriving either too soon or too late. For example, when Charles XII sent out a detachment on the night before the Battle of Poltava, they got lost, which contributed to the army's defeat. Similarly, Prince Eugene's plan to surprise Cremona failed when the Prince of Vaudemont's detachment arrived too late to attack the Po Gate as planned.

Detachments should never be made on the day of battle unless it's done with careful strategy, like Turenne's maneuver near Colmar. There, he presented his first line to the army of Elector Frederick William while his second line moved through narrow passes to strike the enemy's flank, leading to their rout. Another example comes from Marshal de Luxembourg at the Battle of Fleurus in 1690, where he hid a group of infantry in tall corn on Prince Waldeck's flank, and this tactic won him the battle.

Only after a victory, and never before, can troops be detached to protect supply convoys. Even then, they should not move farther than half a league from the main army.

In conclusion, detachments that weaken an army by half or even by a third are extremely dangerous and should be firmly avoided.

Article XI.
Of the Tricks and Stratagems of War.

In war, the skill of a fox can sometimes be just as essential as the strength of a lion, because cleverness and subtlety may accomplish what sheer power cannot. Since brute force can, at times, be countered by equal force, or even bested by clever strategies, we must be thoroughly skilled in both methods. This knowledge enables us to use either force or cunning as the situation demands, ensuring we can adapt and succeed in the face of different challenges.

I won't attempt to recount the countless strategies that have been used in warfare, as they all share a common goal: to mislead and exhaust the enemy by making him move or prepare unnecessarily. When we effectively conceal our true intentions, we keep our enemy guessing, preventing him from countering our actual plans and positioning our forces to advantage. Therefore, it is vital to lead the enemy to believe that we are planning moves that we have no intention of executing. In doing so, we force him to respond to phantom threats, weakening his position and creating opportunities for us to strike effectively.

When we are gathering troops, we often march them in various directions, creating confusion to keep the enemy uncertain about where we truly plan to assemble. By keeping our destination ambiguous, we prevent the enemy from reinforcing his defenses in the area we actually aim to attack. In regions where there are fortresses or strongholds, we choose a campsite that appears to threaten multiple locations at once. By doing so, the enemy may feel compelled to divide his forces, reinforcing several of these areas at the same time. This division weakens his main body of troops, making it easier for us to attack when the right moment arises. However, if he chooses to focus on just one location, this also serves us well, as we can then concentrate our efforts on laying siege to whichever fortress appears most vulnerable.

If our goal is to cross a river or seize a position of particular importance, we begin by withdrawing to a considerable distance from both the crossing point and the position we intend to capture. This maneuver lures the enemy away from our actual target, leading him to believe that he no longer needs to guard it closely. Then, when our troops are fully prepared, and our movements remain hidden, we return quickly to the pre-determined location, seizing control of it before the enemy can reposition.

When we desire a battle, but the enemy shows a clear reluctance to engage, we employ tactics to make him believe we are fearful of his strength. For instance, we may spread rumors that our own forces are weak, diminished, or in disarray. This tactic was effectively used before the Battle of Hohenfriedberg, when I ordered roads to be repaired as though I planned to retreat to Breslau in four columns, at the approach of Prince Charles. His overconfidence worked in our favor, as he pursued us onto the plain, and we were able to achieve victory.

At times, we even shrink the size of our camp to give the appearance of having a smaller force. By keeping detachments out in the open, we make the enemy believe they're of greater importance than they truly are. Such tactics lead him to underestimate us, causing him to overlook chances to attack when they arise. For example, during the 1745 campaign, if my goal had been to take Königgrätz and Pardubice, I would have needed only two marches across the Glatz region toward Moravia. This would almost certainly have alarmed Prince Charles, prompting him to rush to protect the areas from which he drew his supplies after leaving Bohemia, thus leaving other positions vulnerable. By merely threatening locations linked to his supply routes or those connected with the capital, we can create a sense of vulnerability and sow doubt within the enemy ranks.

If we have no intention of engaging in battle, we make an effort to present ourselves as a formidable and confident force, spreading rumors of our strength and readiness. Austria has mastered this approach, turning it into a refined art form where they appear stronger than they are, intimidating their opponents with mere appearances.

By keeping up a bold and determined front, we project the image that we are eager for battle and that we have a daring plan in place. Such a display encourages rumors that we are about to launch a bold, risky maneuver, which often makes the enemy hesitant, fearing the consequences of an engagement. By leading him to believe we have some bold or daring plan in mind, we keep the enemy on edge, making him wary and defensive. Often, this bold appearance alone is enough to make him stay on the defensive, avoiding any confrontation altogether, and ensuring our troops maintain their advantage.

In a defensive war, one of the most important skills is choosing strong positions and holding them until the very last moment. When forced to retreat, the second line of defense should be the first to begin moving back, followed gradually by the first line. With natural barriers, like defiles, in front of you, the enemy will find it difficult to take advantage of your retreat, keeping your forces protected as they withdraw.

Even during the retreat, it is crucial to select positions that are angled and unclear, making it hard for the enemy to understand your intentions. The more the enemy tries to interpret your movements, the more uncertain he will become, while you indirectly achieve your desired objective without giving away your true strategy.

One effective tactic in warfare is to present a broad front, creating an illusion of a large-scale engagement. If the enemy mistakes this feint for an actual attack, he will be caught off guard and will likely suffer defeat. Through these deceptive maneuvers, you can prompt the enemy to send out detachments, taking advantage of his divided forces to strike with precision.

One of the best stratagems is to lull the enemy into a false sense of security, particularly as winter approaches and troops prepare to disperse and settle into winter quarters. By retreating under the guise of ending the campaign season, you can prepare to reassemble your forces quickly and catch the enemy off guard. To do this effectively, troops should be distributed in a way that allows for swift regrouping, enabling a surprise advance on the enemy's quarters. If successful, this strategy can undo the setbacks of an entire campaign within a matter of weeks.

A careful study of Turenne's last two campaigns provides an excellent example of such tactics; they are considered masterpieces of stratagem from this era. Our ancestors' techniques for warfare have largely been relegated to light troops, who still use ambushes and feigned retreats to draw the enemy into narrow spaces where they can be surrounded and defeated. However, generals today rarely fall for such basic traps, having become wise to these older tricks. Yet even skilled leaders can be vulnerable to betrayal; for instance, Charles XII was misled at Poltava due to the treachery of a Cossack chief, and Peter I faced a similar fate on the Pruth due to the failure of a local prince who could not provide the promised supplies.

As for the methods of conducting warfare through parties and detachments, these are detailed extensively in my Military Regulation. Anyone who wishes to refresh their memory on these tactics should refer to that document, as there is little else I need to add on this subject here.

To understand how to compel the enemy to make detachments, we need only examine the brilliant campaign of 1690, led by Marshal de Luxembourg against the King of England. This campaign, culminating in the Battle of Neerwinden, is a prime example of how to keep the enemy divided and vulnerable through strategic maneuvers.

Article XII.
Of Spies, how they are to be employed on every Occasion,

and in what Manner we are to learn Intelligence of the enemy.

If we could know the enemy's intentions ahead of time, we would always have an upper hand, even with a smaller force. This advantage is highly sought by generals but rarely obtained. The use of spies is essential in this regard, and they fall into several categories: 1) ordinary individuals who volunteer for this work; 2) double agents; 3) high-value spies with access to important information; and 4) those forced into this unpleasant line of duty.

The first type, ordinary individuals like peasants, artisans, priests, and others who enter the enemy's camp, can only be used to locate where the enemy is stationed. Their reports, however, are often vague or contradictory, which can increase our uncertainty rather than reduce it.

The intelligence gathered from deserters is usually no more reliable. A soldier may know what's happening within his own regiment but is unlikely to have insight into broader plans. As for hussars, who are frequently dispatched ahead and spend much time away from the main army, they may not even know where the army is camped. Despite these limitations, we still commit all reports to writing, as that is the only way to derive any potential benefit from them.

Double agents, on the other hand, are spies used to feed false information to the enemy. For example, an Italian at Schmiedeberg acted as a spy for the Austrians. When we told him that we intended to withdraw to Breslau if the enemy approached, he hurried to report this to Prince Charles of Lorraine, who came close to being deceived by this misinformation.

High-ranking spies, or those with direct access to critical intelligence, are invaluable assets. The postmaster at Versailles, for instance, worked secretly for Prince Eugene. This unfortunate man would open letters and orders sent from the court to the generals, copying their contents and forwarding them to Prince Eugene, who often received these messages even before the French commanders did. Similarly, Luxembourg managed to win the loyalty of a secretary to the King of England, who then informed Luxembourg of sensitive information. The king discovered this betrayal, turning it to his advantage. He forced the traitor to write to Luxembourg with a report that the allied army would go out the next day on a major foraging mission. This nearly led to the French being ambushed at Steenkerque, and they would have been destroyed if not for their exceptional defense.

Securing such spies in a war against Austria, however, would be highly challenging. This isn't because Austrians are less susceptible to bribery, but because their army is surrounded by a swarm of light troops who inspect all who pass through their lines thoroughly. This challenge led me to consider persuading some of their hussar officers to join our side, allowing us to establish a line of communication in the following way: when hussars engage in skirmishes, they sometimes agree to a brief truce. Such occasions could provide an opportunity to exchange messages discreetly.

In cases where we want to gather intelligence on the enemy or mislead him about our circumstances, we can send a loyal soldier from our camp to theirs to spread whatever information we want them to believe. This soldier might carry handbills encouraging desertion, return by a roundabout route, and bring back any information he can gather.

There is another, harsher way to gather intelligence when less severe measures fail, though I admit it is a cruel method. We identify a wealthy citizen with a large family and considerable property. Then, we assign him a person fluent in the enemy's language, disguised as his servant. This "servant" accompanies him to the enemy's camp under the pretense that the citizen is there to complain of injustices he has suffered. To ensure his cooperation, we threaten that if he does not return within a set time, bringing his servant with him, we will burn his house and harm his family. I had to resort to this tactic once, and it worked as I hoped.

Finally, it's worth noting that when paying spies, we must be generous, even to the point of extravagance. A person who risks his life to provide valuable information deserves to be well-compensated for his courage.

Article XIII.
Of certain Marks, by which the Intentions of the Enemy are to be discovered.

Understanding where the enemy has established his main depot for provisions is one of the most reliable ways to anticipate his intentions before the campaign begins. For instance, if the Austrians set up their supply depots at Olmütz, it's almost certain they plan to launch an attack on Upper Silesia. If they place them in Königgrätz, it's a strong indication that the region around Schweidnitz may be targeted. Likewise, when the Saxons aimed to invade the Electorate's border, the locations of their supply depots—Zittau, Görlitz, and Guben— revealed their intended path, as these towns lie along the route to Crossen.

Therefore, the primary objective in gathering intelligence should be identifying where the enemy has decided to place their supply depots and understanding the positions in which they are established. The French, for example, used a cunning tactic by setting up supply depots on both the Meuse and the Scheldt rivers to obscure their true plans, giving them flexibility and creating uncertainty for their adversaries.

The Austrians, on the other hand, often give away their movements through certain customs. For example, when they are preparing to march, they usually cook early in the morning on the day of departure. If significant smoke is observed in their camp around five or six in the morning, it's a reliable sign that they intend to break camp and move out that day.

Moreover, when the Austrians are preparing for battle, they tend to recall all of their strong detachments of light troops, consolidating their forces in preparation for the fight. If this is noticed, it is a clear signal to stay vigilant and prepare for immediate engagement.

If you are attacking a position defended by Hungarian troops and find it highly resistant to your assault, this may indicate that the main Austrian army is nearby, ready to provide reinforcement. Similarly, if the enemy's light troops maneuver to place themselves between your main army and one of your detached forces, it's a strong indication that the enemy has targeted that detachment, and you should make the necessary preparations to counter this move.

If you consistently face the same general on the opposing side, his tactics and intentions will eventually become apparent. Over time, his strategies and habitual methods will grow familiar, allowing you to anticipate his actions more easily.

After carefully evaluating the terrain of the war theater, the current condition of your army, the security of your supply depots, the strength of your fortified positions, and the potential strategies the enemy might use to capture these resources, it's essential to consider the risks posed by the enemy's light troops. These troops may position themselves along your flanks, rear, or other vulnerable spots or be deployed for diversionary tactics. Taking all these elements into account, you can reasonably assume that an intelligent enemy will pursue an operation that promises to disrupt you in the most damaging way. At the very least, this will likely be his intent, and you must focus all your efforts on countering it to protect your position effectively.

Article XIV.
Of our own Country, and that which is either neutral or hostile; of the

Variety of Religions, and of the different Conduct which such Circumstances require.

War can be conducted in one of three types of territories: our own lands, those belonging to neutral powers, or the land of the enemy. If my sole aim were glory, I would only wage war within my own country, due to the numerous advantages it provides. Every inhabitant becomes a potential informant, making it nearly impossible for the enemy to move undetected.

In our own country, we can safely send out large detachments that can perform any military maneuver with confidence. When the enemy gains an advantage, the local population often takes up arms to resist, just as they did after the Battle of Fehrbellin. At that time, Elector Frederick William saw more Swedes fall to the hands of the peasants than on the battlefield itself. Similarly, after the Battle of Hohenfriedberg, I saw the mountaineers in Silesia capturing and delivering fleeing Austrians to us in large numbers.

When war takes place in a neutral country, both sides have an equal footing, and the main focus shifts to winning the favor and trust of the local population. Achieving this requires strict discipline among the troops, banning any form of looting or theft, and enforcing such rules with severe penalties. It might also help to suggest that the enemy has harmful intentions toward the country, thereby turning the locals against them.

If the country is Protestant, we can pose as protectors of the Lutheran faith, stirring religious fervor among the lower classes, who are often susceptible to our persuasive tactics. In a Catholic country, we promote tolerance and moderation, blaming religious animosities on the priests, who we claim are responsible for much of the existing tensions between different groups. Despite their conflicts, people of different sects often agree on core tenets of faith, which we can use to our advantage.

The size of any detachment we send out must reflect the trustworthiness of the local populace. In our own country, we can take almost any risk, knowing we have widespread support. In a neutral country, however, more caution is required, at least until we're certain that the majority of the population harbors no hostility. Once their trust is secured, detachments can be dispatched with more confidence.

In a thoroughly hostile country, such as Bohemia or Moravia, we must take no risks, sending out no detachments for the reasons previously discussed, as the inhabitants cannot be trusted beyond what we can directly observe. Here, most light troops are best employed to guard convoys, as it's unrealistic to expect any positive sentiment from the population. The Hussites around Königgrätz are the only ones who might offer assistance. Those of influence may appear friendly but are traitorous at heart; nor are the priests or local magistrates any more reliable. With their interests tied to Austria, whose objectives do not entirely align with ours, we should neither trust nor rely on them in any capacity.

Our remaining option in such places is to appeal to religious zeal, stirring up passion for religious liberty and subtly suggesting to the population that their priests and noble leaders keep them under oppressive rule. This, one might say, is a matter of invoking powerful forces to serve our interests.

Since I recorded these thoughts, the Empress-Queen has significantly raised taxes in Bohemia and Moravia. This change could be used to gain the goodwill of the people, especially if we imply that they would be treated more favorably should we take control of the region.

Article XV.
Of every Kind of March, which it can be necessary for an Army to make.

An army moves with specific purposes in mind: advancing into enemy territory, securing a strategic campsite, joining with reinforcements, preparing for battle, or retreating before the enemy. Once the camp is well-fortified, the next priority is to scout the surrounding area and all roads leading into and out of the camp. This reconnaissance allows for precise planning in response to various scenarios.

To achieve this, large detachments are sent out under various pretexts, accompanied by engineers and quartermasters who examine every location that could potentially be occupied by troops. Their job is to analyze the terrain and survey the roads that the army might need to use. Following them are several chasseurs, whose task is to study these roads in detail so they can effectively guide the columns should the general decide to march along those routes.

Upon returning, these officers provide a thorough report on the camp's location, the roads leading to it, the characteristics of the land, and the nearby woods, mountains, and rivers. With this information in hand, the general is equipped to make informed decisions. When the camp isn't too close to the enemy, a specific marching order can be implemented as follows:

Imagine that the camp can be accessed by four different routes. The advance guard, which consists of six battalions of grenadiers, one infantry regiment, two dragoon regiments (each with five squadrons), and two hussar regiments under the command of Mr. N. N., will depart at eight o'clock this evening. All of the army's encampments will follow this advance guard, which will carry only its tents and leave the heavier baggage with the main army.

These troops will march four leagues ahead, securing any important features they encounter—such as defiles, rivers, hills, towns, or villages—until the main army arrives. Once the main army reaches them, the advance guard will then enter the camp that has already been designated.

The following morning, the main army, arranged in four columns, will advance behind the lead of the advance guard. Soldiers stationed as guards in villages along the route will rejoin their respective regiments. The right-wing cavalry, split into two lines and marching on the right, will form the first column. The infantry of the right wing, also in two lines and marching by the right, will create the second column. The infantry of the left wing, filing by the right as well, will establish the third column. Finally, the left-wing cavalry, likewise filing by the right, will constitute the fourth column.

The regiments N. N. of the second line, along with three hussar regiments under General N. N., will escort the baggage, which will follow behind the two infantry columns. Four aides-de-camp will supervise this escort to ensure that the carriages proceed in a well-ordered line with minimal gaps between them.

If the rear guard general requires additional support, he must immediately alert the commander in chief. The chasseurs who initially scouted the roads will guide the four columns to ensure they follow the intended paths accurately.

In advance of each column, a team of carpenters will travel with wagons carrying beams, joists, and planks to construct bridges over smaller rivers as necessary. Column leaders must ensure that each column progresses at an even pace, without moving ahead of one another, and with controlled spacing. Division officers need to monitor their distances carefully, maintaining cohesion.

When crossing a defile, the heads of each column should march slowly or pause intermittently to allow the rear to maintain alignment. This steady pace ensures the entire march remains well-coordinated.

The march continues with this order in mind. When the army encounters mountains, forests, or defiles, the columns should split, allowing the infantry to lead, followed by the cavalry, which will close the march and provide additional protection from behind.

If a plain lies at the center of the area, it should be designated for the cavalry, while the infantry, organized into columns at both ends, should move through the woods. However, this setup applies only when the march is taking place at a safe distance from the enemy. When closer to the enemy, it's sufficient to place a few battalions of grenadiers at the head of each cavalry column to help maintain the battle order.

The most reliable way to ensure a reinforcement reaches us safely is to march along a challenging road to meet it, simultaneously distancing ourselves from the enemy to avoid any confrontation. The advantage gained from the arrival of reinforcements will soon allow us to retake any ground temporarily conceded to the enemy.

When circumstances require marching parallel to the enemy, it should be conducted in two lines, either to the right or left, with each line forming a column and accompanied by an advance guard at the front. The same principles I previously outlined can also be applied here.

All of our marches from Frankenberg to Hohenfriedberg were organized in this manner, consistently moving to the right. I favor these arrangements over others because the army can be easily organized into battle formation by a single movement to the right or left, which is the quickest way to assemble them. This method would always be my preference when engaging the enemy if I had the option, even though I lost the benefit of it at Sohr and Hohenfriedberg. In this style of march, it is essential to ensure that the flank never exposes itself to the enemy.

When the enemy begins a march indicating preparations for battle, it is important to offload all heavy baggage and send it with an escort to the nearest town for safekeeping. The advance guard should then be formed and sent forward to a distance of roughly half a league.

When marching directly toward the enemy, special care must be taken to prevent columns from advancing too far ahead of one another. As they approach the battlefield, the columns should spread out in such a way that the troops occupy precisely the amount of ground they will need in battle formation. This task is challenging, as some battalions often find themselves too crowded, while others end up with too much space.

Marching in lines presents no particular disadvantage, which is why I have always preferred it.

When a battle is expected during the march, extreme caution is required. The general must remain vigilant, surveying the terrain cautiously from one vantage point to another without overexposing himself, in order to develop a clear understanding of different possible positions should the enemy attempt an attack.

Church steeples and elevated areas should be used to gain a view of the terrain, and any paths leading to these vantage points should be cleared by light troops dispatched from the advance guard.

Retreats are typically organized as follows: one or two days before departure, the heavy baggage is assembled and sent off under a strong escort.

The number of columns in a march should be carefully chosen based on how many usable roads are available and, equally importantly, on the nature of the terrain. In open plains, where space is abundant, it is most effective to have the cavalry lead the advance guard, as their mobility and speed make them well-suited for this task. However, if the landscape is more varied, with mixed fields, woods, and potential obstacles, it becomes safer to assign the advance guard duties to the infantry, as they can adapt more readily to varied terrain. When marching in open country, it's typical for the army to be organized into four columns.

In such an arrangement, the right wing's second line of infantry, filing by the right and followed by the cavalry of the same wing, will form the fourth column. Similarly, the first line of the right-wing infantry will also file by its right, followed by its cavalry, forming the third column. On the left wing, the second line of infantry, accompanied by its corresponding cavalry, will make up the second column. Finally, the infantry of the left wing's first line, followed by its cavalry, will compose the first column.

With this formation, the entire rear guard is made up of the cavalry, which provides flexibility and, if necessary, can be reinforced by hussars for added security. The rear guard plays a vital role in ensuring the protection of slower-moving troops and equipment, giving the main body of the army time to maneuver as needed.

During a retreat that requires crossing a defile, it's critical for the infantry to secure the passage the evening before departure. By positioning themselves strategically, they shield the rest of the troops, ensuring that the defile remains open and accessible. In this way, if any resistance or unexpected challenges arise, the infantry can provide cover, allowing the rest of the army to move through safely.

If circumstances require the army to move in only two columns, this will alter the arrangement somewhat. In such a case, the cavalry of the right wing will file to the left, with the second line moving first and taking the lead in the second column. Following this, the second line of infantry will fall into place, with the first line of infantry filing behind them to complete the formation. On the left wing, the second line of cavalry will also file by the left, moving first and taking the lead of the first column. This first column is then completed by the infantry of the left wing, with the second line moving first, followed by the first line.

The rear guard in this arrangement is strengthened by six battalions from the rear of the first line, accompanied by ten squadrons of hussars.

These battalions and squadrons position themselves in a two-line formation at the front of the defile, adopting a checkerboard pattern to secure the area as the army moves through. While the main force passes through the defile, these rear guard troops use their positioning to provide cover fire, protecting those troops still on the other side.

Once the army has fully crossed, the advance guard's first line moves into the defile, passing through openings in the second line. After this first line is through, the second line follows under the cover of the rear guard, which remains stationed on the opposite side to maintain protection until the last units have safely passed.

One of the most challenging maneuvers is to cross a river while in retreat, especially when the enemy is close. An excellent example of this complex operation is our retreat across the Elbe at Kolin in 1744, where careful planning and disciplined execution enabled a successful crossing under pressure.

However, suitable towns or strongholds are not always nearby to support such maneuvers. In cases where two bridges are the only available crossing points, a large entrenchment should be constructed to secure both bridges, with small openings left at the heads of each bridge. Once this entrenchment is in place, several artillery pieces and a designated number of troops should be positioned on the far bank of the river. This opposite bank should have a moderate slope—steep enough to provide a height advantage but gentle enough to permit maneuvering. This elevated position enables these troops to control the crossing area, keeping enemy forces at bay.

With the entrenchment manned by infantry, the main force can proceed with the crossing, beginning with the infantry. The cavalry remains behind, forming a checkerboard arrangement within the entrenchment to act as the rear guard, providing cover for the crossing. Once the majority of the army has crossed, the infantry positioned at the heads of the bridges can take up positions to cover the last stages of the withdrawal.

If the enemy attempts a pursuit, they will be met by concentrated fire from troops positioned at both bridgeheads as well as from the forces stationed across the river. This setup provides a layered defense that can significantly hinder the enemy's advance.

When the entrenchment's infantry has crossed the river, the bridge itself should be dismantled or destroyed, preventing the enemy from following. Those troops who had been stationed at the bridgeheads can then cross by boat, shielded by supporting troops on the far side who are ready to advance and assist if needed. Once the pontoons are loaded onto their carriages, the remaining troops can begin their movement, completing the withdrawal.

At the angles of the entrenchment, fougasses (explosive traps) can be strategically placed. The last grenadiers to cross the river will ignite these fougasses to disrupt any pursuing forces, giving the army time to establish a safe distance.

Article XVI.
On the Precautions necessary to be taken in a Retreat against Hussars and Pandours.

Hussars and pandours may seem terrifying to those who aren't familiar with their methods, but their courage is often superficial. They're brave only when they're driven by the promise of loot or when they can harass others without risking their own safety. Their tactics mainly involve two types of aggression: one directed at convoys and baggage trains, where they seek easy plunder, and the other aimed at troops forced into retreat, where they attempt to annoy and hinder the soldiers' withdrawal.

While our regular troops have little to genuinely fear from these forces, the skirmishing methods of the hussars and pandours can delay our marches. Their attacks are inconvenient, especially since we inevitably lose some men—often at critical moments. For this reason, I will explain the most effective way I know to handle these opponents.

When retreating through open plains, we can typically drive off the hussars with a few well-placed cannon shots, while the pandours can be kept at bay with our dragoons and hussars, who inspire significant fear in them. However, the most challenging retreats occur when our path takes us through forests, narrow passes, or mountainous terrain, as these areas give pandours ample opportunity to inflict damage. In such situations, it is almost unavoidable that we will suffer some losses.

In these difficult environments, the heights should first be secured by our advance guard, positioned with their front facing the enemy. At the same time, we should detach troops to the flanks of the marching column, allowing them to traverse the heights and woods alongside the main body. Additional squadrons should be kept ready to engage wherever the ground allows.

In these scenarios, it is crucial to maintain steady movement without halting, as a stop would only expose some of our men unnecessarily, leading to preventable casualties. The pandours typically lie flat as they fire, keeping themselves well hidden, and when our army's advance forces the rear guard and small detached units to abandon their positions, the pandours quickly occupy these vacated spots. From these concealed positions, often behind trees or on higher ground, they pick off retreating soldiers with relative safety.

Neither musket fire nor cannon loaded with cartridges can effectively target them, as they remain dispersed and hidden behind terrain features like hills and trees.

I faced two retreats under these conditions in 1745: the first through the valley of Liebenthal en route to Staudenitz and the second from Trautenau to Schatzlar. Despite every possible precaution, we lost sixty men killed and wounded in the first retreat and over two hundred in the second.

In cases where we must retreat along difficult paths, our marches should be kept very short, allowing us to stay vigilant and prepared. No march should exceed two leagues, or roughly one German mile. This measured pace reduces strain on the troops, enabling us to respond more effectively to any pandour attacks. If the pandours are careless enough to take refuge in a wood, we sometimes have the advantage of turning their position, forcing them to either flee or face us directly.

Article XVII.
Of the Method in which the Light Prussian Troops conduct

themselves when engaged with the Hussars and Pandours.

When we aim to dislodge enemy light troops from a position, our approach is to launch a swift and forceful attack. Given that these light troops tend to scatter in their fighting style, they are poorly equipped to withstand a direct assault from our disciplined forces, who are trained to engage with full commitment and without hesitation.

To execute this plan, we first detach a few units to secure the flanks of the main force advancing against the light troops. With the flanks protected, we then attack with vigor, ensuring a high chance that the enemy will break and flee.

Our dragoons and hussars, advancing in tightly formed ranks with swords drawn, engage these light troops directly. This type of close combat is something light troops are generally unprepared for and incapable of enduring. In every instance, this approach has proven effective, allowing us to drive them off without concern for any numerical advantage they might possess.

Article XVIII.
By what Movements on our Side the Enemy may also be obliged to move.

It is a grave mistake to think that merely moving an army will compel the enemy to respond by moving as well. Forcing the enemy into action isn't achieved simply by movement; it requires a deliberate and calculated approach in how that movement is executed. An intelligent adversary won't be easily swayed by superficial maneuvers you may employ. Instead, you must take up strategically significant positions that will compel the enemy to think deeply about his options and eventually force him to abandon his own camp.

To execute this effectively, you need a thorough understanding of the terrain, the capabilities of the opposing general, the locations of his supply depots, the towns that provide him with resources, and the areas from which he gathers forage. Only after carefully analyzing these factors can a solid plan be formulated. A general who employs a creative and determined approach to unsettle his enemy will, in time, earn the distinction of challenging his opponent in both skill and reputation.

At the onset of a campaign, the general who promptly gathers his forces, advances to seize a town or occupies a key position will immediately set the pace, forcing his opponent into a reactive, defensive posture. However, there should always be sound strategic reasons behind any attempt to force the enemy to move during a campaign. This may include securing a nearby town close to his encampment, driving him into desolate territory where sustaining his forces becomes difficult, or creating conditions that favor a decisive engagement. With such clear objectives in mind, you begin to develop a plan that considers both the risks and benefits of each maneuver.

It is vital that the marches you undertake and the camps you occupy do not create greater challenges for you than for the enemy. For example, drawing too far away from your depot may expose it to attack by enemy light troops, especially if it is inadequately fortified. Similarly, taking up a position that disconnects you from supply lines or communications with your own country could lead to shortages that force a retreat.

After carefully evaluating these considerations and calculating the potential actions of the enemy, you can then determine your approach. This may include setting up camp on one of the enemy's flanks, moving closer to the regions that provide his sustenance, cutting off his access to his capital, threatening his supply depots, or choosing a position that disrupts his access to essential provisions.

A concrete example of such a strategy, well-known to many of my officers, occurred when I planned to force Prince Charles of Lorraine to abandon Königgrätz and Pardubitz in 1745. Upon leaving the camp at Dubletz, our route should have taken us leftward, skirting the Glatz region and advancing near Hohenmauth. This maneuver would have pressured the Austrians, who relied on supply depots in Teutschbrod and mostly drew their provisions from Moravia, to move to Landscron, effectively conceding Königgrätz and Pardubitz to us. The Saxons, being cut off from their homeland, would have been forced to leave the Austrians and return to defend their own territory.

I ultimately refrained from executing this maneuver because, even if I had secured Königgrätz, it would have been of limited benefit. I would still have needed to send detachments to support Prince of Anhalt if the Saxons decided to return home. Additionally, the supply depots at Glatz could not sustain my entire army for the length of the campaign, rendering such a position unsustainable.

Creating diversions by dispatching troops to separate areas can also pressure the enemy into breaking camp. Generally, any unexpected operation that catches the enemy off-guard has the potential to disrupt his plans, forcing him to abandon his current position. Such operations include crossing mountains that the enemy believes to be impassable or fording rivers without his knowledge.

The campaign of Prince Eugene in 1701 provides valuable insight into these tactics. The disarray of the French army when Prince Charles of Lorraine unexpectedly crossed the Rhine serves as a well-known example of how such maneuvers can unsettle an enemy force.

In conclusion, the success of these operations lies in ensuring that the execution aligns with the intent. As long as the general's plans are carefully crafted and based on solid strategic principles, he will be able to dictate terms to the enemy, forcing him to remain on the defensive. By maintaining this strategic advantage, the general keeps control of the campaign, always a step ahead of his adversary.

Article XIX.
Of the Crossing of Rivers.

When the enemy remains on the opposite side of a river that we aim to cross, brute force alone is futile; instead, strategic deception becomes essential. To understand how to execute a successful river crossing, we need only examine Caesar's crossing of the Rhine, Prince Eugene's crossing of the Po, or Prince Charles of Lorraine's crossing of the Rhine. These generals used detachments to mislead the enemy, obscuring the actual crossing point. They prepared bridges in locations where they had no intention of crossing, thus misleading the enemy, while the main body of the army marched under cover of night to a significant distance away, allowing them time to cross the river before the enemy forces could organize a defense.

Rivers are generally crossed at points where there are small islands, as these natural features provide valuable support for establishing a foothold. It is also preferable to encounter woods or other natural obstructions on the opposite bank, which hinder the enemy from launching an immediate counterattack, giving us time to organize our troops once across.

Such operations demand meticulous planning and vigilance. Boats, pontoons, and all other necessary equipment must be in place by the designated time, with each boatman thoroughly briefed on the typical demands of night operations. Once every component is in order, the troops proceed to cross and secure a position on the opposite bank.

In any river-crossing operation, it is crucial to fortify both bridgeheads, placing ample troops to hold these positions. Nearby islands should be fortified to reinforce the bridgehead defenses and prevent the enemy from seizing or damaging the bridge during the crossing.

For narrower rivers, it is advantageous to select crossing points where the river creates natural angles or bends, with slightly elevated banks that provide a vantage over the opposite side. At such locations, we position as many cannons as the terrain permits, along with a proportional number of troops, to cover the construction of bridges. As the angle creates a narrower stretch of land, we advance carefully and gain ground gradually as the troops cross.

If fords are available, the approach should be smoothed to facilitate the cavalry's crossing, ensuring an effective and coordinated river passage.

Article XX.
Of the Manner in which the Passage of Rivers is to be defended.

Defending the crossing of a river, especially when the area to be covered is vast, is one of the most difficult tasks in warfare, if not altogether impractical. Successfully defending a river crossing requires specific conditions. The section of the river to be defended should not exceed eight German miles in width, as a broader front would be impossible to cover effectively. Additionally, two or three well-placed redoubts must be established along the riverbank within this range, and there should be no fords available elsewhere that might allow the enemy to bypass these defenses and cross unimpeded.

Assuming these conditions are met, adequate time is crucial to properly prepare for the enemy's crossing attempts. The preparations should follow a precise defensive strategy to cover all vulnerabilities.

To begin, gather all available boats, barges, and any other watercraft from the river and relocate them to the redoubt areas. This prevents the enemy from using these vessels to cross the river or otherwise aid in their approach. Next, conduct a thorough reconnaissance of both riverbanks to identify and obstruct any potential crossing points. Every possible location where the enemy might find cover during an attempted crossing must be given special attention, as these areas can offer them protection from our defensive positions.

Once the crossing points are identified, preparations for defense must consider the terrain's specifics. Roads wide enough to support multiple columns should be constructed along the entire defensive front, ensuring that troops can move rapidly without congestion. These roads allow our forces to reposition and reinforce different areas of the defense line without delay, maintaining a flexible but robust defense.

With the defenses in place, the main army should camp at the center of the defensive line, reducing the distance to either end to just four miles, allowing quick access to all points of defense. From this central position, form sixteen mobile detachments commanded by the most diligent and alert officers among the dragoons and hussars. These officers should be handpicked for their intelligence and adaptability. Split the detachments equally: eight assigned to cover the right flank of the defense line and the remaining eight to guard the left flank, each group under the command of a capable general officer.

These detachments serve dual roles. They constantly monitor the enemy's movements, detecting any signs of an attempted crossing, and report any significant activity or shifts in the enemy's positions. During the daytime, guard posts are strategically positioned along the riverbanks to observe any preparations the enemy might be undertaking. At night, patrols should be sent out every fifteen minutes, advancing to the river's edge and remaining there until they have a clear view of the enemy's bridge-building efforts or detect the leading edge of an attempted crossing.

The generals overseeing these detachments, along with the officers in command of the redoubts, must send reports to the commander in chief four times per day. To expedite communication, a relay of fresh horses should be placed between the front lines and the main army to ensure messages reach the commander as swiftly as possible, giving him immediate awareness of any enemy activity at the river. The general must be prepared to respond to a breach in defenses at a moment's notice; for this reason, his baggage should be sent ahead to avoid any delay in his movements.

Each segment of the defensive line should have specific, pre-planned countermeasures ready for activation when the enemy's crossing attempt begins. The commander in chief assigns experienced generals to manage the defense at key points along the river. Upon receiving notice of the enemy's attempt to cross, the army should advance swiftly, with the infantry leading the columns, as it is presumed that the enemy will immediately begin entrenching once they establish a foothold on the other side. Speed and decisiveness are crucial upon arrival at the crossing point; a rapid, forceful attack is the best chance of successfully repelling the enemy and preventing them from establishing a secure position.

Defending the crossing of smaller rivers, though seemingly easier, presents its own set of challenges, often making such defenses even more difficult. If the river contains fords, every effort should be made to render them impassable by blocking them with felled trees or other debris to prevent enemy cavalry from advancing. However, if the enemy's bank is elevated above ours, resistance becomes nearly futile, as they will have the advantage of height for both cover and attack.

Regarding the surprise capture of towns, a successful surprise relies on several favorable conditions. A town susceptible to surprise is often poorly guarded and lacks strong fortifications. If the town's ditches are water-filled, a surprise attack can only succeed during winter, when a hard frost makes the water a negligible obstacle.

Surprises can be conducted by an entire army, as demonstrated by the capture of Prague in 1741. Alternatively, they may result from a prolonged blockade that leads the defenders to a false sense of security, as in Prince Leopold of Anhalt's capture of Glogau. In some cases, smaller detachments suffice for a surprise, as illustrated by Prince Eugene's attempt at Cremona or the Austrian success at Cosel.

The primary rule when planning a surprise attack is to obtain accurate intelligence regarding the town's fortifications and interior layout. Such knowledge allows for a focused assault on specific weak points, increasing the chance of success. The surprise at Glogau stands as an exemplary model of such an operation; it is widely regarded as a masterstroke and provides a worthy example for anyone considering similar endeavors. In contrast, the surprise of Prague, although effective, succeeded largely due to the scale and variety of attacks, which overwhelmed the garrison by forcing them to defend an extensive perimeter. Cosel and Cremona, however, were secured through betrayal: Cosel fell when an officer defected and informed the Austrians that a section of the ditch had not been completed, allowing them to enter and capture the position.

For smaller fortifications, surprise attacks can be directed at the gates. Mortar fire should be used to batter specific gates while detachments are positioned at others to prevent the garrison from escaping. If cannons are employed, they must be strategically positioned to avoid exposure to enemy musket fire; otherwise, the artillery risks being overrun and captured, jeopardizing the entire operation.

Article XXII.
Of Combats and Battles.

The Austrian camp is so densely surrounded by light troops that mounting a surprise attack would be exceptionally difficult. Such vigilance and defensive positioning create formidable barriers against surprise maneuvers. When two armies are in close proximity, a decisive encounter is almost inevitable, unless one side holds an elevated or fortified position that discourages direct engagement and guards against surprise—a scenario that is rare for entire armies but occasionally seen with smaller detachments.

For a successful surprise on an enemy encampment, several conditions must be met. First, the enemy must be overconfident, perhaps relying excessively on the strength of his own troops or assuming his position is too secure to be threatened. He may place undue trust in reports from his scouts or spies or feel assured by the extensive patrols and alertness of his light troops. All these factors create a foundation for complacency, opening the door to a surprise attack. Before forming any concrete plan, however, it is essential to understand the terrain, the enemy's precise location, and the general layout of their camp. Each road leading toward the camp must be thoroughly scouted, allowing us to assess the best approach points and develop a structured strategy tailored to the situation.

Select only the most experienced chasseurs, especially those familiar with the roads, to lead each column. This local knowledge will be indispensable in guiding the troops accurately and avoiding any errors that could expose our movements prematurely. Above all, the operation's success hinges on maintaining complete secrecy; secrecy, as always, is the essence of all surprise maneuvers. To prevent any deserter from betraying our plans, the light troops should lead the march. Beyond ensuring loyalty within the ranks, these light troops will also keep the enemy's patrols at a safe distance, reducing the risk that they will detect our advance too soon.

It is crucial that all subordinate generals receive clear, detailed instructions regarding possible scenarios and know precisely how to respond to unexpected developments. If the enemy's camp is positioned on an open plain, the advanced guard should consist of dragoons. Once these dragoons are joined by the hussars, they can charge into the camp at full speed, creating immediate chaos and cutting down anyone in their path.

The entire army should closely support this initial wave, with the infantry at the forefront. Their primary objective is to target and disrupt the wings of the enemy's cavalry, weakening their defensive cohesion. The advance guard should initiate the attack roughly thirty minutes before dawn, creating maximum confusion at the break of day, while the main body of the army should remain no more than eight hundred yards behind, ready to reinforce immediately.

During the entire approach, absolute silence must be observed. Soldiers should be strictly forbidden from speaking unnecessarily, and all smoking should be banned, as the smallest spark could betray our location in the darkness.

Once the assault begins and dawn breaks, the infantry, organized into four to six columns, should advance directly into the heart of the enemy's camp to support the efforts of the advance guard. No firing should take place before dawn, as the risks of friendly fire in the dark are too high. However, as soon as daylight allows, artillery should target areas where the advance guard has yet to penetrate, especially focusing on the wings of the enemy cavalry. The goal here is to force the enemy cavalry to abandon their horses, especially if they haven't had time to prepare properly, which will throw them into further disarray.

The pursuit should continue beyond the enemy's camp, with the entire cavalry force released to chase the fleeing troops and take full advantage of their panic and confusion. If the enemy has discarded their weapons in their haste to escape, leave a detachment in charge of securing the camp while the rest of the army continues the pursuit, avoiding the temptation to halt for plunder. Pressing the attack to its fullest potential is crucial, as such opportunities to completely rout an enemy are rare. Taking advantage of this moment can allow us to dominate the campaign, dictating the terms of engagement for the foreseeable future.

I encountered a near-perfect opportunity of this kind shortly before the Battle of Mollwitz. We approached Marshal de Neipperg's army undetected, as his forces were scattered across three villages. With the benefit of hindsight, I realize I should have deployed two columns to surround the village of Mollwitz and initiated an assault there. At the same time, I could have sent dragoons to the other two villages, where the Austrian cavalry was stationed, to create confusion and prevent the cavalry from organizing. Following these dragoons, I would have deployed infantry to block the cavalry from mounting. I have little doubt that, with these tactics, we could have effectively annihilated their entire force.

I have already discussed the essential steps for securing our own camp and protecting it from enemy incursions. However, if despite all precautions the enemy manages to approach, the immediate response should be to organize the troops in battle formation on their assigned positions. The cavalry should hold firm, maintaining its position and firing by platoons until dawn. As daylight breaks, the generals should assess the situation, determining whether an advance is advisable based on the condition of the cavalry and the overall state of the field.

In these critical moments, each general must be prepared to act independently, making decisions without waiting for direct orders from the commander in chief. Personally, I am committed to avoiding night attacks due to the inherent confusion that darkness brings. Most soldiers need the oversight of their officers and the motivation provided by discipline to perform their duties effectively, and darkness can undermine both.

Charles XII of Sweden provides an instructive example of the perils of night attacks. In 1715, he launched a night assault on Prince of Anhalt immediately after landing on the island of Rügen. The King of Sweden had specific reasons for this tactic; daylight would have revealed the limited size of his force—only 4,000 men—against the 20,000 troops of his enemy. Despite the element of surprise, this numerical disadvantage ultimately led to his defeat, underscoring the risks of such endeavors.

An unchanging principle of warfare is to secure your flanks and rear while attempting to turn those of the enemy. This strategy can be executed in several ways, but they all share the same underlying goal:

to outmaneuver the opponent and place them in a disadvantageous position.

When faced with the need to attack an entrenched enemy, the assault should be launched without delay to prevent the enemy from completing their fortifications. What may be an advantage today could turn against you by tomorrow if the enemy has time to strengthen their defenses.

However, before committing to the attack, it is essential to personally survey the enemy's position and determine its strengths and weaknesses. This close inspection will help you assess whether your initial plan is feasible or whether the task will require considerable effort and resources. A firsthand reconnaissance ensures that your approach is grounded in accurate knowledge of the terrain and enemy positioning.

Often, the main reason entrenchments are breached is due to inadequate support. Historical examples illustrate this well: the fortifications held by Turenne were captured due to insufficient support, as was another notable entrenchment because Prince of Anhalt could outflank it. Similarly, at the Battle of Malplaquet, the allied forces managed to breach Marshal Villars' left flank by utilizing a wooded area. If the allies had recognized this vulnerability sooner, they could have spared their army a loss of fifteen thousand soldiers.

If a river that can be forded provides support to an enemy entrenchment, then that side of the defense becomes the logical target for an attack. For instance, the Swedish fortifications at Stralsund were overcome because the attack was directed from the sea, where the defenses were vulnerable due to shallow waters.

When the enemy's fortifications are extensive, stretching their forces thin across a broad front, the best approach is to attack at multiple points. If our plans can be concealed from the enemy, preventing them from reinforcing any one area sufficiently, we increase our chances of penetrating their defenses. Such a strategy, when executed well, disrupts the enemy's defensive cohesion and enhances the likelihood of capturing key positions.

Consider the following hypothetical formation for an assault on an entrenched position. Picture a line formed by thirty battalions, with the left wing fortified by the river N. N. The primary assault will focus on the left, where we intend to break through with twelve battalions, while a supporting attack will be carried out on the right with eight battalions. The troops assigned to these attacks will form in a checkerboard pattern, ensuring adequate spacing between units for flexibility. The remaining infantry will form a third line, positioned at the center to reinforce as needed. Four hundred yards behind this line, the cavalry will be stationed, ready to exploit any weakness in the enemy's defense.

The presence of these infantry lines will serve to keep the enemy occupied and prevent them from reinforcing threatened areas. Additionally, the cavalry positioned in the rear will be prepared to seize upon any missteps made by the opposing forces, such as an overextension or shift in defense.

Each attacking force should be closely followed by a contingent of pioneers equipped with shovels, pickaxes, and fascines. Their task is to fill in ditches and clear paths, creating access points for the cavalry once the entrenchment is breached. These support units play a crucial role in ensuring the attack's success by enabling the cavalry to move through the enemy's fortifications smoothly.

The infantry designated for the assault should refrain from firing until they have overtaken the enemy's fortifications and are properly arrayed on the parapet in battle formation. Maintaining silence and restraint during the approach can provide the advantage of surprise and limit the enemy's awareness of our exact position and strength.

Once breaches are made in the entrenchments by the pioneers, the cavalry should enter through these gaps and engage the enemy with force. Timing is critical here—the cavalry must wait until a sufficient number of troops have penetrated the enemy lines and consolidated their position within the entrenchments. Then, with the pioneers' groundwork complete, the cavalry can deliver a decisive blow, exploiting the vulnerabilities created by the infantry's assault.

By executing each phase of this plan with precision and coordination, the assault on an entrenched enemy can disrupt even the most fortified positions, using the advantages of surprise, careful planning, and concerted force to overcome resistance.

If the cavalry is forced to retreat, they should regroup under cover from the infantry's fire, maintaining their position until the rest of the army has moved in, and the enemy has been fully routed. I must emphasize here that I would generally avoid entrenching my army unless a siege is underway or anticipated. Even then, I am inclined to believe it may be more advantageous to advance before the arrival of a relieving force rather than fortify too heavily.

However, if there is indeed a need to entrench, the following approach would be the most effective. In constructing a fortified position, we would establish two or three substantial reserve units positioned to deploy rapidly to any point where the enemy mounts a strong attack. These reserves serve as mobile support, reinforcing sections of the line under the greatest pressure.

The main parapet should be lined with battalions, with a reserve force stationed immediately behind them to provide support when needed. Positioned further back, the cavalry should be organized in a single line behind these reserves, ready to respond swiftly to any breach or weakness in the defense.

The entrenchments themselves must be thoroughly fortified. If there is a river along one side of the line, the ditch should extend into the river, preventing the enemy from easily outflanking the position. Where the fortifications border a wooded area, the defensive line should end in a redoubt, and a thick abatis (a barricade of felled trees) should be created within the forest to further reinforce that side.

Particular attention must be paid to the flanking capabilities of any redans (angled fortifications). The ditch should be dug as wide and as deep as possible, while the entrenchments should be improved daily. Reinforcements to the parapet, palisades at barrier entrances, deepened pits, and chevaux de frise (spiked barricades) around the entire camp all serve to strengthen the position incrementally.

The most significant advantage in defensive entrenchments lies in selecting the appropriate structure and adhering to sound fortification principles, which will force the enemy to attack from a narrow front and focus only on the key points of the defense line. For example, an illustration on Plate 7 shows an entrenched army positioned near a river. Here, the layout angles the front line outward toward the approaching enemy, creating a natural projection. Batteries positioned at the far end of the right flank prevent attacks from that direction, as these batteries would rake the enemy's flank, while a central redoubt would hit the attackers from the rear. Consequently, the center redoubt becomes the only feasible target for assault, but even here, the enemy must cut through a thick abatis before they can engage.

Given these defenses, the fortifications of the center redoubt should be reinforced heavily. By concentrating our attention and resources on one key point, we ensure that this critical part of the defense is as solid and secure as possible.

Alternatively, Plate 8 demonstrates a different fortification style, with alternating projecting and recessed redoubts linked by entrenchments. This configuration requires fewer but strategically positioned redoubts, making it possible to complete the defenses in less time while maintaining strength at the crucial points of potential attack.

In such projecting redoubts, the musketry fire should be planned so that it crosses, creating overlapping fields of fire that trap the enemy in a deadly crossfire. To maintain this coverage, the redoubts should be spaced no more than six hundred yards apart.

Our infantry, defending the entrenchments, should rely on battalion volleys, with each soldier supplied with one hundred rounds. This ammunition supply is complemented by artillery, as many cannons as possible positioned between the battalions and within the projecting redoubts.

When the enemy is still at a distance, we use solid shot, firing to weaken them before they come within effective range. Once they close to within four hundred yards, we switch to grapeshot and canister, intensifying our defense as they near the entrenchment.

If, despite the strong defenses and steady, intense fire, the enemy manages to press forward and make a dent in our line, the infantry reserves must advance to push them back. Should this line of defense falter, the final counterattack rests with the cavalry, who charge forward as a last effort to drive the enemy into retreat.

Entrenchments typically fall for a few critical reasons: poor adherence to established fortification rules, a failure to effectively cover flanks, panic within the ranks, or the enemy's ability to outmaneuver the defenders. The attacking force often benefits from greater freedom of movement and confidence, which gives them a distinct advantage in overcoming fixed defensive positions.

Historical examples have demonstrated that once an entrenched position is breached, the entire defending army can quickly become demoralized and may even retreat in disarray. While I have complete faith in the resilience of my troops and their willingness to rally and repel the enemy, such determination would be wasted if the entrenchments themselves prevent us from exploiting any advantages gained. Entrenchments, while seemingly beneficial, can often impose limitations on an army's freedom of movement, making it challenging to capitalize on unexpected breakthroughs and limiting the possibility of strategic counterattacks.

Given these inherent disadvantages, it stands to reason that continuous defensive lines covering a large front are even more ineffective. These long lines of defense, although popular in recent military tactics, serve more to create vulnerabilities than to offer substantial protection. The style currently in vogue follows the approach of Prince Louis of Baden, who first implemented such defensive lines along the Briel. Later, the French employed a similar approach in Flanders, hoping that extensive lines would deter invasion. I maintain, however, that such defensive lines are more detrimental than beneficial. They require a broader span than the troops can realistically defend, creating gaps and weak spots where the enemy can easily break through. Instead of creating a secure front, these lines tempt the enemy into aggressive attacks and increase the likelihood of failure. Rather than protecting territory, they expose our forces to reputational damage should the line falter under pressure.

In warfare, numerical disadvantage need not lead to defeat, especially when sound tactics and intelligent maneuvering are employed. When facing a larger enemy force, a smaller army should aim to position itself in difficult, mountainous terrain where narrow passes and limited space neutralize the advantage of larger numbers. By restricting the enemy's ability to spread its forces and fully utilize its wings, we effectively level the playing field, making the numerical disparity less relevant. Such terrain provides natural choke points, creating opportunities to ambush the enemy, slow their movements, and limit the effectiveness of their formations. In close, hilly regions, we gain the added benefit of strengthened flanks, a distinct advantage compared to open plains where there is less natural cover. In fact, we secured victory at the Battle of Sohr largely due to our favorable positioning. Although the Austrian forces vastly outnumbered ours, they were unable to break through our flanks, as the terrain kept their superior numbers from becoming an insurmountable threat.

Choosing the most advantageous ground is my first priority, as the right terrain can fundamentally shift the odds in battle. Following the selection of ground, my focus turns to arranging the battle disposition itself. Here, my preferred tactic is the oblique order of battle, an approach that offers a means of both defensive and offensive maneuvering. In this arrangement, we refuse one wing to the enemy, keeping it out of the main engagement, while reinforcing the other wing, which is tasked with leading the attack. Concentrating our forces on a single point enables us to turn the enemy's flank and launch a decisive blow where they are weakest.

An army of even ten thousand men, if its flanks are turned effectively, will find itself rapidly encircled and at risk of collapse. The maneuver centers on the actions of the right wing, where all our offensive power is directed. First, a body of infantry is sent forward to infiltrate the wooded area on the flank, striking at the enemy cavalry from the side and creating a gap for our own cavalry to exploit. Meanwhile, a regiment of hussars charges into the enemy's rear, further destabilizing their line and causing confusion. As the enemy cavalry is broken and begins to retreat, our infantry advances from the woods, flanking the enemy's infantry, while the rest of our forces press the attack head-on.

Meanwhile, the left wing remains stationary, preserving its strength until the enemy's left wing is fully routed. This coordinated approach achieves multiple strategic objectives. Firstly, it enables a smaller force to hold its own against a much larger opponent, as the focus is on exploiting weaknesses rather than matching strength with strength. Secondly, it allows us to concentrate our attack on a single, decisive point that, once breached, has the potential to unravel the enemy's entire formation. Thirdly, if our attacking wing is repulsed, the remainder of our forces remains intact, with three-fourths of our troops still fresh and available to cover a strategic withdrawal, should it become necessary.

When confronting an enemy holding a naturally advantageous position, it is critical to carefully assess both strong and weak points before making any move. The goal should always be to identify the area of least resistance and direct the attack there, maximizing efficiency and minimizing unnecessary losses. Attacks on fortified villages, for example, are often unreasonably costly. Such actions typically result in high casualties among our best infantry, which weakens the overall force. For this reason, I avoid attacking villages unless it is absolutely unavoidable. Villages often serve as a trap, consuming resources and soldiers in a battle for limited gains while risking significant losses.

Some military theorists suggest that the center of the enemy's position is the most effective target, arguing that a successful penetration there will cause the enemy's entire formation to buckle. For instance, if an enemy position includes two large towns and two villages on its wings, then capturing the center will cause a ripple effect, leading to the inevitable fall of the flanks. Plate 10 illustrates such a situation, where a break in the center exposes the wings, leading to their eventual collapse. This approach, when properly executed, has the potential to yield a complete and sweeping victory by exploiting the inherent weakness in the enemy's structure.

Once a breach is made in the center, the attack should be intensified, pressuring the enemy to retreat from both the right and left sides. There is no greater asset in such an assault than the concentrated fire of artillery loaded with cartridges, which devastates the enemy's battalions. The powerful effect of artillery fire was evident during the battles at Sohr and Kesselsdorf, where attacks on well-defended batteries taught me valuable lessons in the complexities of capturing fortified gun positions. For example, let us imagine attempting to capture a heavily fortified battery with fifteen cannons that cannot be outflanked. In such situations, a frontal assault would likely result in devastating losses, as the combined fire of artillery and infantry makes it nearly impregnable. Capturing such a position often depends more on enemy error than on brute force.

In these cases, as our infantry mounts an attack, they are often repulsed, prompting the enemy's defenders to abandon their posts temporarily in pursuit. This movement leaves the artillery momentarily undefended, creating an opportunity for our forces to regroup and push forward. The defenders, realizing their mistake, then attempt to return to their guns, only to find our troops seizing control alongside them.

To improve our chances in such scenarios, I devised a specific maneuver based on experiences from these engagements. The attacking forces are arranged in two lines with a checkerboard formation, supported by a third line of dragoons. The first line advances with a light attack, designed to draw a response without engaging fully. Once contact is made, this line falls back through gaps in the second line, feigning retreat and enticing the defenders to abandon their position to pursue. At this point, we launch a vigorous, coordinated assault, using the defenders' momentary lapse to overrun the position.

This tactic aligns with a guiding principle: never place undue reliance on any single position unless it is unequivocally secure against all foreseeable threats. The primary strength of our troops lies in their offensive capability. Ceding this advantage without sufficient cause would undermine our fundamental tactical approach.

When occupying defensive positions becomes necessary, the priority should be to secure high ground, as elevation offers inherent strategic value. Additionally, reinforcing the flanks is essential to prevent the enemy from finding weak spots. If there are villages situated at the head or on the flanks of our position, it would be prudent to burn them, provided the wind direction does not drive smoke into our own camp. Destroying these villages prevents the enemy from using them as cover and disrupts any planned approach, further strengthening our position and enhancing the defense's overall effectiveness. By adhering to these principles and maintaining flexibility in both offensive and defensive operations, we can maximize our chances of success in any engagement, regardless of the size or positioning of opposing forces.

If there are any solid stone buildings situated in front of the main line, I would station infantry within them to harass and impede the enemy during the engagement. Such structures offer natural defensive benefits and can serve as strong points to delay or disrupt the enemy's advance.

It is critical, however, to avoid placing troops on terrain where they cannot effectively operate. Our position at Grotkau in 1741 was rendered nearly useless because the center and left wing were posted behind impassable bogs. The only usable ground, where any maneuvering could take place, was occupied by a portion of the right wing. This misalignment cost us strategically, limiting the effectiveness of our formation. Similarly, Villeroy's defeat at the Battle of Ramillies occurred because his right wing was positioned in such a way that it became ineffective, leaving the entire French force vulnerable when the enemy concentrated their attack against the unsupported right flank.

While I encourage Prussian troops to occupy advantageous positions as other armies do, these positions should serve a temporary purpose. Once these positions have been used to favor a movement or secure artillery support, the troops must vacate them promptly to engage the enemy directly. Rather than allowing the enemy to initiate an attack, we turn the tables, attacking them instead and thwarting their plans. Any unexpected movement we make in the enemy's presence is almost certain to yield positive results, particularly when directed against a weak or exposed point.

I consider battles fought in this manner to be among the most effective engagements. On these occasions, I would order the infantry to refrain from firing as it only slows their advance. Victory in these encounters is not measured by the number of casualties inflicted but by the extent of ground gained. The surest path to victory is to march forward swiftly and in tight formation, continuously advancing and pressing the enemy. When moving through challenging, broken terrain, it is customary to allow an interval of fifteen yards between squadrons.

However, on even ground, the line should be unbroken, forming a solid front.

For the infantry, the spacing should be just wide enough to allow room for the artillery. Exceptions are made only in certain scenarios—such as assaults on entrenchments, batteries, or villages, and in forming the rear guard during a retreat—where cavalry and infantry are arranged in a checkerboard formation. This pattern allows the second line to immediately fill any gaps in the first, providing support and enabling an orderly retreat, with each unit able to cover the other as they withdraw. This principle is fundamental and should never be overlooked.

This discussion provides an opportunity to outline some core principles for arranging an army in battle formation, regardless of the terrain. First, select prominent landmarks as reference points for aligning the wings. For instance, the right wing might align itself with a particular steeple designated as point N.N. The commanding general must exercise extreme caution in ensuring that the troops do not establish their positions incorrectly, as even a slight misalignment can disrupt the entire formation.

It is not always necessary to delay the attack until the full army is ready to engage. At times, opportunities arise that can be exploited swiftly, and hesitation could result in losing a strategic advantage. While a large portion of the army should generally be engaged in the battle, the first line should receive primary consideration when establishing the order of battle. If any regiments in the first line are unavailable, they should be replaced with an equal number from the second line to maintain continuity.

Special attention should be given to the wings, especially those expected to bear the brunt of the engagement. In open terrain, where the enemy is free to maneuver, it is essential to maintain a uniformly strong order of battle throughout the line. The enemy may hold back a reserve force, which they could deploy to disrupt our formation, so all parts of the line must be equally prepared to respond to potential threats.

If one wing lacks adequate support, the general commanding the second line should immediately dispatch dragoons to extend and reinforce the first line, without waiting for formal orders. Meanwhile, hussars from the third line can take the place of the dragoons, ensuring that the reinforcement does not weaken the second line's overall integrity.

This maneuver is critical because, should the enemy attempt to flank the first line's cavalry, the dragoons and hussars will be in position to counter the enemy's move and return the threat, ensuring that our forces remain adaptable and resilient in the face of unexpected developments.

To support the left wing, I recommend positioning three battalions in the interval between the two lines, as this will provide additional security. In the event that our cavalry is repulsed, these battalions will serve as a barrier, preventing the enemy from advancing directly onto the infantry—a tactic that proved effective during the Battle of Mollwitz.

The general in command of the second line should maintain a distance of three hundred paces from the first line. If he notices any gaps or intervals forming in the first line, he should promptly deploy battalions from the second line to fill them. This proactive approach ensures continuity in the battle formation, preventing weaknesses that the enemy could exploit.

In an open plain, it's advantageous to station a reserve cavalry unit behind the center of the infantry battalions. This reserve should be led by a capable officer who can operate independently, either reinforcing a pressured wing or flanking the enemy in pursuit if they manage to disorder one of our wings. This reserve gives the cavalry a moment to rally and reorganize while protecting the main force.

To initiate the engagement, the cavalry should charge at full gallop, while the infantry advances briskly toward the enemy. Commanding officers must ensure their troops penetrate and break through the enemy lines entirely. It is crucial that no one fires until the enemy is clearly routed, as premature firing can disrupt the momentum of the attack. Should any soldiers fire without orders, they must be immediately commanded to shoulder arms and resume their march without pausing. Once the enemy begins to falter, we can allow firing by battalions, which, when coordinated, can bring the engagement to a swift conclusion.

This formation includes a unique feature where small bodies of infantry are positioned at the extremities of the cavalry wings. These battalions provide support by using their own cannons, along with those on the cavalry wings, to target the enemy's cavalry from the outset, giving our cavalry an advantage as they prepare to charge. Additionally, if our wings are forced to retreat, the enemy's pursuit will be deterred by the risk of being caught between two fires—our main line and these supporting battalions.

When our cavalry appears to have gained the upper hand, this supporting infantry should advance toward the enemy's infantry. The battalions positioned in the intervals between the cavalry units should then quarter-wheel, moving to the flanks and rear of the enemy infantry, allowing us to surround and decisively engage them.

The victorious cavalry wing must prevent the enemy's cavalry from regrouping, pursuing them in orderly fashion and cutting them off from their own infantry. As confusion overtakes the enemy, the commanding officer should dispatch hussars to pursue the routed troops, supported by our main cavalry force. At the same time, dragoons should be sent along the roads the enemy infantry is using to retreat, capturing as many as possible and disrupting any organized escape.

This order of battle introduces another element—integrating dragoon squadrons with the infantry of the second line. In past engagements with Austrian forces, I observed that after approximately fifteen minutes of musket fire, Austrian soldiers tend to gather around their colors in small, dense formations. During the Battle of Hohenfriedburg, our cavalry exploited this tendency by charging these clusters, capturing many prisoners in the process. With the dragoons positioned nearby, they can immediately charge into these groups when the opportunity arises, leading to effective captures and disrupting enemy cohesion.

Some may argue that I appear to rely heavily on artillery over small arms in these dispositions. My response is that one of two outcomes is nearly inevitable: either our infantry will fire despite orders not to, or they will hold fire, waiting for the enemy to waver. In either case, the moment confusion is observed among the enemy, the cavalry should be ordered to charge. Facing flanking attacks on one side, a frontal assault on the other, and a cut-off line of retreat, most enemy troops will inevitably surrender or be captured.

In such a situation, the battle becomes less a contest and more a complete rout, especially if no natural obstacle, such as a defile, exists to shield the enemy's retreat.

In marching to battle, whether advancing by the right or left, the battalions or divisions must remain closely aligned, ensuring they are ready to engage as soon as they deploy. If advancing in a broad front, careful attention must be paid to maintain appropriate spacing, so that units are neither too tightly clustered nor too far apart.

There is also a distinction between positioning heavy artillery and field pieces attached to battalions. Heavy cannons should be stationed on elevated terrain, while the battalion field pieces should be set fifty paces ahead of the infantry. All artillery, regardless of type, must be well-aimed and consistently fired to maximize impact.

As the line advances to within five hundred yards of the enemy, field artillery should be moved by hand, allowing for uninterrupted firing. Once the enemy is in full retreat, the heavy artillery should also advance, firing a few more rounds as a parting blow to ensure their departure remains chaotic.

Each piece of artillery in the first line should be manned by six gunners, along with three regimental carpenters to maintain and operate the equipment efficiently. At approximately three hundred and fifty yards, artillery should switch to firing cartridges for maximum effect as the enemy is within critical range.

Victory in battle requires more than defeating the enemy in the immediate sense; it demands understanding how to capitalize on that victory fully. To spill blood needlessly, without securing a strategic advantage, is wasteful and inhumane. Pursuing a retreating enemy to heighten their fear and capture prisoners not only determines the current engagement but influences the course of future encounters. However, practical limitations—such as a shortage of provisions or troop exhaustion—may sometimes prevent a full pursuit. These factors must always be weighed carefully to balance immediate gains against the needs of sustaining the campaign over time.

It is ultimately the responsibility of the commanding general if an army finds itself lacking in provisions. When he chooses to engage in battle, he does so with a specific purpose in mind; and having such a purpose obliges him to ensure that all necessary preparations are in place to achieve it. This includes having a sufficient supply of bread or biscuits to sustain the army for eight to ten days. Such planning is essential to maintaining momentum and avoiding logistical setbacks that could undermine the success of the campaign.

As for the physical demands on the soldiers, any hardships they endure should not be given undue consideration if those exertions contribute to the attainment of victory. In times of exceptional opportunity, it is expected that the troops will be called upon to perform extraordinary feats, accepting the rigors of such efforts as part of their duty.

Once victory has been decisively secured, I recommend dispatching a detachment from among the regiments that have suffered the greatest losses. This group's mission would be to care for the wounded, prioritizing our own but extending basic care to enemy casualties as well. These soldiers should be transported to the hospitals, which, ideally, have already been set up in advance, demonstrating foresight in caring for the casualties.

Meanwhile, the main army should not hesitate to press on and pursue the defeated enemy to the nearest defile. In their state of panic, they are unlikely to maintain control of such positions if they are immediately pursued. The pursuit must be relentless to prevent the enemy from catching their breath and regrouping; otherwise, they might turn these natural defenses to their advantage.

After securing this initial victory and attending to the aftermath, it is time to establish the camp. When doing so, strict adherence to established rules and security measures is essential; overconfidence can be a grave miscalculation. Even when the victory appears complete, we should not assume that the enemy has no fight left. They may still have the resources or cunning to seize upon any negligence or error in our ranks, and vigilance is crucial to prevent this.

In cases of an absolute victory, additional steps can be taken to maximize the gains. Detachments may be dispatched to intercept the enemy's retreat routes, seize their supply depots, or even lay siege to multiple towns simultaneously. Here, specific strategies depend largely on the situation at hand, as circumstances beyond control often influence the best course of action. One must remember that as long as there is more to accomplish, the task is not finished. A sharp-minded, defeated enemy will seize any opportunity to exploit lapses in our conduct.

I earnestly hope the Prussian forces will never know defeat and am confident that, with sound leadership and rigorous discipline, they will avoid such a fate. However, should such a misfortune befall them, there are specific actions that can help mitigate its impact and restore the army's footing.

When it becomes evident that a battle is lost and that the enemy's advances are unavoidable, immediate steps should be taken to secure a controlled retreat. First, the second line of infantry should be sent to any nearby defile to establish a defensive position, utilizing the principles outlined in the section on retreats. Along with the infantry, as many cannons as can be spared should be stationed at this point to strengthen the line.

If no such natural chokepoint is available, the first line should retreat through the intervals in the second line, reforming into battle formation approximately three hundred yards behind. This spacing allows for an orderly fallback, providing a buffer for regrouping. The remaining cavalry must be consolidated and, if desired, can be arranged into a square formation. Such a formation offers greater defensive resilience, shielding the retreating forces from enemy incursions.

History offers notable examples of this tactic. After the Battle of Frauenstadt, General Schullembourg used a square formation to lead his forces across the Oder River without interference from Charles XII. Similarly, after the first Battle of Hochstädt, the Prince of Anhalt deployed his forces in a square to withdraw across a two-league plain, deterring the French cavalry from engaging them. These cases illustrate how, even in defeat, maintaining composure and using strategic formations can protect an army's integrity during retreat.

Finally, I emphasize that a defeat does not necessitate a long and frantic retreat of forty leagues or more. Rather, the army should withdraw only to the nearest advantageous position, rallying there to regain cohesion and morale. By taking up a defensible position and projecting confidence, the army can gather its scattered ranks and provide reassurance to those who are disheartened. This immediate regrouping prevents an initial setback from devolving into a complete rout and keeps the army poised for future engagements.

Article XXIII.
Of the Reasons which should induce us to give

Battle,and in what Manner it is to be conducted.

Battles shape the fate of nations. It is essential that they be decisive, whether the goal is to free ourselves from the ongoing burdens of war, place the enemy in a disadvantaged state, or resolve a conflict that might otherwise persist indefinitely. A wise commander will not make any movement without a sound reason, and a general should never engage his forces in battle unless he has a strategic objective of considerable importance. If he finds himself forced into battle by his opponent, it is likely due to previous errors that have allowed the enemy to dictate the terms and place him at a disadvantage.

Reflecting on my own experience, I do not claim infallibility. Out of five battles fought by my troops, only three were intentionally planned, while in two instances, circumstances forced me into conflict. At Mollwitz, for instance, the Austrians had positioned themselves between my army and Wohlau, where I kept my provisions and artillery, necessitating a battle to maintain access to essential resources. Similarly, at Sohr, the enemy had cut off my route to Trautenau, leaving me no choice but to fight or risk the loss of my entire force. The contrast between battles we choose and those imposed upon us is striking. The premeditated battles of Hohen-Friedberg, Kesselsdorf, and Czaslau yielded brilliant victories, with the engagement at Czaslau even leading to a negotiated peace.

In setting forth these guidelines for battle, I do not deny that I have made my own share of errors through oversight. However, I expect my officers to learn from these mistakes, and they can be assured that

I am committed to rectifying them through diligent study and improved tactics.

There are instances when both armies may desire engagement, leading to a swift and decisive resolution. However, the most advantageous battles are those in which we compel the enemy to fight against his will. It is a fundamental principle of warfare to force the enemy into actions he would rather avoid. Since our interests and the enemy's are naturally opposed, it is unlikely that both of us desire the same outcome from a confrontation.

Numerous factors might compel us to engage in battle: the need to force the enemy to lift a siege on a strategically valuable location, to drive him from a province he occupies, to penetrate further into his territory, to gain the upper hand in a siege, to press him toward peace negotiations, or to capitalize on any mistake he has made. For example, if we maneuver to threaten a town of importance to him or sever his lines of communication, the enemy may be forced into a confrontation to protect his interests.

In conducting such maneuvers, however, we must be cautious not to place ourselves in a similar predicament, as overextending our forces or occupying a position vulnerable to counterattacks could give the enemy the same opportunities against us. Engagements targeting an enemy's rear guard often carry the least risk, as they can disrupt his movements without exposing our own forces to undue danger.

If such a strategy is pursued, the most effective approach is to encamp near the enemy and wait for an opportunity when he attempts to withdraw through defiles or narrow passages. At that moment, we can strike his rear guard, potentially securing a decisive advantage with minimal risk. Small-scale engagements like these can yield substantial gains and often produce outcomes disproportionate to their scope.

There is also the tactic of harassing the enemy to disrupt his ability to consolidate scattered forces. The purpose of this strategy is justified by the objective at hand, although a skilled enemy may counter it with a rapid forced march or by positioning himself in an advantageous spot to avoid interception. On occasion, we may also find ourselves drawn into battle by the enemy's missteps. When the opposing force makes an error, it is our duty to capitalize on it, as every fault in the enemy's plan presents an opportunity to punish his lack of prudence.

Moreover, it is essential to keep in mind that our wars should be as brief and decisive as possible. Prolonged engagements are not in our interest, as they gradually weaken discipline, deplete the population, and exhaust the nation's resources. Consequently, Prussian generals should strive to conclude campaigns with a balance of prudence and urgency. Success should not tempt us to delay; instead, we must act efficiently to secure a quick and strategic conclusion.

The Marshal de Luxembourg's response during the Flanders campaigns is a cautionary tale. When his son suggested that they could capture yet another town, Luxembourg replied dismissively, "Hold your tongue, you little fool! Would you have us go home to plant cabbages?" Such complacency risks prolonging conflict without purpose. Rather, we should adopt the philosophy of the Hebrew leader Sennacherib, who believed it better to sacrifice one man than to risk the well-being of an entire people.

There are instances in military history that illustrate the principle of exploiting an enemy's mistake. In the Battle of Senef, the Prince of Condé seized the opportunity to engage the rear guard of the Prince of Orange (or possibly Prince of Waldeck) when he failed to secure the entrance to a defile, making his retreat vulnerable. The battle accounts of Marshal de Luxembourg's unnamed victory, as well as the Battle of Raucoux, provide further examples of how adept generals have capitalized on enemy errors.

In sum, battles are complex affairs with far-reaching consequences, and every engagement must be approached with purpose, preparation, and a readiness to exploit any advantage. By understanding and applying these principles, we can increase our chances of achieving not only victory in battle but also a swift and favorable resolution to the larger conflict.

Article XXIV.
Of the Hazards and unforeseen Accidents which happen in War.

This discussion would become unmanageably lengthy if we delved into every possible mishap a general might encounter in war. To summarize, a general needs both skill and good fortune to succeed. Generals face far more challenges and scrutiny than most people realize. Their actions are judged by the public, often based on nothing more than a brief report in the gazette, while the very readers passing judgment may lack even the basic experience to lead a small detachment, let alone command an army.

I don't aim to excuse generals who have made errors—my own campaign in 1744, for instance, had its share of missteps. But while I've often made mistakes, I have also undertaken successful operations, such as the siege of Prague, the defense and retreat at Koelin, and another strategic retreat in Silesia. I won't detail these campaigns further here, but it's important to acknowledge that some misfortunes cannot be avoided, no matter how well-planned or carefully considered the strategy may be.

Since these notes are intended for my generals, I'll focus on lessons from my own experiences rather than other examples. At Reichenbach, I planned a forced march to reach the Neiss River, intending to cut off General de Neuperg's communication by positioning my forces between his army and the town of Neiss. All preparations were in place, but heavy rain turned the roads to mud, stalling our advance guard and preventing the pontoons from moving forward. A dense fog compounded the issue, leaving village guards lost and unable to rejoin their regiments. The conditions were so poor that, rather than arriving at 4 a.m. as planned, we reached the river at midnight. By that time, the element of surprise was lost; the enemy had already prepared for our approach, and the opportunity slipped away.

Disease can also derail the best-laid plans. During our campaign in Bohemia in 1741, poor provisions led to sickness among the troops, forcing us into a defensive position. In another instance, at Hohen-Friedberg, I dispatched an aide-de-camp to instruct Margrave Charles to command the second line, as General Kalckstein had been detached to lead the right wing against the Saxons. Unfortunately, the aide misunderstood and instructed the Margrave to reorganize the first line into the second, a miscommunication that could have thrown our lines into complete disarray had I not discovered it in time to correct the error.

These examples underscore the importance of staying vigilant and recognizing that a single poorly executed order can disrupt an entire strategy. If a general commanding a critical detachment falls ill or is killed, it can create substantial complications for the overarching battle plan. Offensive maneuvers, in particular, demand generals of both sound judgment and unwavering courage, qualities that are rare; in my entire army, I count no more than three or four such individuals.

Even with the best precautions, losing a critical convoy to the enemy can ruin a plan, requiring either a significant pause or a complete reevaluation. Should circumstances necessitate a retreat, the troops may become demoralized. While I have fortunately not experienced such a setback with my entire army, I observed this effect at the Battle of Mollwitz. After a setback, it took considerable effort to revive the spirits of the troops, especially the cavalry, which was so shaken that they seemed resigned to defeat. To restore their morale, I sent out small detachments to give them a manageable task and gradually ease them back into combat readiness. It was not until the Battle of Hohen-Friedberg that our cavalry regained the confidence and effectiveness they continue to exhibit today.

The discovery of a significant spy within the enemy's camp can deal a severe blow to one's intelligence efforts. Without such informants, a general must rely solely on personal observation, a limitation that restricts insight into the enemy's movements and intentions.

The carelessness of officers tasked with reconnaissance can also create distressing complications. Marshal de Neuperg, for example, was taken by surprise when a hussar officer, assigned to keep watch, neglected his duties, allowing our forces to approach undetected. Similarly, an officer from the regiment of Ziethen failed to conduct his night patrol properly, enabling the enemy to build bridges at Selmitz and surprise our baggage train.

War is fraught with unpredictable challenges, and while one must be prepared for setbacks, many factors remain beyond a general's control. That said, by anticipating potential issues, staying alert to changing conditions, and instilling responsibility in subordinates, we can better navigate the many hazards of command. Through these reflections, I hope to equip my officers with the resilience and adaptability necessary to mitigate the effects of unforeseen setbacks, maintaining both the integrity of the army and the momentum of the campaign.

This illustrates the importance of my belief that the security of an entire army should never rest solely on the vigilance of a single officer. Entrusting such a consequential responsibility to one man, particularly a lower-ranking officer, is an unwarranted risk. Remember carefully the guidance I have given on this matter under the topic "Of the Defence of Rivers." It is essential to rely not solely on patrols and reconnaissance parties, but on strategies that provide stronger, more reliable safeguards.

Of all the disasters that can befall an army, treason is the most perilous. A notorious example occurred in 1733 when Prince Eugene was betrayed by General St. . . ., who had been bribed by the French. I, too, have felt the sting of betrayal; the fortress of Cosel was lost due to the treachery of a garrison officer who defected and led the enemy directly to it. Such examples serve as a stern reminder that, even when fortune seems firmly on our side, we should be wary of complacency and refrain from letting success breed overconfidence. Instead, we should remain mindful that any skill or foresight we claim is, at best, subject to the whims of unforeseen events—forces beyond our control that seem determined, for reasons unknown, to humble even the proudest of human plans.

Article XXV.
If it be absolutely necessary that the General of an Army should hold a Council of War.

Prince Eugene once remarked that "if a general does not wish to fight, he only needs to hold a council of war." His point is well-proven, as councils of war tend almost universally to vote against engaging. In these settings, secrecy—so essential to military operations—is often lost, as too many opinions and details are shared openly.

A general, entrusted by his sovereign with command of the army, should act independently and decisively. The confidence placed in him by his king justifies such an approach. Yet, while a general must lead firmly, he should not disregard the counsel of even the lowest-ranking officer. In matters concerning the nation's welfare, a true patriot sets aside personal pride and considers all suggestions, valuing advice that may lead to the successful outcome they all strive for.

Article XXVI.
Of the Manoeuvres of an Army.

The principles outlined in this work shed light on the theory behind the maneuvers I have instilled within my troops. These tactics are designed with the primary goal of maximizing every possible moment, enabling us to resolve engagements more swiftly than has been customary, and ultimately to overwhelm the enemy through the relentless momentum of our cavalry's charge. This intense, impetuous force ensures that even the most reluctant soldier is swept along, compelled to perform his duty alongside the bravest, making every trooper an active participant in the assault. Success relies heavily on the vigor of the attack.

With this in mind, I am confident that each general, fully appreciating the necessity and benefits of strict discipline, will prioritize its preservation and enhancement, both during wartime and in periods of peace. I am often reminded of the inspiring words of Vegetius regarding the Romans: "And finally," he declared, "Roman discipline triumphed over the hordes of Germans, the strength of the Gauls, the cunning of the Germans, the vast barbarian hosts, and conquered the entire world." Such is the importance of disciplined forces to the flourishing and security of a state.

Article XXVII.
Of Winter Quarters.

When a campaign concludes, the focus naturally shifts to organizing winter quarters. This requires careful planning and must align with the unique circumstances at hand. The first priority in establishing winter quarters is to construct a robust protective chain around these positions. Such a defensive line can be created in several ways, depending on the available natural and constructed defenses: positioning the line behind a river, leveraging mountainous terrain for added security, or taking advantage of nearby fortified towns to serve as protective barriers.

During the winter of 1741-42, for example, when my forces wintered in Bohemia, we set up behind the Elbe River, with our protective chain beginning at Brandeis and extending through key points, including Nienbourg, Koelin, Pojebrod, and Pardubitz, eventually ending at Konigingraetz. However, it is important to remember that rivers are not impenetrable barriers. When frozen, they can be crossed at numerous points, which highlights the need for constant vigilance. For this reason, hussars should be stationed along the full length of the chain to observe the enemy's movements carefully. These hussars are responsible for patrolling frequently, monitoring for any unusual activity or signs of enemy troop gatherings in the area.

Beyond the infantry chain, additional brigades of both cavalry and infantry should be stationed at strategic intervals. This arrangement ensures a rapid response and provides reinforcement to any section that might require immediate assistance. In the winter of 1744-45, we secured our quarters by establishing a defensive line along the mountain range separating Silesia from Bohemia. We guarded this line meticulously, aiming to maintain peace within our quarters. Lieutenant-General de Trusches, for instance, oversaw the front of Lusatia up to the Glatz region, covering crucial posts from Sagan to Schmiedberg, extending to Friedland, where redoubts were fortified for additional defense. Additional fortified posts were constructed along the vital routes of Schatzlar, Liebau, and Silberberg, bolstered by a reserve unit, ready to assist any post that might come under attack.

To add further strength, abbatis were set up in the surrounding forests, creating blockages on all routes leading into Bohemia and thereby limiting enemy movement. Every post was also equipped with hussars, assigned specifically for reconnaissance duties, ensuring that any attempt by the enemy to advance would be immediately detected. General Lehwald similarly protected the Glatz region with his own defensive arrangements, fortified positions, and prudent precautions. He and General Trusches coordinated their efforts to provide mutual support. Thus, if the Austrians moved against General Trusches, General Lehwald could counter by advancing into Bohemia from the rear, and General Trusches would do the same if Lehwald's forces were threatened. This network of mutual defense ensured that neither general's position could be easily overwhelmed.

Tropau and Jagerndorf were significant posts in Upper Silesia, and the main line of communication with Glatz ran through Zeigenhals and Patchskau, while another route through Neustadt connected to Neiss. It is also prudent to avoid excessive reliance on mountainous terrain for security, as we must remember the adage, "Where a goat can pass, a soldier can follow." For those winter quarters that benefit from proximity to fortresses, Marshal Saxe's arrangements provide an excellent model. Yet, we cannot always choose the ideal positions, as our defensive lines must adapt to the geographical realities of the terrain we occupy.

It should be regarded as a fundamental principle that we are never to consider any location entirely safe from enemy incursions. A constant state of readiness is required to maintain security within our winter quarters. Another important practice is to assign regiments by brigades, keeping them under the direct supervision of their respective generals. Where possible, generals should remain close to their own regiments, providing oversight and ensuring that discipline and readiness are maintained. However, exceptions to this rule may be necessary at times, depending on the broader strategy and the army's needs, which the commanding general is best positioned to assess.

There are also logistical considerations to be addressed regarding the upkeep of troops during winter quarters. If circumstances demand that we take winter quarters within our own territory, captains and subordinate officers should be compensated to match what they would typically receive in occupied winter quarters. Additionally, the soldiers should be provided with bread and meat at no cost to them, ensuring that their needs are met without imposing undue strain on their resources.

If, however, our winter quarters are in enemy territory, resource allocation follows a distinct structure. In this scenario, the commanding general receives an allowance of 15,000 florins, while generals of cavalry and infantry receive 10,000 florins each. Lieutenant-generals are allocated 7,000 florins, major-generals or camp marshals receive 5,000, cavalry captains are given 2,000, infantry captains 1,800, and subaltern officers between 1,000 ducats and 400-500 florins. Soldiers are provided with bread, meat, and beer without charge, though they are not issued money directly, as this could increase the risk of desertion.

The commanding general must closely monitor this allocation to prevent looting and to maintain order. Some leniency may be afforded to officers if they can secure small, fair gains, but plundering should be strictly controlled to maintain discipline and prevent resentment among the local populace. When stationed in enemy territory, the general must also ensure that an adequate number of recruits are obtained. The distribution process should be organized so that each district, or "circle," supplies a certain number of regiments. Ideally, each circle should be subdivided to match our cantonment arrangements, thereby streamlining the recruitment and training process.

If local authorities willingly supply recruits, that arrangement is preferable. If not, firmer methods may be required to meet recruitment needs. The early arrival of recruits is crucial, as it allows sufficient time for them to undergo training and become combat-ready by the spring. Captains should still send out additional recruiting parties if necessary to meet the numbers required.

The general must oversee all logistical aspects, such as securing artillery horses and other necessary supplies, either directly from the region or through compensation. Equipment maintenance is vital, and all military gear, from baggage wagons to basic supplies, should be repaired or replaced at the enemy's expense. This includes specific attention to the needs of the cavalry, whose officers must ensure saddles, bridles, stirrups, and boots are maintained in peak condition. Infantry officers, meanwhile, should ensure their men are supplied with adequate shoes, stockings, shirts, and gaiters for the next campaign. Soldiers' blankets and tents must be repaired, and cavalry swords sharpened, while infantry arms should be inspected and readied.

Additionally, artillery teams must prepare ample ammunition, especially cartridges for the infantry, to ensure our forces are fully equipped for the spring campaign. By attending meticulously to these logistical details, we can enter the next season with a well-prepared, well-provisioned, and confident army, ready for whatever engagements may come.

It remains essential for the general to ensure that all troops assigned to form the defensive chain are adequately supplied with powder and shot, and, indeed, that no essential provision is lacking for the entire army. Should time permit, it is highly advantageous for the general to visit various quarters himself. By doing so, he can assess the condition of the troops firsthand, ensuring that officers are diligently overseeing both the training and welfare of their men. Such oversight is vital, as regular drilling is necessary not only for recruits but also for seasoned soldiers to keep them sharp and ready for the demands of combat.

At the start of each campaign, the arrangement of cantonments is adjusted to align with the expected order of battle. Typically, this involves positioning the cavalry on the wings and placing the infantry at the center. These cantonments often extend nine to ten leagues (or about four to five miles) forward, with a depth of approximately four leagues (or two miles). As the time for encampment approaches, it becomes necessary to draw these cantonments inward slightly, consolidating the positions in preparation for rapid deployment.

A well-organized structure within the cantonments can significantly enhance the efficiency of command. I have found it highly practical to assign command responsibilities to the six senior-most generals. For instance, one general should oversee the cavalry on the right wing of the first line, while another commands the left. Similarly, two additional generals can command the cavalry of the second line, each responsible for a wing. This approach facilitates swift communication and execution of orders and enables the troops to assemble into columns for camp or combat with greater ease and precision.

Concerning the subject of winter quarters, I must once again advise great caution in entering them prematurely. It is imperative to confirm beyond doubt that the enemy's forces have fully disbanded before settling into winter positions. Let the misfortune of Elector Frederick William serve as a reminder: he was caught off guard and surprised in his quarters in Alsace by Marshal de Turenne, suffering a setback that might have been avoided with greater vigilance.

In sum, these strategies are not mere formalities but are fundamental to preserving the army's readiness, security, and overall effectiveness, ensuring that our forces are always prepared for rapid mobilization or engagement should the need arise.

Article XXVIII.
Of Winter Campaigns in particular.

Winter campaigns are particularly taxing on troops, not only due to the illnesses they often bring but also because they demand constant movement, preventing soldiers from being adequately clothed or reinforced. Such campaigns also strain the transportation of ammunition and provisions. Even the best-trained army cannot sustain prolonged winter campaigns without severe consequences. For these reasons, winter campaigns should generally be avoided, as they are among the most punishing and challenging forms of warfare. Yet, circumstances may arise where a general has no choice but to undertake them.

Reflecting on my own experience, I believe I have undertaken more winter campaigns than any general of this era, and it may be useful to outline the motivations behind these decisions. In 1740, following the death of Emperor Charles VI, Silesia held only two Austrian regiments. Determined to assert my family's rightful claims over this duchy, I launched a winter campaign, aiming to capitalize on the advantageous conditions and quickly advance toward the Neiss. Had I waited until spring, the war front would likely have settled between Crossen and

Glogau, necessitating three or four grueling campaigns to accomplish what we achieved with a single, well-timed march.

Another example is my winter campaign of 1742, when I attempted to protect the region from the Elector of Bavaria. That endeavor fell short, but not due to the season itself; rather, it failed because the French acted foolishly, and the Saxons proved untrustworthy. My third winter campaign, in the winter of 1741-42, became necessary when the Austrians invaded Silesia, forcing me to drive them back during a time of year when most would avoid warfare. In the winter of 1745-46, both the Austrians and the Saxons aimed to invade my hereditary lands, intending to wreak havoc. As was my custom, I decided to act preemptively and initiated a winter campaign within the heart of their territory, seizing the advantage by taking the war directly to them.

If I were to face similar conditions again, I would not hesitate to repeat such actions, and I would commend any of my generals who chose to follow this example. However, I must caution that without compelling reasons like these, a winter campaign should never be undertaken lightly.

For the logistics of winter campaigns, certain precautions are essential. Troops must be stationed as closely as possible in their cantonments, concentrating their strength in larger villages or towns whenever feasible. Ideally, two or three regiments of cavalry, mixed with infantry, should be housed together if the village is large enough to accommodate them. On some occasions, as when the Prince of Anhalt quartered his forces at Torgau, Eilenbourg, Meissen, and several other small Saxon towns, all infantry regiments may be gathered within a single town to maintain a more cohesive force, with the general remaining nearby in an encampment.

When we approach enemy territory, a rendezvous point should be established for all troops, who will then proceed in multiple columns. At the moment of any critical movement, whether preparing to storm enemy quarters or advancing to confront the enemy directly, the troops should arrange themselves in battle formation. In such circumstances, they may remain in open fields overnight, each company lighting large fires to endure the cold. Yet, these maneuvers demand great endurance, and their duration must be minimized. Swift, decisive action is key in winter warfare. Hesitation is a luxury we cannot afford; plans must be formed with boldness and executed with unwavering resolve.

If possible, winter campaigns should be avoided in regions dotted with fortified towns, as the season's constraints prevent a prolonged siege. Attempting to take well-defended positions by surprise is often doomed to fail, as the logistical challenges of winter make it nearly impossible to sustain such efforts.

In the ideal scenario, troops should be allowed to rest as much as possible during the winter months. This time can be used to strengthen the army and make any necessary preparations so that when spring arrives, our forces can move out with a renewed advantage over the enemy.

These principles outline the key aspects of large-scale maneuvers in winter warfare, as comprehensively as I am able to explain. I have endeavored to make these guidelines as clear as possible. If any part seems ambiguous, I welcome you to communicate these concerns to me, so that I may either elaborate further or acknowledge if your insights exceed my own.

Through my experiences, limited as they may be, I have come to understand that war is a complex art, one that can never be fully mastered. It continually rewards those who study it with dedication, offering fresh insights to those who remain attentive. If this account encourages my officers to deepen their understanding of military science, I shall consider my time well spent. Such knowledge opens the surest path to glory, allowing men to lift their names from obscurity, achieving renown, and securing a legacy of immortal fame through bold and distinguished deeds.

Thank You for Reading

Dear Reader,

We hope this timeless classic has sparked your imagination and enriched your literary journey. Now that you've turned the final page, we want to share a vision for the future of reading—one where every classic you've ever wanted to explore is at your fingertips, in a format that best suits your life.

We'd like to invite you to gain immediate, unlimited digital & audiobook access to hundreds of the most treasured literary classics ever written—along with the option to secure deluxe paperback, hardcover & box set editions at printing cost. Together, we can spark a new global literary renaissance alongside our small, independent publishing house called "The Library of Alexandria."

Thousands of years ago, the Library of Alexandria stood as a beacon of knowledge—until it was lost to history. We aim to reignite that spirit of preservation and discovery right now, in the modern age—only this time, it's accessible to all, in every language and every format.

Picture a world where every timeless classic, novel, poem, or philosophical treatise is not only available to read but also updated for today's readers—modernized, translated into any language or dialect, and ready to enjoy in any format you choose, whether that is in an eBook, audiobook, paperback, or deluxe hardcover & box set version a printing cost.

By joining our movement to rebuild the modern Library of Alexandria, you become part of an unprecedented mission to offer:

- **Unlimited Audiobook & eBook Access to the Greatest Classics of All Time**

  Instantly explore thousands of legendary works, from Plato and Shakespeare to Jane Austen and Leo Tolstoy. All are instantly ready to read or listen to, giving you a complete literary universe at your fingertips.

- **Paperback & Deluxe Editions at Printing Costs:**

  Purchase any title in a paperback, deluxe hardbound, or deluxe boxset edition at printing costs, shipped right to your doorstep. Curate your personal library of Alexandria with editions worthy of display—crafted to last, designed to captivate, and delivered straight to your door.

- **Modern translations for Contemporary Readers in all languages and dialects**

  Discover a vast selection of classics reimagined in clear, current language—no more struggling with outdated phrases or obscure references. Next to the original versions, we aim to offer translations in as many languages and dialects as possible.

  As we continue our translation efforts and add new languages, readers everywhere can connect with these works as if they were written today. By bridging linguistic divides, you're contributing to ensuring that these timeless stories become more meaningful, accessible, and inspiring for people across the globe.

- **Your Personal Library of Alexandria:**

  Over the months and years, you'll curate a unique physical archive of classics—each volume a testament to your taste, curiosity, and love of knowledge. It's not just about owning books—it's about curating a cultural legacy you'll cherish and pass down for generations to come.

- **Join a Global Literary Renaissance:**

  Your support fuels an ongoing mission: allowing us to reinvest in offering deluxe print editions (including special boxsets) at their true cost, broaden the range of available formats and translations, and extend the reach of these works to new audiences worldwide. By joining today, you're not just preserving a legacy of masterpieces; you set in motion a powerful wave of literary accessibility.

  We are more than a publisher—we're a movement, and we can't do it alone. Your support lets us scale our mission, preserving and reimagining history's greatest works for tomorrow's readers.

Become a Torchbearer of knowledge.

Thank you for picking up this book and allowing us into your literary journey. As you turn the pages, know that you're part of something larger: a global effort to keep these stories alive, share their wisdom across borders and generations, and spark a true cultural revival for the modern era.

If this resonates with you—please consider taking the next step by visiting:

www.libraryofalexandria.com

With gratitude and a shared love of knowledge,

The Modern Library of Alexandria Team

Visit:

www.libraryofalexandria.com

Or scan the code below:

www.ingramcontent.com/pod-product-compliance
Lightning Source LLC
Chambersburg PA
CBHW011426010726
47494CB00011B/2530

* 9 7 8 1 8 0 6 2 9 4 2 4 4 *